W.S. Harrison

**Sam Williams**

A tale of the old south

W.S. Harrison

**Sam Williams**
*A tale of the old south*

ISBN/EAN: 9783337089177

Printed in Europe, USA, Canada, Australia, Japan

Cover: Foto ©Andreas Hilbeck / pixelio.de

More available books at **www.hansebooks.com**

# SAM WILLIAMS:

## A TALE OF THE OLD SOUTH.

BY

## W. S. HARRISON.

———

NASHVILLE, TENN.:
PUBLISHING HOUSE OF THE M. E. CHURCH, SOUTH.
BARBEE & SMITH, AGENTS.
1892.

# PREFACE.

The existence of slavery in the South for more than two hundred years, and in the Southwest from the earliest settlement of the country, developed a unique condition of society. There were three distinct classes: the slave owners, the laboring white people, and the slaves. The line was sharply drawn between the slave-holding and nonslave-holding classes. As a rule, they lived apart, occupying different characters of soil. One class rested supinely on slave labor; the other toiled incessantly in competition with that labor. Their manners and "manner of speech" were different. The slave-owning class was highly educated, and spoke the purest English; the other was less cultured, and used idioms which at once evinced the earnestness and independence, the mental force and acumen of these toiling millions.

Then there were the slaves. Grafting the half-acquired English on the peculiarities of their native tongues, and following the natural bent of their vocal organs, they had in the generations of slavery developed a dialect peculiarly their own. This dialect is all the more interesting because it is passing away. Just as the old-time darkey is soon to become extinct, so his speech will shortly be heard no more. And this is true of all the phases of society which existed in the South before the war. The upheaval has been so complete that the old life is now a memory, and will soon belong to tradition. To aid in rescuing this life from oblivion the writer hopes is not the chief merit of this volume. The rendering of the dialects, both of the blacks and of the " po' white trash," as well as the representation of the manners and thoughts of the generation gone, or rapidly passing, he hopes will be accorded the charm of usefulness. As a Southerner " to the manner born," and having lived among the characters represented, he claims the right to speak. But beyond this he hopes the book, on account of its contents, will be found worthy of perusal.                    W. S. H.

Starkville, Miss.

(3)

# CONTENTS.

(5)

# SAM WILLIAMS:

## A TALE OF THE OLD SOUTH.

---

### CHAPTER I.

#### The First Important Event.

THE first if not the most important event in every life is to be born. Whether or not that event is important depends on what follows. I am sure that in many cases the credit side of the world's balance sheet, representing the sum of human happiness, would have been larger if that part of the life had been entirely omitted.

The wisdom of this remark finds proof in the large number of suicides, in the wrecks of life, and in the wrecking wish so often expressed, and always with a deep sigh: "O that I had never been born!" You see I am only rising to confirm the opinion of those most immediately interested. But what per cent. of human lives stands respectively on the debit and credit sides of the world's ledger I am not prepared to say.

But whether for good or ill, I was born. I can hardly plead the verity of an eyewitness, but I am positively certain of the fact. If the occasion

made any impression whatever on memory's tablet, the vital forces have so far failed to bring it to
the recognition of consciousness.   The evidence
to my own mind was a thing of growth.   As the
years passed by it dawned upon me as the shadow
of a great reality.   But the first clear statement of
fact was made to me by mammy.

The reader, whether gentle or otherwise, will
bear in mind that I do not now refer to my mother.
Mother was white; mammy was black.   Mother
taught me propriety and good manners; mammy
laughed at my whims and inflated my vanity.
Mother insisted that my face and hands should be
washed, at least occasionally; mammy permitted
me to play in the mud, and taught me how to make
pots and pies of that material.   Mother had me
placed at the table in a tall armchair, with bib and
napkin properly arranged, and fed on food suited
to my age and station; mammy took me to the
kitchen and allowed me to fish corn dumplings out
of the pot and drink pot liquor out of the ladle.
Mother tried to make me respectable; mammy
made me happy.   Mother wanted me to be wise;
mammy thought I was already so.   I had great respect for mother, and great love for mammy.

In that early period of my life mammy was to
me an important personage.   She was about five
feet high and about three feet through.   Her broad,
woolly head sat far back on a splendid bust, and
was ready to carry anything, from a pail of water
to a basket of vegetables.   Her fat, jolly face was

the very home of good humor, and wore in its natural attitude the breaking movements of a half-
born smile. Her little black eyes constantly
twinkled with good nature.

Mammy's most important business in life was to
look after " ole missus's chillerns.''   As I was the
last of the tribe, she had nearly outlived her occu-
pation, and seemed to have no regrets in the matter.   She enjoyed a monopoly of the business, and
as the perquisites of the office remained the same,
she had no reason to complain of the decline of
the work.

Our relation was one of mutual influence, each
half commanding and half obeying.   It is so delightful to yield to a power that will always bend
at least halfway to our own wishes.   She was in
the lead, but was oftener led.   We were like bi-
nary stars revolving round each other.   She was
my first interpreter, and my infant mind unfolded
to the simple ideas so delightfully seasoned with
unfailing good nature and constant appreciation.

Besides keeping me somewhat in the bounds of
reason, mammy gathered vegetables for the kitch-
en, and assisted Aunt Daphne, the cook, on special occasions, and lent a helping hand about the
housekeeping.

There was one occasion on which mammy always came to the front in fine feather.   That was
hog-killing time.   Mammy was the commanding
genius when it came to saving the lard.   Whole
troops of women were at hand to do the work,

but mammy did the commanding! A general
hog-killing called for the suspension of all other
work. All hands up and astir long before day!
How the fire roared in the frosty air! How the
darkies moved! It was, in fact, a moving time.
A hundred and fifty hogs at a killing was not unusual, and the work was fairly under way by daylight. The man with the ax, from long experience, was expert. He of the knife never failed.
How the men handled the nimble porkers!

Uncle Mike was supreme at the scalding vat.
With two or three assistants, the work went rapidly on. As soon as he pronounced it "good," the
hog was heaved from the vat out on the long platform of rails, and then a half dozen black hands
snatched the loosened hair. The porker was kept
moving down the "run," to make way for others;
and by the time he reached the lower end, the hair
was off, and he was ready for the gambrel stick.
One by one the dressed carcasses were suspended
on long poles. It was a high day for me. How
I reveled among the busy throng! What blowing
up of bladders! For days I sniffed the odor of
cooking lard and fresh meat, till for once I had
enough of the kitchen.

Another important duty for mammy was to make
up the family soap in the spring. This she did
admirably, provided she could get the moon in
proper position; and provided, also, she could pro-
cure a good sassafras stick with which to stir.
There was another considerable trouble with which

she had to contend, and that was to keep the urchins from stirring the pot the wrong way.   That
was stirring it back to lye.

That is what a party leader in Congress does
when he applies the party lash to the members of
the House for having, through mistake, voted for
some good measure contrary to party principles.
The little negro was apt to catch a flogging for
such backwardness, but the Congressman often
owes his reëlection to roundabout practices.   But
my business is with mammy, and not with the Congressman.

Whenever she could manage to get all the conditions in line, and somehow she generally suc-
ceed in that, she always turned out a good supply
of soap.

While engaged in this very important domestic
industry one beautiful spring day, and while holding up the sassafras stick to see the hot fluid drip
off in order to judge of its consistency, it was in
answer to a childish question which mammy
thought was very smart, and which, in her estimation, indicated future greatness, that she exclaimed:
"Law, yes, hunny, you was borned; I minds it
well.   Hit was jest ten years arter the stars fell."

Mammy was in the habit of dating events from
the time the stars fell.   The intelligent reader, if
any such should ever chance to read these pages,
will remember that the great shower of meteors
occurred in 1833, and this will give sufficient intimation as to the time I first saw the light.

The event here recorded, viewed latitudinally, is of very little importance; but longitudinally it is worthy of the very first consideration. The latitudinal view is that which sends out rays of relation on each side, and has reference to all events of simultaneous history. In this view, the birth of a child, as it is but one of thousands of such events taking place every day, is rarely of sufficient importance for any record whatever.

But viewed longitudinally—that is, running along the thread of my own life—it is, for me at least, of the very first moment. It is of such magnitude that it could occur but once. The wise saying that history repeats itself probably does not refer to biography. It evidently does not apply in this case.

From the foregoing remarks it will be seen that human life is comparable to a journey from the equator toward the pole, from the flowery tropic of childhood to the chilly regions of old age and death. "Jest ten years arter de stars fell" I started on this momentous journey.

I was the youngest of the children. My oldest brother, having married, was living some miles away. My oldest sister was the wife of a planter, and lived in another state. I found many advantages in bringing up the rear of the family. I loved to be petted, and much of this fell to me in consequence of my position in the household. I loved liberty. Father and mother, as is often the case, had, as age advanced, become more lenient both to children and servants. In consequence,

many privileges came to me that would have been
denied to an older son. Whether such indulgence
was at the expense of the bone and sinew of character I cannot say. It was certainly very pleasant, and, so far as I know, the sweets of life have
come about as readily to me as to those better dis-
ciplined.

The burden of this chapter is worthy of some
reflection. I sometimes think the fact here recorded is the most surprising part of the history
to be written. Not so strange, perhaps, that people should be born, but marvelously so that I
should have emerged into individual consciousness and separate activity. A failure in any single link in the long chain of events from the beginning of the world, and may be for endless cycles before that, would have resulted in my non-
existence. Millions of people might have been
born, but not I. When there are so many millions
of chances against the occurrence of an event, and
only one chance out of all the millions for it to
happen, is it not strange, wonderfully strange,
that it should ever come to pass? I am therefore
astonished that I was born.

Our earthly existence is a mystery. "Of the
earth earthy," we are built of very common materials, such as are found in rocks, in water, in
plants, in mud, and dust. Yet we are none of
these. Here are the ethereal elements of mind;
the strange thinking faculty, the capacity of link-
ing thought to thought and fact to fact, making a

chain of convictions that no power can break. Then here is the light, fantastic, the boundlessly soaring, the endlessly combining faculty of imagination. Then back of all this is the wonderful will power strangely hedged in beyond the reach of physical force. These splendid faculties are constantly fed by the earth, and yet are immeasurably superior to earth's dull activities.

Nature has given to the different things suitable length of tether. The plant rooted in the soil is intensely local in its dependence. The animal is more at large, roaming about in search of food, and may change his habitat as the conditions of life may require. The animal man is still more independent, as he can prepare and transport his sustenance with him, and is thus able to traverse the great Sahara, the trackless ocean, and even to navigate the air. He claims the whole earth and the fullness thereof as his own abode, and occupies the different apartments at pleasure.

But the mind has a still larger range; its tether is immeasurably extended, so that it gathers food from afar. It unwraps the covering from around the most obscure secrets of nature; it weaves into the web of poesy the beautiful images of manifold being; it makes the impressible atmosphere resonant with the grandest harmonies of music; it analyzes the materials of the great luminary of the heavens by day, and then walks forth among the stars by night, the appreciative observer in the remote depths of space.

Thus is man anchored to the earth, yet lives in all the realm of nature's wide domain. What means this fetter and this freedom? Will the great earth which feeds these faculties claim them as his own and draw them back to himself? or does nature give us such length of strand to encourage the hope and faith that she will finally cut the earthly tie and let us live apart forever? Are not our very best faculties more than earth can give? Then should not Heaven claim his own?

We are all hastening to solve these problems, each for himself in the destiny of his own being. These considerations make life momentous. Man is such a wonderful being that the story of any life must be of thrilling interest. The waking desires, the rise of aspirations, the birth and growth of hope, the genesis and development of love, together with the ripe fruition of life, are themes worthy of any tongue or pen.

# CHAPTER II.

EVERY boy has a budding season. He buds ideas, oddities, and mischief. From this trinity of resources the character of the future man is to be produced. If ideas prevail, the boy develops into a wise man; if oddities, he becomes an eccentric man; if mischief, then comes the disagreeable man. If ideas and oddities are both strongly developed, we have a strong, angular man, a man of sharp corners, apt to be conscientious, and always forceful. If ideas and mischief blend together in large proportions, we have the dangerous man, the revolutionist, or the sharper. If oddities and mischief make up the man, they turn out the scoundrel or the scapegrace.

The boy makes the man as surely as the tadpole makes the frog, and the making is well or ill according to the materials used in the construction.

I suppose I was about an average boy, as these qualities were developed in me in about equal proportions. All these attributes were indicated by the number, variety, and absurdity of questions. My inquisitiveness levied tribute upon the patience of everybody in reach.

A boy thus constituted becomes a veritable, living interrogation point. The very crook of his
(16)

finger is suggestive of that punctuation character. And when he is lying flat of his back on the carpet, with his feet waving in the air, he looks like an interrogation point which has fallen down to laugh at the absurdity of his own questions.

Good health, perfect digestion, and complete assimilation, in a boy, are wonderfully productive of questions. Beef, pork, mutton, chicken, biscuit, butter, molasses, and almost anything else, turn out a large supply. A healthy, growing boy will ask more questions in a day than a dozen query editors of our great papers could answer in a week.

The questions in my case pertained to every department of life and every secret of nature. They were especially noted for frequency, persistency, and audacity. To worry, to puzzle, or to embarrass somebody seemed to be the chief concern of life at that period. I could always worry mother, and generally puzzle mammy, and sometimes embarrass Will Benson, my sister Mary's lover. In asking these questions I was performing the true functions of a boy's life, growing in body and mind, and having a good time. Mammy used to say that I was then " eating my white bread," by which she meant that I was having the happiest time of my life.

This sage remark of mammy's, so often repeated about the white bread, was always a puzzle to me. I had never seen any other than white bread, and why the eating of that should be a symbol of good

2

times was what I could not understand.  In latter
life I have concluded that the phrase originated at
the time when white or sifted flour had not yet
come into general use, but was the food of only
the favored few.  To be able to eat white bread
was then the evidence of superior condition in
life.

But the idea conveyed that I was then seeing
my best days was also a puzzle.  To my mind
nearly everything good was in the future.  While
I had everything necessary to my comfort, still it
was a period of unrest.  I was too eager to get onward to permit intense enjoyment of the present.
It is always so with youth.  The dim figure of
prophecy marches ever before the young.  The
pillar of cloud by day and the pillar of fire by
night are always to the front.  The grand endeav-
or, the brilliant achievement, the successful life
are all in the future.  The manliness of independence, the joys of love, and the rewards of bravery
sparkle like scintillations of hope along the paths
trodden by the young.  Those who walk forth
amid the roses still fresh with the dews of life's
early morning are always looking to the brighter
and richer joys of the midday splendor.  To them
the garden of Eden is still in the future.

When we reach the borders of age, we are apt
to find that our Eden has shifted to the past.  Instead of anticipation we have reverie; memory instead of hope.  Thus it is ever the same in every
age: " the young men see visions and the old men

dream dreams.'' If the genius ever comes to give to the world by chisel or brush the true ideal of youth, it will be a figure of manly beauty, young in years, bending forward in the attitude of rapid walk, with vigorous energy in the step, the countenance lighted with a smile of hope, and the eyes beaming with intense desire, as they peer into the uncertain future.

Surely the hopes of youth are not all, and always, futile. The bright visions are not all delusions. There is no good reason why the bud should be sweeter than the fruit, unless the fruit is of the bitter kind. Surely it is the pessimistic view of life to regard childhood as its best or happiest stage. It is only in lives that are failures that this is true. Men in the haunts of vice, or in the penal cells of confinement, may well sigh for a return to the innocence of youth. The man who meets the demands of life bravely and performs his duties faithfully has no occasion to wish to go a second time over the pains and sorrows of the past. After mature deliberation I conclude that for once mammy was mistaken. Those were not my best days.

One very annoying trouble I had in my early days was that mother insisted on putting me to my book. It was not books in those days, but book. Noah Webster's blue-back speller was the rack on which every child's pleasure had to be tortured. It seemed to me that every time I became particularly interested in play mother or sister would call

out: "Sammy, come say your lesson." Mother
said that she wanted no boobies in her family, and
would hear no excuse. Thus early she began my
education—that is, she began to round off the
oddities, suppress the mischief, and develop the
ideas. As the young ideas began to shoot, she
began to train them through the trellised letters of
the old speller. These branches in time became
stout and self-sustaining, but needed support at first.
The tree of knowledge grows all the more straight
and comely because of proper training. Such a
tree will sometimes grow wonderfully strong and
towering, without apparent help, but is apt to be
rugged and crooked. The man of well-rounded
intellect, correctly poised in moral strength, who
is able to stand forth as a successful champion of
the right, is apt to be the man whose early training has not been neglected, and who shows in the
lineaments of his intellectual character the unmis-
takable traces of a mother's hallowed influence.

# CHAPTER III.

## The Home.

THE greatest blessing of childhood is to have a home. Not simply a place to stay, a locality where he may grow in stature, and perhaps in wickedness, but a real home; a home where parental authority guides, and where the graces of virtue and wisdom preside; a home where love reigns supreme, and molds the home manners; a home where God is recognized, and duty is supreme, and pleasure is not forbidden; a home from whose altar the incense of true worship daily ascends to the great giver of life. Such homes are the nurseries of the church and the bulwarks of the state. Here the better instincts of life are developed, and virtue and wisdom spring forth like angels of peace to make the world better and brighter.

If the home is in the country, all the better. Then if this country home is in the South, all the conditions are complete, and childhood's days are bright indeed. Some of the sweetest recollections of life cluster around the dear old country home in the land of sun and flowers. Home! the place where the soul unbends and the mind grows calm; the place where manhood puts on the armor for the battles of life. No other spot can inspire such sentiments of devotion. No other place is half so sweet with the fragrance of genial love. The love of home is the taproot of patriotism, and from it grows the grand old trunk of national independence.

Those were sunny days: the days of youth on a Southern plantation. Surely no other land could be so productive of reverie and daydreams. What delightful pictures pass in bright procession through the halls of memory as the scenes of childhood come afresh from the stores of the past!

"The First Steps in Geography" with me was to become acquainted with my father's plantation. It was such a delightful study that I must tell the reader its important features. The house sat far back from the road in the midst of grand old forest trees. I am grateful even yet to the original settlers for leaving about forty acres of woodland not to be encroached upon by the ever greedy cotton fields. Through the center of this woodland a wide avenue led from the large gate on the road to the house. The trees, shrubs, and vines of this forest were of nature's own planting. Here were deep shades and tangled masses interspersed with more open spaces, as we are apt to find in wild forest growths.

Around the borders of this wood in the early spring the little meadow blue-bells sprinkled the green earth with tiny gems of beauty. Everywhere, even in the deeper shades, the violets grew in great profusion. Other flowers in succession, as the season advanced, lent beauty to the scenes. In their season the white blooms of the dogwoods, the red ones of the red buds, and the yellow ones of the poplars were objects of special admiration. When the linden trees were in bloom, they gave not only beauty to the scenery, but a rich fragrance to the atmosphere. They attracted the honey bees in such numbers as to produce a constant hum, like a swarm of bees passing through the air.

Animated nature added charms to this wood. There squirrels lived and rabbits hid. Coveys of partridges found retreat in the underbrush, and the limbs of the trees were often loaded with blackbirds. Little wrens and bluebirds sported along the ground. Gay redbirds and beautiful robins played among the foliage. The soft cooing of the dove and the harsh voice of the blue jay mingled in strange contrast. All bird notes were heard, from the sweet, variable songs of the mocking bird to the cawing of the crow. Many a time, while the bright sun peeped down through the leaves and the soft breezes of the south fanned the cheeks of nature, I have for hours lolled on some grassy knoll watching the birds in their loves and the flowers in their beauty.

The avenue from the gate to the house was nearly level. Off to the left, as we approached the dwelling, the land was gently undulating, while to the right it broke into deep hollows. Near the corner of the woodland, in one of these hollows, a cool spring flowed out from under the bluff. The spring

was several hundred yards from the house, but not
so far from the quarters.

Our dwelling had been built with a view to comfort in the Southern clime. It had broad halls and
spacious verandas, where the cool breezes made
leisure delightful. The spacious yard abounded
in shrubbery and flowers; the rich garden teemed
with vegetables; the outhouses were many and
convenient; the quarters, the rows of white houses,
with street between, where the servants lived, were
located a convenient distance from "de big house,"
while near by were the lots and barns for the care
of mules and other stock.

In the rear of the buildings the broad fields extended for more than a mile. The cultivated land
was gently undulating, thus giving proper drainage
and a pleasing variety as to elevation. A broad
valley ran through, giving richness and beauty to
the farm. It looked as if the broad waves of some
mighty ocean had been suddenly arrested in their
action and hardened into solid ground. The large
fields of cotton and smaller ones of corn in summer presented a pleasing variety of living green.
In autumn the cotton fields were white with open
bolls. The fleecy rows looked like banks of snow
in underbrush.

Such was the home of my childhood; a home
to memory dear, and made dearer still because of
a fact which very early came with peculiar force to
my consciousness. That fact is germane to the
truth of this history. It was the existence of

another home near by.   Just beyond the woodland, and almost in front of the big gate on the road at the terminus of the avenue, in a grove not so large as ours, was the home of Mr. Brantlett.   His daughter Susie was just two years younger than I.   The Brantletts were our friends.   The relations between us were never strained.   We interchanged visits informally, and our intercourse was always cordial.

To my childish imagination the bright Southern sun became several degrees brighter on the days when Mrs. Brantlett came over to spend the day and brought Susie, as was always her custom.   I remember well one such day.   It was a perfect day in early summer.   With delight and tender care I led the way to the most cherished retreats in the forest.   Here were mossy banks and there were wild flowers; here the dense, cool shade, there the grapevine swing.   With leafy bowers we constructed playhouses, floored them with moss, and decorated them with flowers.   Let Burns talk about "the golden hours on angels' wings;" I had my angel with me, and took no note of the flying hours nor the texture of their wings.

The spirit of prophecy often hovers about each life.   Sometimes with grim visage, lurking in the shadows, crying, "Woe, woe;" and sometimes with the radiance of hope, whispering, "Peace, peace."   Hence it sometimes happens, we know not why, that our brightest days have a semblance of a shadow and a tinge of sadness.   Sometimes

our joy is intensified by the subtle presence of a
delightful forecast. So it was with me. Some
sweet angel's finger was toying with my spirit's
happiness and painting the riper joys on the far-off
horizon of the future.

But hours, however golden, will, after awhile,
bring us around face to face with some of our oft
returning wants. To us they brought intense
thirst. This, of course, suggested a trip to the
spring. With what joy I assisted Susie down the
steep declivity, while the air grew refreshingly
cooler as we descended!

From the "time to which memory runs not
back" a stake stuck in the ground had held a
crooked-handle gourd by that spring. With what
simple gallantry I took the gourd and handed water
to Susie! Her unfeigned relish for the cool beverage made me glad. The deliciousness of the
water from that gourd! it refreshes my memory
still.

We always had special orders not to play in the
spring branch. As usual, that which was forbidden
was powerfully tempting. I cannot say we were
entirely exemplary. We lingered too long in the
atmosphere of enticement. Among the vivid pictures of those early days, preserved on memory's
scroll, none are more vivid than those of Susie's
little hands playing in the clear, cold water, or her
little, disobedient feet wading in the spring branch.
But our transgressions were cut short by mammy's
watchful eye. We could depend on mammy to

keep our secret and to make us presentable at the
" big house," so that " ole missus " would know
nothing of our playing in the water.    Up the steep
ascent, a narrow path, worn deep by many footsteps,
led us out of the deep ravine.    The air was sensibly warmer as we ascended from the cool water.
We returned home as demurely as if no temptation
had befallen us.    But Susie was too conscientious
for concealment.    A tearful repentance, an honest
confession, and a vow of obedience in the future
put an end to our disobedient wading in the water.
But I must confess that it was hard for me to see
the harm in a transgression so delightful.    'Tis
always so; sin comes with oiled point so smooth
that the sting at first gives only a sensation of
pleasure.

# CHAPTER IV.

## Our Neighbors.

AS I grew older the boundaries of my geographical knowledge extended. In all directions from our home, except north, there were farms like our own. These were joined by others, so that for many miles there was a succession of highly cultivated fields, with intervening reservations of woodland. About a mile and a half south of us, in a lovely grove, was situated Conway Chapel, the church we attended. About halfway between our home and the church was the neat little academy where the young ideas of the neighborhood were woven into the web of culture.

Maj. Allen lived southeast of us on his large plantation. He had two sons, Ben and Joe. They were playmates of mine. Their little sister Minnie was about the age of Susie Brantlett. South, between our house and the academy, lived Maj. Jones. He was a man of excellent culture, and this, in some degree, made up for the smallness of his farm. He worked only about a dozen hands. Southwest lay the magnificent home of Col. Parker. He worked more hands than any other man in the settlement, and was therefore much respected, and his friendship greatly prized. His only son, Adolphus, was a well-grown, fine-looking boy,

(28)

and rather overbearing. He moved about among us boys with the conscious air of great possessions. West was the plantation of 'Squire Benson, whose hopeful son Will was a frequent and not unwelcome visitor at our house. East, just beyond the woodland, as I have before noticed, was the pleasant little home of Mr. Brantlett. Beyond that, old Mr. Webb lived on his large estate. The children were all married and settled in homes of their own. The old people lived in the old homestead in great peace, and greatly respected by all their neighbors. These were our nearest neighbors. Except Mr. Webb's, their plantations joined ours. We were people similarly situated in life, and of similar tastes, and therefore we were congenial and friendly. Our parents visited each other often, and we children were frequently together.

Of course our acquaintance and our neighborly friendships extended further. There were the Smiths, Murphys, Browns, Bufords, Conways, and others. We frequently met these more distant neighbors at church and elsewhere. We occasionally visited each other, and thus maintained friendly relations. But the families to whom I have specially referred were our intimate friends.

North of us was a stretch of hill country, unsuited for large farms. Ours was frequently spoken of as a "border plantation." I very early had a desire to know something of that hill country. One pleasant day in winter I received permission to take two negro boys and go rabbit hunting. I

called up Dick and Jake, who responded with alacrity. As soon as they learned that a rabbit hunt
was on the tapis they began to yell for the dogs.
There was no scarcity of this article on our place.
Nearly every negro had his dog. Here they came,
" mongrel, puppy, whelp, and hound, and curs of
low degree." "Tray, Blanche, Sweetheart, the
little dogs and all," all ready for the fray. With
dogs yelping and jumping, and boys in high glee,
we made toward the hills. Passing the quarters,
we encountered a group of small darkies. One little kinky-headed fellow, grinning out of a round,
black face, ventured the question: "Whar's y'all
gwine?" Each one of them in succession repeated the very same question: "Whar's y'all gwine?"

Dick, showing his white teeth, acted as spokesman for the hunters: "Us's gwine ter ketch a
Molly cottontail." This was his name for rabbit.

We rambled over the hills chasing "har's," as
some of the negroes called them, until we were
more than a mile from home. Dick and Jake
each sported a " Molly cottontail.'

From a lofty eminence we looked down a long
hollow and plainly saw a house. It was a double
log house, or perhaps it would be more properly
classed as a comfortable cabin. In the narrow
valley beyond was a small field cramped in between the hills. White people were passing about.

" Dem's not our sort o' folks," said Dick.

" Dat fiel' ain't no bigger'n a turnip patch," replied Jake.

We at once became explorers. Guided by the sound of an ax, we soon came in sight of a white man cutting wood. A white boy was piling the brush and otherwise helping. The boy was about my age. We judged them to be father and son. They wore coarse clothes, and were evidently used to work.

This was all a revelation to me. I had never heard of these neighbors of ours. Then it was so strange to find them doing work that I had seen colored men do. The man and the boy looked at us kindly enough, and I think would have spoken to us if we had not been so shy.

That night, after we returned home I asked mammy about these people.

"O dem's po' white trash," she said, "moved in down dar; you's mighty wrong, hunny, to go dat fur f'um home, an' 'mung dem folks."

This was not very satisfactory. Next morning I hunted up Uncle George, the carriage driver, and inquired of him.

"Hit's dat feller Henderson I 'spects you seed, sunny," said the old darky kindly. "Heap o' dem po' white folks live over on Plum Creek."

So we had new neighbors. I determined as opportunity offered to find out more about them.

# CHAPTER V.

## In the Quarters.

NEVER was a boy raised on a large plantation in the South who did not love to revel in the quarters. The reader will understand that this is the name universally applied to the village where the servants lived. A boy reached his utmost importance down in the quarters. Smiles and kind words greeted him everywhere. He was "hunny," "sunny," or "young massa," was at full liberty to bound into any cabin unannounced and unceremoniously, and was everywhere welcomed and flattered. The old servants loved to put their hands upon him, or their arms around him, and tell how much he "favored ole massa," or "Mas' George" or "Mas' Charlie," alluding to his uncles or older brothers. The young servants were always ready for a romp "wid young massa."

The most delightful time to study the negro character in the quarters was in autumn by moonlight. The evenings were long, the weather bracing, and life was at full tide. Of course mammy was expected to keep watch over me; but mammy was as fond of the freedom of the quarters after the busy rush of the day was over as was her charge. Then where could I be safer than among her own people? Mammy usually settled

(32)

down in a comfortable corner with Aunt Sally or Aunt 'Lindy for a season of quiet repose, amid whiffs of tobacco smoke and plantation gossip, while I romped around with the "young fry" from one cabin to another with great hilarity.

One such visit I now recall, and will describe. I had not more than reached the grounds and sniffed the signs of fun, when a great commotion in the lower part of the quarters attracted my attention. I heard pious Aunt Lizzie say: "Long Jim is sarvin' de debel, an' leadin' dem young niggers to 'struction." This was probably meant as a warning. But for me it was more than an invitation. It lent speed to my feet.

Sure enough, Long Jim had out his fiddle, and its moving strains were fairly inspiring the devotees of such music. He was surrounded by about thirty negroes, male and female, mostly young, all out in the bright moonshine. They were having, as they expressed it, a regular "breakdown." Such music, accompanied by such dancing! The whole performance was a law unto itself. It was hampered by no rules of art. It was above art. It was genius. The music was like an all-pervading nerve center actuating every movement. Such spirit, such energy, such exuberant life! It was the poetry of motion set to music. It was the rhythmic riot of physical energy prancing in the harness of delight. Among no other people in any part of the world could such a scene have been witnessed. The artificial dances practiced

3

by the *élite*, as compared with this, are like the faint echoes of the far-off reality.

Not far from this group was a much smaller one, actuated by a similar spirit, as if it were a side-show in the wake of a circus. Here was a man sitting on the doorsteps of his cabin making music, or at least keeping time, with two gourds by knocking them together. Two boys were dancing. As they danced, one sang, and both accorded their motions to the words:

> " Fust upon de heel tap, den upon de toe,
>     An' eb'ry time I turn aroun'
>   I jump Jim Crow."

At the other end of the quarters another group was gathered in and around the door of a cabin, singing with a pathos which seemed to be born of the recollections of long ago:

> " O carry me back, O carry me back,
>     To ole Virginny's shore."

Right across the grounds a man or boy came bounding along with a " hop, skip, and a jump," and singing a solo as he went:

> "Jenny crack corn, I don't keer,
>     Ole massa gone away."

In another part of the quarters a lot of boys were turning somersaults, jumping flat-footed, going half-hammered, making three jumps, running and jumping, jumping backward, and otherwise testing strength and skill.

Finally Long Jim's concert made a halt, probably for a rest before taking another heat. As if moved by a common impulse, they struck up with a full chorus of melodious voices:

" Way down upon de S'wanee Riber,
    Far, far away,
Dar's whar my heart is turnin' eber,
    Dar's whar de ole folks stay."

Especially when they reached the chorus there was a swell of voices which was truly inspiring:

"All de worl' am sad an' dreary,
    Eb'rywhar I roam;
O brudder, how my heart grows weary,
    Sighin' for de ole folks at home."

Why words which imply sadness and isolation should be so much in favor with people in such a high tide of social life is a psychological problem I leave the reader to solve.

In one of the cabins several men and women were singing religious songs. One acted as leader by chanting two lines of the hymn, and then all joined in the singing.

All this time talking went on as if nothing else was on hand. They always talked in loud tones, with constant effort at wit and repartee, though of course they knew nothing of these words. It was no uncommon thing for conversation to be carried on by persons on opposite sides of the street. They had no disposition to talk in undertones. A white man will walk fifty yards to talk in low tones to a friend for two or three minutes, about the most trivial matters, rather than put forth the exertion of his vocal organs to make himself understood at that distance. He does this because it

saves labor. Not so with the big-lunged and glib-
tongued slaves of the olden time. For them to
talk was not labor; it was rest and pastime. On
this moonlight night motion and noise had full
sway.

Passing by Uncle Ned's cabin, I saw that he
was holding family worship. If Long Jim was
"sarvin' de debil," not a few of these old negroes
were trying to serve the Lord. They were faithful in their prayers and pious songs. No amount
of mirth in the quarters could interrupt their religious services. It was the general rule with the
negroes in their devotions to pray for " ole massa
an' ole missus " and all their family.

My associations with the servants in the quarters were by no means all demoralizing. Noble
sentiments, spiritual aspirations, patient endurance,
lasting friendships, constant recognition of divine
Providence, and humble submission to the divine
order were prominent characteristics of many of
these truly pious old slaves. Their influence on
me was strong and durable. I was constantly impressed with the thought that if slaves could have
noble qualities of manhood a freeman should have
more. Their religious fervor acted as a powerfully conservative check on the waywardness of
young masters, I am inclined to think that their
influence was afterward felt in the religious tone
of the Confederate armies. They have a genius
for religion, and may yet render the world important service along this line.

# CHAPTER VI.

## In the Fields.

THE cotton fields of the olden time were unique. They were characteristic of the system then regnant. They showed plainly the labor of many hands directed by one mind. There was none of the patchwork division peculiar to lands cultivated by small, independent farmers. Each season had its own peculiar labor, and all was of interest to me. The broad fields gave ample range for my boyish feet. The winters were so mild the men could generally be out at work, and I was apt to be out at something, probably chasing rabbits or baiting traps for birds. Snow fell only occasionally, and then soon melted away. The early part of the winter and sometimes more was occupied in picking cotton. It was always a great desire with us to get the cotton out by Christmas. Then the holidays were enjoyed with more zest. These lasted one week, including Christmas, and ending with the last day of the year. Then came the time for opening ditches, repairing fences, and clearing up land for a new crop. The clearing up was done mostly by the "trash gang." This was made up of women, youngsters, and old men. The able-bodied men had more robust labors.

(37)

The "hands" enlivened their work by songs, jokes, and laughter. In their bright, open faces there was scarcely a trace of care. Their cheerfulness was ever an attraction for me. Whether their jokes were stale or new, they never failed to provoke mirth. These people had the happy faculty of laughing at their own fun. I never knew one to make a repartee that he did not clinch it with a laugh. Often when separated into squads, working in different places, they would respond to each other in song. The squads singing alternate stanzas; or one squad would do the singing, while the others would reply in a kind of chorus. They were a talking, working, singing race. The seasons succeeded each other, bringing a variety of labors, but their cheerfulness continued always fresh.

Behind the "trash gang" came the plows, bedding up the land into long ridges some three or four feet wide. Afterward, when the dogwoods were in bloom, the planting began. The seed were hauled out in wagons and thrown in piles about in the fields as they would be needed. The ridges were opened with a very small plow and the seed sown mostly by women and boys. Each sower had a sack in which the seed were carried. This sack was suspended under the left arm, by a strap over the right shoulder, after the manner of a hunter's horn. The mouth of the sack was within easy reach of the right hand. The seed were sown in great profusion, often covering the whole top of the ridge. A board or light harrow was run over them, and thus the new crop was planted.

Soon after this came " cotton choppin' time," universally recognized as a busy time, a time when " Gineral Green " had to be conquered. Then came the " trash gang " with hoes to the front. The immense fields were cultivated like a garden. I have romped over the soft loose soil after " de secon' goin' ober," and could scarcely find a sprig of grass. It was delightful to look over the broad fields of undulating and varied green. The corn and cotton were of different shades, the corn being darker. Then each had shades of its own. As a rule the crops on the lowlands were darker than those on elevated positions. But the age of the crops, the degree of moisture at the time each piece had been worked, all tend to break the monotony of color, and give a pleasing variety to the aspect of cultivated nature. All the negroes look forward to a season of relaxation or comparative rest after " layin' by time."

All through the long summer days the cotton was blooming. Conditions being favorable, the fields looked white in the morning and crimson in the evenings with the blooms. The cotton bloom is the creature of a day. It is full blown early in the morning, and is then a rich cream color; by night it has turned to red. The next day it is withered and a new set of blooms is undergoing the same changes. Thus the cotton is making a new crop of bolls each day through the blooming season. The bountifulness of the crop for the year depends largely on the fortune that attends the plant during the making season.

Early in the autumn, or rather while the summer yet lingers, the busy picking season comes on. At break of day the hands, each with a large "hamper basket," partially inverted and with the edge resting upon his head, might be seen in long single file making haste to the fields. This was the busiest season of the year, and the meals were usually sent to the fields to save time. As soon as the hands were fairly under way with the picking, the gins started. What a blessing Whitney conferred on the world when he invented the cotton gin! The gins were a perpetual source of interest to me. I remember with what delight I first caught the idea as to how the brush wheel took the lint from the saws. Then the big cotton press with its long levers sweeping around in the air! I have always been sorry that the famous Don Quixote did not encounter one of these old-fashioned cotton presses. It would have been a giant worthy of his bravery. But he and Rocinante might have fared badly, and poor Sancho would have had fresh cause to lament.

The starting of the gins was the signal for the wagons to take the road. In those days before railroads the cotton had to be hauled some thirty miles to the river. Three wagons were usually put on the road. Each wagon had six large mules.

It was grand to see this wagon train put in trim, with every convenience for traveling and camping out. At least two mules in each team were decorated with bells. Four or five small bells were suspended from a brass bow which extended in a semicircle above the withers, being attached to the mule's harness. I never knew the use of the bells, unless it was to keep the mules from being frightened at unusual noises. But whether for use or ornament, they were the pride and joy of the wagoners. Jack was the chief wagoner, and to him was intrusted the oversight of the whole train. His was a position of trust and honor, and he appreciated it most highly. Jack was of yellow complexion, stout build, sinewy and muscular. Intelligence was stamped on every feature. Never did an engineer bound into his cab and lay his hand on the lever with an air of more importance than that with which Jack mounted his saddle mule and drew the line over his leader.

Amid the jingle of bells and the flourish of whips the wagons, each carrying six bales of cotton, started for their destination. It was desirable that the wagons from several plantations should go together for mutual protection and help. The return of the wagons was an event to be noted. With what dignity Jack drove in his team and reported to "ole massa!" Then what stores of sugar, coffee, molasses, tea, mackerel, and sometimes oysters! The wagon train was the connecting link between us and the outside world. It brought tidings as well as good things from afar. And Jack was chief of that train! Jack was a hero; he was a traveled man, and had seen the world. He talked about the big river and its wonderful mysteries, about fine steamboats and their all-powerful captains. The young negroes on the place looked to his position as the youths of America look to the presidency: as the highest position it is possible to reach.

Other industries were carried on which, though not so prominent, were, nevertheless, valuable. Quite a number of women, from various causes, did not go regularly to the fields. These did the spinning, weaving, and sewing for the hands. Thus the plantation was a community of itself. The necessaries of life were raised or manufactured. Few things needed to be bought. There was very little extravagance, no dissipation, no wasted energy among the members of the little community. Good export crops were grown every year. No wonder the signs of prosperity increased on every hand.

As I remember those early days of simplicity and constant work, they were days full of contentment and cheerfulness. On the return of the wagons in the early fall, when, as a special favor, some of the luxuries of life, such as sugar, coffee, a larger ration of molasses, and sometimes (for we were not yet wise on the temperance question) a " leetle ob de critter to raise de sperits " were issued to the hands, the quarters became scenes of unusual mirthfulness.  Long Jim's concerts would take on new proportions, but would even then be almost rivaled by squads of young bucks "patting juber."  This last exercise was one for a boy to remember.  They would pat themselves with both hands, frequently slapping their hands together, making a rythmic sound to which others and sometimes the patters themselves would "trip the light fantastic."

The amount of activity to be gotten out of this performance was wonderful.  When once fairly under way, they would pat themselves from the shoulders all the way down to the feet.  Every muscle was in lively exercise, even the tongue contributing to the effect: "Juber dis an' juber dat, an' juber killed de yaller cat."  Thus in the absence of all instruments the negro's love of music was gratified.

# CHAPTER VII.

## AT THE MEETING.

FATHER always insisted that the colored people should have religious privileges. They always enjoyed such privileges on our place. The missionary came round regularly every month. There was always some colored exhorter or preacher to hold meetings on the intervening Sabbaths. Services were generally held in the afternoon. I frequently went with mammy to these meetings. They were never without interest. The simple and abiding faith of these people seemed always to insure the divine presence. They lived constantly on that plane of humility where God most readily touches humanity. Their prayers were direct appeals to the ever present God. Sometimes their exhortations had an unction born of a mighty faith. Their songs were a benediction. Their shouting, in which exercise they were not wanting, was as the triumphs of Israel over his enemies. Their spiritual enjoyment was born of a divine life in the soul.

Father sometimes attended their meetings, and they always did him the honor to call on him to pray. This was generally at the close of the services, for they seemed to think it indecorous to call on "ole massa" to pray in the midst of confusion,

(44)

and therefore waited till the emotional excitement had mostly subsided. Father's prayers were short, fervent, and adapted to the occasion. The next morning after one of these services, I heard mother ask Joe, the man who made fires and waited about the house, what sort of meeting they had last night. " O, mighty fine, missus, mighty fine," he said. " We allus has a good time when John preaches and I 'zorts and massa 'cludes meetin'."

But the great time with them was when the missionary came round. Then there was a general turnout and more interest was manifested. There were several of the more intelligent men, and I mention Jack the wagoner as one of them, who did not much care to listen to the home talent. They wanted something better—wanted instruction. As a natural result the home talent was not pleased with them and held them in some degree of suspicion. The home preachers thought the cause should be sufficient inspiration, and to wait for the missionary was to distrust God and take too much to man. Thus it was among them as among all people: intelligence looked for the means of feeding intelligence, while ignorance became sore and sensitive on account of supposed neglect.

Their worship was not of the silent sort. Cries of " Dat's de truff," " Yes, Lord," " Hallelujah," " Bless de Lord " were frequently heard from all parts of the house, especially from " de amen cornder." They had a peculiarity in their worship I have never heard of among any other people. It

was a sort of humming in rhythmic measure. No
words were spoken, but a semivocal sound was
prolonged into a tune in which large numbers
would join. This frequently ended in open shouts
and hallelujahs.

On all occasions they were ready to " speak out
in de meetin'." Uncle Sam was especially noted
in this regard—in fact, he was a noted character.
He was a stout old man, of great dignity of manner and of excellent character. His white head
and massive features and solemn mien marked him
as a patriarch of the Church. He always occupied
a prominent seat near the pulpit. His outspoken
sanctions, comments, or observations were sometimes embarrassing, but most generally helpful to
the preacher. On one occasion the missionary
was dwelling with happy effect on the text, " They
desire a better country." He was describing that
country as fairer than anything mortal eyes had
ever beheld when Uncle Sam asked: " Brudder,
who lives in dat country?" The preacher at once
caught on a higher strain as he told of Abraham,
Isaac, and Jacob, of the prophets, apostles, and
martyrs, of the great company which no man could
number, of every nation and race, including our
own loved ones gone before, all living happily in
that blessed country. " What is all dese folks
doin' in dat country?" In response to this question the preacher told how the people were resting
under the shade of the trees by the river of life;
how they were shouting, singing, and praising

God; how they wore the robes of white and waved the palms of victory over sin and sorrow. "Is dat a healthy country, brudder?" The preacher replied: "No doctors in that country; nobody was ever sick there. There never was a funeral in that country, and never will be. Those who live there will live forever." "Now, brudder, please tell us," the old negro's lips quivered as he asked the question, "Now, brudder, please tell us, can a poor man what ain't got no money git a home in dat country?" This question was too much for the audience and almost upset the preacher. Feeling had grown more intense with each question and answer. It now reached white heat. The preacher could scarcely keep control of his congregation or himself while he explained that homes were obtained in that country without money and without price.

The scene that followed is not easily described. It was one in which intense feeling found expression in motion and noise. By stamping or patting with the feet on the floor, and striking the benches with the hands, a constant noise was kept up. All this racket seemed naturally to fall into measured time and rhythmic flow, in exact accord with the feeling of the occasion. They had music in their souls, and every motion fell into that line. All over the house nodding heads kept time to the song of the soul. Several women were up jumping and shouting, but this seemed to bring no disturbance to the harmony of the occasion. Two or three

strong men sprang up and threw themselves reck-
lessly backward into the audience, but were caught
by strong hands, so that no one was hurt.

This exercise was followed by a more subdued
feeling, more calm and mellowed expressions.
Just at this time a party struck up a lively air—a
real dancing tune. Several women sprang to their
feet and danced to the music in a manner that
would have been no disgrace to one of Long Jim's
moonlight performances. Aunt Lizzie, the very
woman who said Long Jim was "leadin' de young
niggers to 'struction," was one of the dancers. I
do not know how she would have explained the
matter. She would probably have said: "Dat
was de debil's work, and dis is de Lord's sarvice."

It was quite the fashion for the young couples on
the place to marry in the church. There was a
very awkward, gawky fellow by the name of Ike.
Ike wore a skin that must have received the last
shade of the dark continent. Its glossy finish was
a sufficient evidence of its purity. Ike was not deficient in features, especially as to nose and lips.
One thing redeemed him from ugliness, and that
was his pearly white teeth. Altogether he did
not seem to be very taking. But considering the
strange freaks of a woman's love, it is not very
surprising that Ike succeeded in winning the hand
of a very plump, saucy-looking girl of eighteen
summers. As usual, the wedding was appointed for
Sunday afternoon. Ike seemed even more awkward at the hymeneal altar. When the preacher

ended the ceremony by which the twain were made one, Ike stood with his big lips sprung apart and was at a loss how to act. His big hands seemed to be wonderfully in his way. His big feet looked like they were glued to the floor. The suspense was biting, but was soon broken by a lusty voice from the audience: "Why don't you salute de bride, nigger?" This was the signal for a general laugh and much handshaking. And the meeting broke up in great good humor.

John was at times strangely eloquent. Considering that he was a regular field hand, doing full work every day in the week, I was astonished at the way he could preach on Sunday. I was the more interested in him because he used to want me to read the Bible to him. I have often heard him make the most effective use of the very passages he learned from my reading. On one occasion in particular he seemed almost like one inspired. It was Sunday afternoon. All the people were out, and many from the neighboring plantations were present. It was an important funeral occasion. A very good man on the place had died. The name of the man was Tom. As he came from the Weaver estate, he was called Tom Weaver to distinguish him from another Tom on the place.

I give only the concluding part of the sermon. Excitement was running high as the preacher reached the peroration:

"Ole Massa above is callin' us home. ["Yes, Lord."] Tom Weaver's done hyerd dat call an'

4

gone. ["Yes, Lord."] He's no more gwine to de
fiel's at daylight; but is singin' an' shoutin' all day
among de angels an' tellin' how Jesus helped his
po' soul outen de sinful worl'. ["Truff, Lord,
hallelujah!"] Night afore las' Sis' Lizzie an' me
was down to Tom's house, an' Tom says to me:
'Brudder John, I's almos' home. [Audible crying.] I wants you an' Sis' Lizzie to pray to Jesus
to help me ober de ribber.' Hit was pas' midnight,
an' de candle was a burnin' dimlike on de hath,
and Sis' Lizzie an' me we got down an' we prayed
an' prayed, an' de Holy Ghos' jes' come down in
our souls. [Cries of "Bless de Lord!"] An' Tom
he lifts his han' all a tremblin' an' p'inted right up
toward heben. We knowed de Lord was a
comin' for Tom. Sis' Lizzie she fetch de candle,
an' sich eyes as Tom did have! He looked like
he was a lookin' right up inter glory. [" Bless de
Lord!"] An' hit appeared dat de chariot ob de
Lord come right down in dat cabin and Tom went
up to glory. [Cries of " Hallelujah!"] Bless de
Lord, I's been happy eber since dat night. [Gen-
eral shouting; but the preacher rose above the
noise and continued.] Tom's an angel now.
["Dat's so; bless de Lord!"] Jes' look at him
ober dare!" The preacher seemed rapt as seeing the invisible, and pointing the way his eyes
were looking he repeated: "Jes' look at him ober
dare!" He's a lookin' right up in de face of Jesus
an' singin' de song ob Moses an' de Lam'. [" Hallelujah!"] Dis [pointing toward the corpse] is not

Tom Weaver. Dis is de ole hull arter de cotton is done picked out. ["Dat's de truff!"] Tom's up yonder! [" Pointing again toward the invisible."] How his face do shine! Dat looks like Tom when all de sin an' sorrow an' crime has done been taken f'om him. Dat's Tom, done changed to an angel. ["Glory! glory! glory!"] Dis [pointing to the corpse] is Tom's ole cabin lef' down here for de Lord to make a mansion outen. [Shouting all over the house. But above the roar of the shouts of victory the preacher's voice rang out clear and distinct like bugle notes as he continued.] Dat is Tom Weaver [still pointing to the invisible] wearin' de crown ob glory. See dat harp in his han'! Don' you see he favors Jesus? Jes' see him wave dat palm! Shout on, Tom. Dese ole han's o' mine will arter awhile grasp a harp an' wave a palm! Yes, bless de Lord, I's comin'.

> Sink down ye separatin' hills,
>   Let sin an' death remove,
> 'Tis love that drives my chariot wheels,
>   An' death mus' yiel' to love."

It was a long time before the excitement mellowed down. Then the honored negro was laid to rest in the silent grave, and the mourners, in the dusk of evening, returned to their quarters.

# CHAPTER VIII.

## IN THE KITCHEN.

WAS ever a boy raised who did not love the kitchen? As well try to find a magnet without polarity. The magnetic part of boy is his stomach, and it is as true to the kitchen as the needle to the pole. I feel the need of some domestic muse to sing the charms and the mysteries of my mother's kitchen. But from the " vasty deep" or elsewhere the Muses come not to the hapless man who has no voice to sing. Therefore, in prosaic periods, I must tell of the scenes which so often ministered soothing palliatives to my tender youth.

Than a growing boy no animal on earth can, on short notice, get up an appetite of keener edge; such appetites without a kitchen would be a calamity. And a kitchen without appetites would be useless. Appetites and kitchens fit each other like framework dovetailed together. In most things we are coworkers with the divine nature. So in this case; God gives the appetite; man or woman has devised the kitchen. But a hungry boy has no time for such speculations. However crooked in his ways, he is always straightforward in his route to the kitchen. However tardy his disposition or his feet in the path of parental requirements, he is ever prompt to obey the calls of hunger.

(52)

But the boy is not alone in his weakness on the side next to the kitchen.    It is a trite, but alas! too often it is a true saying, that the nearest course to a man's heart is by way of his stomach.    The man of splendid dinners is apt to be popular. Many schemes of state policy have ridden into favor on roast meat and blushing wine.    Puncture human nature anywhere, and the cuticle of selfishness is the first thing you touch.    And of all the component parts of that wonderful nature this cuticle is the most sensitive.    The nerves not only of appetite, but of pride, ambition, greed, lust, and love, spread themselves there into an intertwining network so compact that not even the needle points of honor and justice can penetrate without a sense of pain!

But I am moralizing away from the kitchen. Grand old kitchen!    Memory stands with bared head and bending form looking through a wreath of smiles, down the aisle of years gone by, to the picture of my childhood's happy hours in the dear old kitchen!    Aunt Daphne, black, fat, and jolly, with laughing face, was the presiding genius. There is the fireplace with its immense wood fire. In one corner stands the iron crane ready to swing the "pots" on and off the fire.    On the long side table are two whole pigs thoroughly roasted, each with a red apple in its mouth.    Two rabbits, each suspended by a cord, are roasting before the fire. An attendant is keeping them saturated with gravy. Simmering by the fire is the great kettle containing a meat pie nearly large enough to feed a regiment. Great "pones" of light bread are stacked about. There are cakes of all sizes and varieties. Negroes great and small, each wearing a white head cloth, are running here and there doing this and attending to that with an alacrity that makes labor a delight. Aunt Daphne sits as a queen in her own dominion giving orders and guiding the destinies of things. This is the picture of the reality I saw on a Christmas eve day in the home of my childhood. The servants, as well as their masters, were to have a feast on Christmas, and this was the preparation for the great occasion.

It was a day of great expectations. A week of holiday after the steady work of the year was something to be prized. Then many of the servants had reason to expect additional favors. The negro's natural talent for cheerfulness and hilarity reached its maximum swell on Christmas eve. At night the Christmas frolic began. Long Jim was the hero of the hour. He knew it, and magnified his opportunity. Uncle Sam the patriarch, John the preacher, and Joe the exhorter were for the time relegated to places of honorable retirement. The young negroes said:

> "We's got Chris'mas in our bones,
> De fiddle's got Chris'mas in its tones." ·

A lover of music might have gratified two senses at once: the fiddle playing music to the ear and the feet speaking music to the eye. The "sound of revelry" continued far into the night—in fact, some of the negroes were up so late and others so early there was scarcely a lull in the hilarity during the whole night.

About daylight troops of servants gathered about " de big house;" old reliable hands on the place behaving with the gravity becoming their position, young lads full of life and fun, "small fry" leaping and prancing with excess of joy. A constant murmur of suppressed vociferation, of gay and festive impulses, showed that they had come with Christmas greetings. As soon as a door or window was thrown open they began to shout " Christmas gift" to " ole massa" and " ole missus," to " young massa" and "young missus," and to everybody else who happened to be present. Gifts were distributed, while some of the older men and women were invited around to the closet and treated to a Christmas toddy. This was a mark of special favor, and was so received.

That Christmas day the weather was delightful. My older brother and his wife, my older sister and her husband, with the little ones of both couples, were on a visit to the old home. It was to be a feast day, and two neighboring families, the Allens and the Brantletts, had also been invited to dine with us. I was glad at any time to have a day of pleasant romp with Ben and Joe Allen. Their sister Minnie was a pleasant little girl. But I was most delighted that Susie Brantlett was of the company; her very presence was joy. Then she took it so much as a matter of course that I appropriated so much of her company to myself. We children took great interest in all that was going on, especially in what was being done in the kitchen. Things there were growing constantly more to our taste. In the midst of all the confusion we could see a method laboring to an end. These indications we regarded with special delight.

A side table in the dining room became the center of attraction. It was spread with a cloth of snowy whiteness and decorated with flowers from the greenhouse. A large China bowl or tureen was in the center containing a silver ladle. Mammy was presiding here, and officiated with the dignity of a sibyl offering oblations to a sylvan deity. When all was ready, " ole massa " was called in to give final directions. Following him were two little negroes, one bringing the decanter and the other a basket of eggs. The design was evident. The Christmas eggnog was now to be made. The proceeding was watched with peculiar interest by all the servants who could venture up close enough to see. The interest thus manifested was not without a reason; for on this annual festival it was the custom to distribute the eggnog among all the servants who were supposed to be old enough to love it. Our fathers indulged in this convivial custom with never a thought that they were sowing the seeds of fearful temptation for the generations following.

We were all well pleased—especially was this true of my sister Mary—by the arrival of Will Benson to take part in the festivities. Will was a genial, good fellow, and added much to the *bon-homie* of any company. But somehow it appeared to me that he was not particularly concerned about the company that day.

Keeping an eye as usual on the kitchen and its annex, the dining room, we found that things there were rounding to a beautiful consistency. A side table in the dining room the exact image as to its top dressing of the larger one was set for the children. We little men and women very keenly appreciated this token of respect. With' mammy to wait on us, and with Susie by my side, and with little companions to appreciate the hospitality, it could not fail to be a high day with me.

Ours was not the home of oppressive ceremony. From the times to which my memory runs not back, three courses at dinner were regarded as amply sufficient for any occasion: first soup, then meats and vegetables, and lastly cake and fruit. These courses, with coffee or milk as per taste, enlivened by genial and general conversation, made a meal which lords and ladies might have enjoyed.

Next to enjoying a good dinner is to see some one else enjoy one. So when the company left the table, the ladies to gossip, the gentlemen to discuss politics, and Will and sister to revel in love's sweet dreams, we boys repaired to the kitchen to enjoy the relish with which the servants received their dinner. As they all could not eat in the kitchen, temporary tables had been prepared in the back

yard, and loads after loads of provisions were carried out.   The older servants had charge, and the
utmost decorum prevailed.   It was a pleasure to
see how the young bucks bowed reverently to their
seniors and anticipated every wish of the dusky
maidens.   They probably had never heard of
Cupid, but the principle represented by that gay
little deity was as active that day as he could have
been in any similar assembly in any part of the
world.   Fewer preliminaries lay in the way of consummated love with these than with any other people.   Good nature, light-heartedness, the absence
of all care, the entire exemption from anxious
thought were plainly visible in every face.

The perfect picture of placid contentment which
has clung to memory through all these years was
presented by old Mike.   He was a large, good-
natured old fellow, evidently the man to enjoy a
good dinner and a good rest after it was eaten.
The dinner he had enjoyed.   To make it more
complete, it had been spiced with a cup of good
coffee.   He had managed to save over his mug of
eggnog, or, which is more probable, had succeeded in getting a second supply.   He was sitting
in his chair with his chest thrown back, one leg
stretched out at full length, while a permanent
smile rested on his placid countenance.   Saying
but little while hilarity was holding high carnival
around him, he was sipping the delightful beverage
in a way to prolong the taste.   It was not in his
nature to sigh for a long neck, but he did the more

sensible thing of lengthening out the potations. He was the very expression of contentment.

" Hello, Uncle Mike," said a pert youngster, " is yer gwine ter git tipsy on yer eggnog?"

" Go on, nigger," was Uncle Mike's reply, " you ain' wuff a ni' pence nohow;" and with this good-natured thrust Uncle Mike's face lighted up with a still richer glow of satisfaction.

# CHAPTER IX.

## CARE OF THE SICK.

THE negroes were a remarkably healthy race. T he invalid was practically unknown. They frequently had colds in winter, but consumption was very rarely found. Their diseases were mostly the result of a malarious climate. The soil was full of *humus*, rich and moist, and produced chills with nearly as much certainty as it produced cotton. But the chills were usually of a mild type and easily cured. The negroes were substantially fed, comfortably clothed, and had prompt medical attention when needed. Such conditions, with the absence of care, were conducive to health. Nevertheless the country practitioner was a familiar personage in the quarters. He was promptly called when a case seemed to be serious.

It was father's rule to see that the hands had proper attention when sick. The milder cases were attended to without the aid of a physician, as father had from long experience become expert in the management of ordinary diseases. Much of his success was due to faithful nursing. He would rise at any time of night, if necessary, to see that medicines were properly given. A supply of drugs was always on hand, so that in cases of emergency, as well as in milder attacks of sickness, suffering might be relieved. Both humanity and pecuniary interest prompted to this course.

Many of my errands to the quarters were in the interest of the sick. I was sent to carry simple remedies or to inquire about a patient. Many were the profound, if not wise, discourses and dark intimations to which I have listened concerning diseases, and their causes and cures. There was a strong tendency among the negroes to be fatalists. Calamities came by divine appointment. Disease and death were unalterably fixed in the plans of Providence. The negroes rarely ever looked to imprudence or local causes to account for these things. God willed it so, and they could only submit.

But there was a class of diseases, so the negroes thought, that was not in the order of God's providence; disease not reached by the doctor's medicine. Man was to a great extent, through some evil influence, responsible for much of the discomfort to which man is liable. The old superstition of the evil eye seemed to be rife among them. Alf said: "No sooner'n ole Ned looked at me, I felt de pains in de hip j'ints." This is but a sample case. They believed in a sort of witchcraft known as "conjuring." Some people, so they thought, had the power of producing spells. This was accomplished in some profoundly mysterious way by a mummery of senseless words over a rabbit's foot, a snake's head, or certain bones of an

animal. When one felt sick and did not know what
was the matter, he was apt to conclude he was
"tricked." This led to many broils and many
estrangements. So true is it that imaginary ills
make up no inconsiderable part of those that flesh
is heir to.

Some of the negroes encouraged a belief in their
supernatural power. True, that made them objects of suspicion and aversion. But they were
feared; were often a cause of terror. The innate
love of power asserted itself. We all have a natural longing for a connection with the invisible
and spiritual. This is especially true of the negro
race. This feeling usually led to noble aspirations
for communion with God. But a few turned to
the darkly mysterious, and hence here and there
a man or woman was found carrying about some
mysterious charms, as heads of snakes or lizards,
or the bones and feet of some small animal.

And many were their victims, and strange were
their complaints. Those who imagined themselves
affected could feel lizards and scorpions and even
huge serpents crawling through their bodies. I
remember one man of robust frame and ordinary
intelligence, pointing to his large forearm, and
telling me that he saw a snake come down his
arm just under the skin. It came down to his
wrist and then doubled back and crawled away
into his body. I questioned him closely, and he
said that he actually saw and felt the snake. It
was some three feet long and an inch in diameter,

and it was at that very time running riot in every part of his body.   Another negro, a blacksmith, a man of more intelligence than an ordinary field hand, said that he had no doubt these things were so.   He had been troubled himself.   He just the other day while at work drew his hand across his forehead to wipe away the " sweat," and brushed a full-grown lizard from his brow.   He could not be mistaken, he said, for he saw it plainly when it fell to the ground.   It remained in sight but for an instant, but long enough for him to get a good look at it,   These superstitions were realities to them.   The least encouragement would lead them on to tell a whole train of evils, evils no less af- flictive because imaginary.   It is one of the great blessings of enlightenment that we get rid of so many imaginary ills.   How many yet remain, even among educated people !

Superstitious diseases called for superstitious remedies.   Rabbit foot against rabbit foot.   Cer- tain persons had power to remove " spells." There were always " spells " to be removed, and some of the cures were marvelous.   Thus a double practice went on in the quarters.   The man of sci- ence looked at the tongue, felt the pulse, and measured his powders or applied his opodeldoc. The man, or oftener the woman, of superstition mumbled over the lizard heads, spoke unmeaning words, and looked mysterious.   Cures generally followed in either case.

With what tenacity superstition clings to the

mind! It is like some indelible tracery on fine linen, which, after many efforts to remove, may still be dimly seen. Reason did not avail. The more I argued the more they asserted. What they had felt and seen with confidence they told. Ridicule was better. The man who gets the laugh on his side has more than half gained the victory. But victories over superstition are apt to be temporary. When the mind settles back to its normal quietude, the dark streaks, though dim, are still to be found there. The stern authority of the master was best of all. That at least stopped the complaints. Father had no patience with such folly.

Amusing instances sometimes occurred. One day Short Jim came in with the backache. It was in the midst of the busiest season. This was natural: aches have a tendency to assert themselves at such times. The case was duly reported at the house, and father went down. As I had no important engagements just at that time, I followed after him. Jim was a short, fat young fellow, the very picture of health. I stopped by the way and asked Aunt Lizzie what was the matter with Jim. Emphasizing her opinion in advance by a very significant grunt, she replied: "Dat nigger is jes possomin." I found Jim doing some very ostentatious grunting. Father's manner was very much in accord with Aunt Lizzie's opinion. Fortunately, for aches father had one great remedy—that was the Jew David plaster. Jew David was the specific in all backaches, sideaches, and aches in general. Everything but the toothache. This plaster came on in little tin boxes, and had to be heated and spread on a cloth to be used. Jew David had at least one noble quality, the same which a presiding elder so highly prized in some of his preachers: stickability. It settled down with an air of something that had come to stay. Be it said to its praise: it "sticks to its business." Faithfulness was probably not its only virtue, but it was certainly one of the chief.

Father always went about the preparation of the plaster with the manner of a man who knew that he was doing the proper thing. There was an air of precision and alacrity. He knew exactly how it should be done. I remember so well how he placed the thumb and forefinger of the left hand on opposite corners of the cloth, and then, with knife in exact position, the hot plaster was taken from the box and spread. He said that the plaster should be applied hot. Heat was a great advantage. The plaster stuck better, and was more effective. If it blistered, all the better. That was counter irritation, and counter irritation was the thing. If the plaster blistered, it also cured the blister by excluding the air. Well, the plaster was prepared in due form, and heated to a pitch every way satisfactory. Jim was ready, so there was no loss of caloric in transit from fire to back. The effect was magical! Jim's exclamation, "O massa!" would require at least five exclamation points to give the reader an idea of the surprise it ex-

pressed. But his right hand was still more de-
monstrative. Catching the plaster by one corner,
he snatched it entirely off. It fairly popped as it
loosened its hold. Now father did not like trifling
where Jew David was concerned. So, reaching
for a shingle, he gave Jim a few lively spanks
which restored him to calmness and reason.

Jim said that he was entirely well, never felt better, and was only too anxious to go to work. But
father quietly remarked that the plaster would keep
him well. It was duly heated again, and Jim received it meekly, and went cheerfully to work. It
was evidently his first experience with the plaster,
and was likely to be the last for some time. The
negroes were wonderfully interested in Jim's backache. For several weeks they scarcely missed an
opportunity to ask him about his back. I think
the back got to be a sore subject with Jim. But
somehow it seemed to afford a good deal of amusement to the others. In this case, as in many others, Jew David maintained its high reputation. The
cure was instantaneous and permanent.

# CHAPTER X.

## THE FUNERAL.

ONE day the quiet of our homes was disturbed by the arrival of a messenger bringing news that Mr. Webb was very sick. Uncle George was ordered to get the carriage ready, and mother took me and went over. When we arrived, we found some of the neighbors already in attendance. Two doctors were present, the servants moved about with anxious faces, spoke in low tones, and went on tiptoe when they had occasion to enter the chamber of the sick. Mrs. Webb was completely broken down with apprehension. All indications pointed to the worst. When I fully comprehended the situation, a chill of gloom came over me. I had never before been so near face to face with the grim monster. By the bedside of the sick man stood his faithful old foreman, Uncle Ephriam, anxious to anticipate every wish in his power to alleviate his master's suffering. The servants were all attentive, grief-stricken, and seemed anxious to be told to do something; so solicitous were they to assist, if possible, in turning aside a calamity so much dreaded.

As it was not necessary for mother to sit up, we returned home in the evening; but continued our visits every day. The members of the family met

(67)

the emergency by all the tender and soothing attentions which love and veneration could suggest. This was natural, and was to be expected. But I was deeply impressed with the solicitude manifested by the servants. They were of a different race, occupied the place of menials, and held in perpetual servitude by a force they were unable to resist. Now the very man who more immediately represented that force to them, and in whose service they had grown up from infancy, was passing away. I doubt whether any of them would have been more concerned if one of the dearest of their own kindred had been about to die.

The third day there was apparently a change for the better. The sign of hope was plainly visible on the faces of all the servants, even more than upon those of the whites. It looked like a bright morning was about to dawn after a night of terrors. Old Ephriam looked almost rejuvenated. But the hopes of the faithful old servant were of short duration. That night a change for the worse was so decided that death ensued before morning.

The day following was one of great sadness. The servants were almost in despair. Their loss was truly great. The loss of a good master was about the greatest loss a slave could sustain. The expression of mingled grief and anxiety so visible on every face made a lasting impression on my mind. Their grief was genuine; their anxiety was not without cause. They loved their master.

His death had touched the wellspring, and every wrong had been forgiven and every complaint forgotten. They followed him to the grave with a sorrow that was as real as it was pathetic. They knew full well that his death would bring changes to them. The old home and the old associations would probably all be broken up. Relations that had subsisted from infancy were now to be dissolved. New masters, younger and more vigorous, would now take charge. Young masters are apt to have fortunes to make, and the negroes knew that the making would be required of them. It was therefore natural that anxiety should mingle with their sorrow. I was also impressed with the simplicity of their trust in an overruling Providence, and with what promptness and force their religious convictions came to their support in this hour of distress.

But while I was musing upon these things, my spirit shadowed by the signs and cries of distress around me, a familiar carriage was drawn up, and I saw that Mrs. Brantlett had brought Susie. The little creature was overawed by the solemnity of the occasion, and saddened by the moans of grief, but her presence was sunshine to me. I soon contrived an excuse for a walk in the garden. There, among the flowers and shrubbery, gloom and sadness melted away like snow in summer. Though almost in the very presence of death, and still hearing the sounds of sorrow which ever and anon came up from the quarters, our spirits brightened in

the glow of life's bright youth and budding hopes.
Extremes had met. The winter of gloom and the
sunshine of spring lay alongside of each other.
There in the house were age and death and sorrow; here in the garden were youth, love, and joy.
It was like certain places in Switzerland where
winter rules with a frozen scepter in undisputed
sovereignty over the giant mountains, while spring
crowns with brightest flowers the vale below.

'Tis ever thus in the world's broad history. The
tears of sorrow and the smiles of joy are bathed
in the same bright sunshine and fanned by the
same gentle breeze. The wedding march and the
funeral procession often keep step to the same
strain of nature's music.

But the hour for interment came, and we formed
a procession out to the family graveyard, where,
with appropriate ceremonies, the remains were laid
to rest. Some stout, young servants came forward
with spades to fill the grave. They looked as if
they were burying their own hopes beneath every
spadeful of dirt. After the grave had been taste-
fully decorated with flowers and evergreens, and
the white people were turning slowly and sadly
away, the servants gathered closely around the
tomb. Some of them had brought flowers, with
which the freshly raised mound was strewn. I
was surprised, if not amused, to see the kinds of
flowers they brought. They were pinks, holly-
hocks, poppies, bachelor's buttons, and touch-me-
nots, such as grew around their cabin doors; but

they were the tributes of real affection. Others fell down in complete *abandon* of sorrow, and some found relief in tears. Some were praying aloud, and others with silent grief. After awhile they seemed to find some relief in singing a song peculiarly pathetic and sadly appropriate. One stanza of that song I now remember:

> Down in de co'n fiel',
> Hear dat mo'nful soun';
> All de darkies am a weepin':
> Massa's in be col', col' groun'.

# CHAPTER XI.

## ATTENDING CHURCH.

ONE Saturday our family was thrown into a flutter of delightful expectancy by a visit from the pastor, who informed us that the bishop, in passing, would spend a couple of days at our house, and would also preach at Conway's Chapel tomorrow. As we had never had the honor of entertaining one of our bishops, this was rare news, and at once rare preparations were made to receive the distinguished guests. I say guests because the bishop was accompanied by another distinguished preacher, who was looking after some important interest of the Church. The great simplicity, the air of homelike familiarity, and fatherly bearing with which they entered our home put every one of us at ease. We at once grouped about them in the attitude of listeners, while they did the talking. And such talking!

Their stay at our house was to me an intellectual epoch. It was the uplifting of the soul; a clearing of the mental vision; an expanding of the imagination! They were acquainted with every part of the Church. They talked about the work along all the Mississippi and its tributaries; along the Alleghanies; on the Atlantic and Gulf coasts.

(72)

They had been much among the Indians. Many were the incidents related in the lives of these strange people. The bishop had even been to California, following the people in their mad rush for gold. To see and hear a man who had been to that distant country was about like contact with a being from another sphere. The bishop had gone by water, and this added much to the interest of the narrative. They talked about the mission in China, and the prospect of converting the world to Christ. Such comprehensive views I had never before heard. Here was a man at the center of a mighty movement, planning, thinking, and working for the good of others. In my imagination I could see the preachers of his appointment following the settlers into every part of the great West, while they were holding forth the beacon lights of knowledge to the people in the East, and seeking the salvation of the slaves on the rice, cotton, and sugar plantations of the South. They were penetrating the forest to the homes of men who had settled in the lonely swamps or pitched their habitations on the rugged mountains. Whether the people were white or black or red, whether they lived in pleasant homes or in huts or in wigwams, whether they were intelligent or ignorant, whether they were refined or rude, with the same untiring zeal they were sought and instructed.

I could see that here was a system that worked; that was forceful, elastic, and far-reaching. Here were men in vast numbers, moved by a common

impulse, ready to go, and go cheerfully, anywhere;
to follow Indian trails or take their way through
the trackless forest, to swim rivers, to sleep in huts
or camp in the woods; to brave diseases or the
skulking savages, to endure hardships and priva-
tions of every kind; yea, to defy death itself that
they might accomplish their important mission.
Vital in every fiber of the movement was a power to command the allegiance and inspire the
energies of the soul. It was an organized force
against ignorance and wrong, and instinct with an
uplifting and cleansing power. It appeared to me
that no President could command such service,
and no king could count on such fidelity. Here was
life full of purpose; it was life worth living. Such
was the impression that these kindly, fatherly men
made on my mind. Their conversation was full
of reminiscence, full of hope, and richly spiced
with anecdotes. They seemed so kindly disposed, so ready to talk, so gentle and persuasive
in manner that I ventured a question or two.
The dignified simplicity with which they con-
descended to my young capacity was truly gratifying, and, as I have since learned to appreciate
things, a most decided evidence of true greatness. That visit has been to me an intellectual
and moral benediction.

Sunday morning Uncle George brought out the
carriage in more than the usual good trim. The
horses were of fine appearance, and had those qualities so highly prized: mettle and bottom. Every

movement showed that they had been well kept and properly groomed. Every planter prided himself on the good qualities of his carriage horses. The carriage of that day has long been extinct. Then it was a badge of respectability, and indicated some degree of wealth. Nearly every family in good circumstances had one. They were costly concerns, many of them costing as much as their drivers. Ours cost about twelve hundred dollars. In general shape it was something like a steamboat on wheels. It was rounded in the front and at the rear, and the bottom sloped up at each end as if intended for the water. Then the top was oval, so as to shed water every way from the center, very much after the style of the covering on boats. Trusting entirely to memory, I judge that the " ladies' cabin " was about six feet long, and four feet wide, and five feet from floor to ceiling. It was entered from either side, by a door. Each door had a large panel of glass to admit the light. In the front and rear were mirrors fixed in the wall, so that ladies sitting *téte-a-téte* could see themselves while riding. The carriage, on the inside, was finely cushioned throughout. Padded pendants made of soft material hung at the sides. Some of these pendants hung in a loop, and others with a tassel. They were intended mostly for ornament, but might be used as supports for the hand. The carriage was a luxury, and was built for elegance and comfort. I have seen no palace car with finer finish. The driver's seat was

perched high on the front, and placed the " likely fellow " several feet above his horses.  George
drew up in front of the gate in fine style.  With
a flourish of dignity, he nimbly alighted from his
place of honor, opened the door, and unfolded the
steps.  The steps were neatly folded up just inside
the door.  When unfolded they reached nearly to
the ground, each outward and downward-bound
step becoming smaller.  This was necessarily the
case, as they folded into each other.  They were
so firmly hinged into each other as to hold a person's weight without apparent strain.  Of course
Will Benson was on hand, to help sister Mary into
the carriage.  It was quite an accomplishment for
a lady to mount the carriage steps with becoming
dignity, and I noticed that the help of a gentleman
always aided very much in the accomplishment of
the feat.  The bishop and his companion rode in an
open carriage.  As they had taken a fancy to me,
they invited me to ride with them.  This invitation
I was delighted to accept.  All being ready, the
boat on wheels led the way, and we followed.
This comparison of the old family carriage to a
steamboat was probably suggested by an amusing
incident which occurred long after the time of
which I am writing.  As the great civil war was
dragging its dismal length near to a close, the Federal soldiers were making a raid through the country.  It was along a lonesome road through the
pine hills in the western part of Calhoun County,
Mississippi.  Under a shelter near the roadside,

and near a home that had once known better days, one of these old carriages had found rest for the last three years. Some of the foremost cavalrymen, pointing to the antique symbol of departing glory, cried out " Gunboat!" and made a wide curve in the line of march, as if afraid of the monster. The whole line took up the cry, and with great glee made the curve around the harmless relic of a once powerful aristocracy.

Will was conspicuous as he cantered along close behind the carriage, ready for any emergency, especially to be ready to assist sister from the carriage and escort her to the church door. That was the exact thing to do under the circumstances. As we drew near the church, we saw carriages coming from all parts of the country. Behind each carriage was a young man in a fair canter to keep up. To a cynical eye they might have suggested the idea of sharks in the wake of ships. Behind one carriage there were two young men speeding along as if in a race. The reason was soon apparent. There were two young ladies demanding attention. Ladies and gentlemen did not sit together in church in those days. So the ladies were simply escorted to the door. It appears to me that the young gentlemen of that day were more easily satisfied with the amount of the young ladies' company than are the lads of our times. Now the young gentleman takes his sweetheart in a buggy all to himself, takes any circuitous route in getting there, and then sits by her side while the

minister conducts the services, or at least takes
some part in the exercises.

The services in church that day were just such
as might be expected from the able men who conducted them. There was no effort at display, no
airing of great philosophical questions, nothing to
suggest or invite skepticism. The truth was presented with such persuasive unction and simple
purity of diction as at once to win the assent of
the mind and the affection of the heart.

To me the occasion was one of delight. I sat
by mother and she sat near Mrs. Brantlett and
Susie. I was between two sources of inspiration:
Susie and the bishop. Faith went out toward the
pulpit, and love toward Susie. Heaven and earth
had charms equally attractive. Fortunately, in
my view, the charms were not incompatible. I
saw no reason why heaven and earth might not
embrace and kiss each other, and that I should be
the center of the meeting. Duty thrilled from the
pulpit; love rose gently from the pew. As these
lines lay out before me, I could see that they were
not parallel, but soon became identical.

The visit of the good bishop to our house was
made more memorable by the fact that Will Benson took occasion by it to bring his suit for the
hand of sister Mary to a happy consummation.
Will had for some time been urging this matter,
and had the consent of all who had a right to be
consulted. But mother wished to postpone. She
liked Will. She knew he was a gentleman, and

Mary was doing well. She did not make wealth a special consideration, but I noticed that she generally mentioned the fact that Mr. Benson had a fine plantation and worked many hands. But why not wait just a little. Will had consummate skill in the management of feminine instincts. It would be so nice, he said, to be married by the bishop. And such an opportunity would never again occur. He had learned that the bishop could be induced to stay and rest until Tuesday morning. Why not now, as well as any time? Mother was fairly caught. To have her daughter married by a bishop was evidently taking. Father saw the effect, smiled at the young man's ingenuity, and said: " Yes, as well now as any time." So Tuesday morning the private, simple wedding took place. Only a few of the neighbors witnessed the happy event. The distinguished ministers went on their way. Will and sister Mary blessed their coming, as did every one else.

# CHAPTER XII.

## On a Visit.

WHEN I was about twelve years old, a very memorable event occurred. It was a visit to the family of my older sister. Capt. Johnson owned a large plantation in Louisiana. Mother had often planned a visit down there, and now it was to be realized. Great were the preparations, and great the expectations which ushered in the day of our departure. Mother, mammy, and I were the principals in the movement; while trunks, boxes, and bundles were, according to sister Mary's idea, entirely too numerous for respectability. Mother said she didn't think it necessary to take much baggage, but of course we must have several different suits. We would meet strangers, probably desire to make some visits, and possibly wish to attend church. Our wardrobe had to be equal to all these possibilities. Then there might be changes in the weather, and it would be better to have wraps. We might by some accident all get wet, and some heavy cloaks and oversuits would be needed. Then Mary, Fannie, and Willie, sweet little things, must all have some special presents from grandma. Father ventured to remark that we had better not overload the boat, for in that case we might not need the clothing. Mother's

(80)

reply indicated that there was apt to be a very fair margin between what men know and what they think they know. So with much debating and deliberating the number of packages to be taken was definitely settled. It was also settled that father was to go with us to the river, and see us comfortably on the boat.

As there was a convenient stopping place about halfway to the river, it was determined to make the trip by easy drives in two days. The auspicious morning finally came, and George brought out his span of blacks in splendid order. The carriage fairly glistened in the morning sun. George was dressed for the occasion. He sported a suit of second-hand black. It was a composite suit, the different parts having been furnished by different originals, of different sizes. The pants were tight at the knee, and wide at the shoe, reminding one of an inverted lily. The coat was remarkable for extravagance in length and economy in breadth of tail. His boot heels added about one and a half inches to his height, while his head was crowned with a narrow "beaver" nearly a foot long. I took his picture with my eye, by the instantaneous process, while he was mounting his seat on the front end of the carriage, and just as his rear foot was on the last step, and his front one on the foot rest of the driver's seat. In this position he has served ever since to remind me of a crane climbing up a corner of a cliff at the angle of a mill pond.

6

It was in early morning in May when we finally waved adieu to familiar scenes, and took our course westward to the river.   As a special favor, I was allowed that bright spring morning to ride out on the seat with George.   We were soon skirting along the edge of Mr. Benson's farm; then away into the wooded country where birds greeted us, and ever and anon a squirrel was seen to jump from limb to limb amid the leafy bowers of his native home.   All nature glowed in a broad sheen of sunshine, leaf, and flower.   It was a time for thought and reverie.   For once my tongue was silent, and my reason active.   On that beautiful morning my young imagination was held in a sweet thraldom by the blending sensations of sight and sound.   Mother nature was humming in my reason's ear a delightful song to the praise of the ever present Deity.   Beneath the calm surface of beauty my mind was reading an underlying purpose of divine love and protection.   There was before me in all its complicated beauty the problem of all ages, the problem of existence.   The lesson it spelled out to me was one of trust and hope. Looking back at this distance, I do not see how my mind could have been better employed, or my conclusions more just; for surely he sees nature "through a glass darkly" who fails to see in her manifold phases the ever present finger of purpose pointing to the invisible Power whose presence is felt in every atom of existence.

But my reverie was checked or turned into a new

channel by the sight of something far down the road coming slowly toward us, while we were moving rapidly toward it. It was like a covered wagon, but somehow we could see no team or driver. Finally there was the appearance of a boy's head right in the middle of the slowly moving mass. Then there seemed to be a horse's head peering out in front. At last George discovered that it was a boy carrying a huge bag of wool rolls in front of him on a horse. "Dar's a wool-kyardin' mersheen down on de road head uv us." When we met the lad, I was surprised to see the same boy I had seen piling brush for his father when I was out last winter rabbit hunting. It was evident the family was beginning thus early to manufacture clothes for the coming winter. "Dat's John Henderson," said George. "He's a son uv John Henderson, the kyarpenter. His paw's named John an' he's named John." There was a contemptuous slur in George's voice. This was because of the boy's lowly condition. Such is the force of thought when it is ground into us by daily experience. George had an utter contempt for a freeman whose condition compelled him to do the work a slave was bound to do. Freedom and idleness, slavery and work, were so connected in George's mind that they were correlative conditions. But the boy had a bright, winning face, and I desired to know more about him. We soon arrived at the "kyarding mersheen," as George called it, and finding a good spring and a good chance to water and rest the team, we drew up for lunch. As we were in no hurry to get away, I had an opportnnity to satisfy my curiosity in regard to this wool-carding machine. It was driven by water applied to a breast wheel. The wheel was some twenty feet in diameter, and had " buckets "—that is, receptacles for the water—all around its rim. These buckets were about two feet long, reaching across the face of the wheel. They were about four by five inches in breadth and depth. The water ran into the buckets from a flume about half the height of the wheel, or " breast high." Hence the name. The buckets were filled in succession as the wheel moved slowly around. The machinery was driven by the weight of the water in the buckets. The wool, after being thoroughly washed and picked, thus being freed from dirt and burs, was placed on a feeder and thus carried regularly into the machine. The wool, being well carded, came out in rolls about a yard long. These were taken up in bunches, and so looped that they could be packed in large bags for transportation. That was one of the bags we had seen carried by John Henderson, " de kyarpenter's son."

Next day about 1 o'clock we reached the river. The great father of waters had taken on royal proportions. As we went through a cut in the bluff down to the landing, it seemed to me we would drive right into the world of waters at our feet. I could hardly assure myself that there was no danger, and that the water was some distance off. The boat was expected to arrive soon, as she was due to leave at 4 o'clock that afternoon. My fears subsided very rapidly, and my curiosity rose in like ratio. It kept mother and mammy both busy to keep me out of danger. Two trading boats were cabled at the landing, and seemed to be doing well in trading dry goods and notions. These floating stores were novelties to me; and had my cash been equal to my questions, I would have been a much desired customer. Several skiffs were tied to stakes at the water's edge. To get in them and feel the motion of the waves seemed to me an innocent pastime, but mother and mammy were constantly perturbed lest the little boat should get adrift with me.

But attention was now directed to the noise of a steamboat. Of course we thought it was *our* boat, and we looked anxiously up the river to catch sight of her. It seemed to me she was a long time making her appearance. As the sound became more distinct, it seemed that the boat was coming up the river. So we impatiently waited, looking first up and then down the river. The beauty of the scenery now began to dawn upon me. Our landing seemed to be just in the center of a grand bend, as the river flowed round at our feet. On the opposite side, a fringe of willows, kissing with lips of green the river's rippling face, made a graceful and beautiful curve, receding from us in either direction, until it obstructed our view of the great stream. Thus the river seemed to end in points about six miles above and below. It looked as if we stood on the outer rim of a great crescent of water, looking down into either horn. The mellow sunshine, like the spirit of peace, added yet brighter charms to this scene of beauty.

Above the green foliage we could at last see the smoke of the steamer as she was coming round the bend below. Presently she glided into view, seeming to emerge from some recess in the green forest. A glance up the river showed that our boat also was in sight. The scene was splendid. A magnificent crescent of water, glistening with a silvery sheen, lay before us, while the two boats looked like gems set in either tapering horn.

The boat coming up seemed to court the farther shore, and made no motion to land until about opposite us, and then came directly across. This was to avoid the swift current on our side. The other boat, having the current in her favor, came the nearest way to the landing, and " rounded to," throwing her prow up the stream in fine style, and was cabled and her gang planks run out over the gunwale to the land sometime before the up bound steamer reached the shore. It was amusing to hear the boats' crews exchange salutations and then unite with peculiar gusto in their songs, while each took on the freight as directed. These boats were packets, and both belonged to a line between Cincinnati and New Orleans. Thus the reader will see there was a " Queen and Crescent Route " long before the days of railroad combinations.

We were soon comfortably situated in the ladies' cabin. The deep-toned bell rang out the signal for departure. Father bade us adieu with his best wishes for a pleasant trip and a safe return. The gangways were drawn in, the great wheels began to revolve, the boat backed out into the river, turned her prow to the south, and we were afloat on the great Mississippi. The constant quivering of the boat, and her forward movement as the ponderous wheels revolved, were new and delightful sensations to me. That there was a sense of danger seemed only to heighten the joy. For a time my attention was absorbed by the magnificent scenery which was constantly coming into view, and changing as the boat sped on her way. The waters were high, filling the channel, and in many places overflowing the low lands. The banks were everywhere covered with living green. From the tallest trees in the background to the surface of the water there was unbroken foliage, varied in shades of green, as different trees entered into the make-up of the scene. Occasionally long tongues of green jutted out from the shore, far into the great stream. These were willows growing on sandbars, now covered with water.

As the sun went down one shore was wrapped in voluptuous sunshine, while a deep shade rested on the other. Finally the evening shades crept across the waters and climbed the heights on the other side, and a spirit of rest came down on everything except the ever restless waters and the swift-moving boat consigned to their mercy. All colors were lost in the dark outlines which indicated merely the forms of things on either margin of the river.

But light, life, and animation prevailed within. The passengers were mostly well to do planters bound for New Orleans on business or pleasure. A few from the cities far up the river lent additional charms to the conversation. It was an intelligent, cosmopolitan company, talking of politics, religion, literature, business, and pleasure. But good health, satiety of animation, and regular habits invited me to repose, and I was rocked to sleep by a method I had not known before.

Next morning the scenery along the river was different. Immense levees ran along on each shore, to protect the country from overflows. It was strange and surprising to look down on the growing sugar cane, and to see hands at work on farms that would be under water but for the levees. The boat sped on, and in due time "rounded to" at the landing near where my sister lived.

# CHAPTER XIII.

## In Louisiana.

OUR reception was most cordial. Captain Johnson and sister were both at the landing to extend a welcome. As they lived only a few hundred yards off, we were soon at their fine residence. In the shade of its broad verandas the breezes were delightful. In the two weeks we spent there I think I must have lived about two years, so vivid were the impressions, so glowing were the emotions! Everything was new and full of interest. But the one thing that never failed to engage my thought and elicit my admiration was the great river. It lived in my thoughts, and has crystallized in my memory. No other impressions of my visit have been so enduring. It awoke the enthusiasm of my soul, and has been a delightful theme for reflection ever since.

In those days the commerce of all the upcountry, from the Alleghany Mountains westward, flowed through this great steamboat highway. The river was the great artery of Western trade, and was just at that time in full, healthy action. Much of the produce from the head waters of the seminavigable streams had been waiting for the spring rise to find its way to market. Flatboats from the interior had met steam crafts far up these rivers, and the rewards of waiting and patient industry were now to be realized. The supplies for the planters, and the summer goods on the way to country and village stores now gave full work, and boats were almost constantly passing.

What a revel of thought these steamers produced! Imagination was turned loose, and invested the beautiful steamers with sympathetic interest. One day—it was a perfect spring day, when all nature united in the production of the best—I was lying prone on the floor of the upstairs veranda. I was looking out on the majestic river, lost in a sense of its grandeur and beauty, when a magnificent steamer came in sight. A few scattering trees in the foreground, along the margin of the river, added tone to the picture. The scene was inspiring. The great river was as calm, apparently, as an infant in slumber; yet the swiftly moving trash and foam, showing the sweep and velocity of the current, revealed a mighty energy hidden beneath the unruffled surface. It was majestic power in grand repose.

With the gracefulness of a swan on a placid lake, the boat glided over the waters. I felt my own life *en rapport* with the manifold life on board the floating palace. There were the passengers, many of them from homes up the country, like my own. Some, probably, were on their first trip, and enjoyed the flavor of novelty, as they drank in the shifting beauty of ever changing scenery. Maybe a boy like myself was on board, with receptive

faculties all ajar; or a little girl like Susie, ab-
sorbing the poetry of the passing views. In their
new sensations of mingled pleasure and apprehension I felt a kindred glow. Then the boat's
crew! What a strange life they lived! This
great, mysterious river was their only home. I
wondered if the stream held its fascination over
their minds, or had it by constant association become tame. The roustabouts, who were so often
taking on and putting off freights; who loaded
cord wood, worked the pumps, and kept generally
so busy; I wondered if they loved their work.
And the cabin boy, whose youth was spent on the
ever moving vessel; I wondered if he ever had a
home like mine, and where were his father and
mother. I felt strangely drawn toward the boy of
a strange destiny. Then the great man who had
charge of all, the captain; my! wasn't he born
to command? How everybody moved when he
was about! But to me, the most interesting man
of all was he who worked the wheel in the pilot
house. From his lofty position, constantly looking over the waters and picking out the path of
the steamer where no path was visible; he was to
me the very genius of progress. Thus I mused
till the boat passed by and glided out of sight.

One bright morning I went out to the river
and threw myself on the grass, on the slope
of the levee, to commune with things about
me. On the other side of the levee, just a few
yards away, the waves were breaking in a delight-

ful murmur. In the tree above the birds of rich
plumage were singing their sweetest notes. Before me was the home of my sister. The splendid
residence, the extensive quarters, the capacious
barns, the sugar mill in the distance, and the broad
expanse of growing cane spread out as far as I
could see, waving in the pleasant breezes fresh
from the Gulf. The scene was poetry without a
bard, and music without a master. I felt that nature was just then tuning all her harps to one common melody, and giving to my spirit's finer sense
an unworded song of vast significance; and
strange were the echoes awakened in my plastic
mind.

But of all the harps of nature then giving music
to my soul, the great river, the harp of a thousand
streams, was out of all comparison the most engaging. To this music I turned with special delight. I rose from my place of reverie and took
position on the levee, with the broad expanse of
waters before me. My eyes feasted on the scene;
the river had me fascinated; to give it study was
pleasure. In studying the sources of this mighty
stream, my geographical knowledge assumed new
significance. In this great volume of water, held
in abeyance by the narrow embankments of earth
on which I reposed and thought, how many great
rivers and smaller streams were commingled on
their way to the Southern Gulf! From the con-
fines of New Mexico, in the Southwest, along the
Rocky Mountains to the British possessions in the

Northwest; from the neighborhood of the great lakes of the North, from New York, in the Northeast, the empire State of the North, thence along the Alleghany and Cumberland Mountains to Georgia, the empire State of the South; the waters from all this vast region were gathered here. I never before so fully realized the greatness of my native land. And I felt a young patriot's pride of country. In the imperial domain from which these waters came might be merged a score of European principalities, over whose destinies men have fought and heroes have died, and still there would be room for more. The waters from every vapory cloud, the torrents from every raging storm, the tricklings from melting ice and snow, the gurglings from the million springs in all this great country, were here passing by with energy irresistible and yet with murmurings soft as an infant's laugh. Waters collected from the broad prairies, from the mountains, swamps, and forests; from the trails of the buffalo, the warpaths of the Indians, and the furrow of the hardy settlers; from the haunts of the wild beasts and the cities of busy men; were here singing to me a song of my country's greatness and her noble destiny.

I had a new conception of the vastness and certainty of the Western empire. When this immense territory shall have a population equal to its full capacity to maintain, then the flag of ascendancy will have crossed the Atlantic and be floating here. Such a country has only to bide its time to rule the destinies of the world. Surely the land of Washington is to be the guiding star of the nations. Such were my thoughts that morning as I communed with nature, and drank deep of the prophecy of my country's progress.

All too soon the time came for us to return home. It was in the early morning we assembled on the levee to await the landing of the steamer. She was a magnificent boat. My heart beat with quickened force as she came up, seeming all the times to increase in size, till she stopped at our very feet. We were soon on board; farewells were said, and once more I was enjoying the strange sensations produced by the steamer's motions. I was glad we were to make so much of the trip this time in daylight. The scenery along the river was beautiful, and I never tired of the changing views. As the waters were high, the boat took several short routes called " chutes," thus saving the distance around long bends in the river. In some places the water in these chutes was shallow, and the vessel had to feel her way along. At such places two men with sounding lines, one on either side of the boat, sounded for the bottom. As they stood at the gunwale and threw out the lead they kept up a monotonous cry, "no bottom," "five feet scant," "mark twain," and other phrases I failed to remember. The captain stood on the upper deck and repeated their words to the pilot, with the additional information as to the side of the

vessel from which the message came.   The boat
veered as the depth of water was ascertained, thus
creeping along the bottom till she passed over the
bar.

I witnessed another method of economizing time
by the up-bound steamers.   Instead of landing to
take on wood, they fastened to the side of the
steamer a loaded wood boat kept in readiness at
the wood yard for the purpose, and unloaded as
they went, till finally the empty flat, with its small
crew of two or three men, was set adrift to float
back.

Our boat's crew were all white men.   On the
boats plying exclusively on Southern rivers the
crews were composed mostly of negro slaves.   I
was told that it was no longer safe for slaves to
land in the free states North, and that was why
boats plying in those waters employed only white
men.

We reached our landing in the night, and met
father, who had come with the carriage; and next
day, by an early start and long drive, we arrived
safely at home.

# CHAPTER XIV.

## GOING TO SCHOOL.

AFTER our return from Louisiana life at the old home went on as usual till autumn, when I started to school. Up to this time I had been taught at home. Mother said she had me far enough advanced to risk me in the hands of a teacher. Father said he wanted me to go school to take the conceit out of me. He was of the opinion there was nothing equal to boys to take the conceit out of a boy. Thus one parent was willing for me to begin school because my education could not now be readily spoiled; the other because it would keep me from being spoiled. Father thought that much of the practical education which a boy needs to prepare him for usefulness in life is gained by daily association with his equals. Boys demand of each other fair dealing and evenhanded justice, and are even more ready than men to denounce any undue assumption. The petted boy, fresh from the parental roof, is apt to hear things of himself he had not heard before. By the frankness of his companions he may see himself as others see him.

School life was rather irksome at first, but I had been taught to study. I soon saw that I had an advantage over others who had been going to school for some years. I shall always be grateful

to mother for laying the foundation of my education at home.   It was to me a kind stroke of fate
that Susie Brantlett began school at the same time.
She too had been taught at home, and was right
well advanced for one of her age.   Her presence
was to me a source of joy, a safeguard against
mischief, and an inspiration to study.   A tender
regard for purity is purifying; the admiration of
nobility is ennobling.   These qualities in Susie
were to me a constant reproof and a perpetual encouragement.   Under such influences the man
that is in us is constantly struggling, with fair
chances of success, to gain the mastery over ignoble selfishness and contemptible littleness.   This is
Heaven's method of developing manhood.   Thus
I gained at school a culture not included in the
teacher's curriculum.

Twice each day the scholars were drawn up in
line for spelling.   Almost the entire school, without regard to age, sex, or proficiency, was in the
spelling class.   When we stood up in line, we
reached entirely across the schoolroom, and had
to double round at the foot of the class.   The first
day we took position by lot.   As I was never lucky
at games of chance, I drew up far down toward
the foot.   I was glad to see that Susie was near
the head.   The first word was missed by the first
three spellers.   Dick Webb was fourth, and
spelled the word quickly, with an air of intelligence, and took his place at the head of the class,
as one born for the position.   Susie was next, and

7

spelled her word with a modesty and independence all her own. There was constant change of place during this first spelling, the good spellers going toward the head, and the bad ones toward the foot of the class. At the close Susie was third, and I sixth. It was evident that there was to be sharp competition for the first place, and that this part of our daily routine was to be very interesting.

The second morning, when most of the scholars had arrived, and we were waiting for the teacher, Mr. Dunbar, to come and open school, we were surprised to see a strange man and boy come riding up, with evident intention of stopping at the schoolhouse. It was a source of open and indecorous merriment that they both came on the same horse, the boy riding behind. I knew them at a glance. They were the Hendersons. My first impulse was to speak to the man, and call him by name. But partly from timidity and, it must be confessed, partly from fear of ridicule, I was silent. But I had the indiscretion to tell some of the boys I knew them. At once, with laughter and jeers, the words were bandied around, " These are some of Sam Williams's acquaintances." Dolph Parker stuffed his hands in his pants pockets and stepped around like a turkey cock on a plant bed in spring time, as he said; " Sam, why don't you bring up your chum and introduce him?" The laugh that followed was very provoking. I knew I had done nothing to provoke laughter, and I felt my blood boil; but at this time Mr. Henderson

came up and inquired if the teacher had come.
Adolphus had turned off with an air of contempt,
the other boys were chuckling over his wit at my
expense, and I was sulking with indignation. I
felt that our silence was rude, and I was turning
to speak, when Susie, who had spied the teacher
coming over the hill, replied: "The teacher is
coming, sir." This was timely and brave. The
dread of unmerited contempt was now all gone,
and I went up to John and asked if he was coming
to school. His replies were manly and straightforward. He seemed to appreciate the situation,
and was drawn toward me because he saw that a
right motive had prompted my familiarity. From
that hour we were friends.

Mr. Henderson had come to place his son in
school. It was three miles to walk, he said, but it
was the best he could do. So John Henderson
was enrolled as a pupil. The boys manifested a
shyness, if not contempt, for the boy who had to
walk three miles to a school, and who wore coarse
clothes and brogan shoes. Other boys came as
far, but they had horses to ride, and if at any time
they wore coarse garments or heavy shoes, it was
largely a matter of choice. It matters little what a
man wears so everybody knows he could do better.
But with John the hard conditions were of necessity. He was doing the best he could; therefore
he was the subject of dislike and ridicule.

When the school was called into line to spell just
before dismissal at noon, it was to be seen that

most of the larger scholars had risen toward the
head of the class, while the smaller ones had settled toward the foot, so that the class was tapering
in size, something like a pig's tail. And when they
doubled around at the foot the likeness became
still more striking, as it seemed to give the final curl,
not for ornament, as on the pig, but for want of
room. John, being a new scholar, had of course
to take his place at the foot. As he was much
larger than any others down there he looked like
something stuck on the extreme end of the pig's
tail to represent a grand flourish.

The class had now become more settled. Of
course changes occurred, but they were less frequent. John missed his first word. Dolph, from
his position up near the head of the class, enjoyed
this with a savory relish. John was a little embarrassed, but the miss was not wholly attributable to
that. He was rather backward in his studies.
His opportunities had been poor. But no boy in
school had more resolution and determination
stamped on his countenance.

The contest for the first place in the class was
sharp between Dick Webb and Susie Brantlett.
Dick was two or three years older; but if he had
the mastery, he held it by a very uncertain tenure.
Dolph and I kept pretty well together, about sixth
and seventh from head. John gained some, but
held position near the foot. It seemed to be taken
for granted all around that this was in accordance
with the fitness of things.

On the playground a new trouble arose. Dolph
Parker and Dick Webb were selected as cham-
pions of the game of ball. They were to choose
alternately among the boys until all had been
chosen. The choosing went on until every boy
large enough to play had been chosen, except
John. It was Dolph's time to choose. He made
it his opportunity to snub. With an air of super-
cilious disdain, he said he had no use for any further material in reach. Webb proposed to make
an exchange and himself take John. But Dolph
would hear to nothing of the kind. The boys felt
the injustice, and many of them were indignant,
but they did not like to have a rupture with Dolph
Parker. He was stout, revengeful, overbearing.
Besides, he was the richest boy in school. Wealth
is very apt to claim some social advantages and
exemptions, and such claims are generally allowed.
I remembered the brave words of Susie in the
the morning, and how I had felt the sting of
Dolph's taunt. Fortunately I was on Dick's side.
My resignation would make the game even. So
I said to Dick: "I don't care to play; I'll pull
out and make you even." As I walked off, Dick
made earnest protest; but Dolph, with a contemptuous wave of the hand, said: "Let him go with
his equal." I hurled back, in defiance: "If I do,
I'll not be found in your company."

Things had now gone as far as they could go
without being recognized by the teacher. I went
down to the spring, and, sitting at the root of a

tree, in the dense shade of the forest, let the ministries of nature help to cool down my indignation. I could hear the boys at play, and wondered if they were thinking of John and me. When I thought playtime was nearly over, I went back, going round the playground to the schoolhouse. There I found John poring over his lessons. The sympathetic concern on his face as he looked at me was something to remember. He looked like he wanted to say something, but knew not what to say. I affected to appear as if there was nothing wrong, picked up a book, and pretended to study. But the awkward suspense was soon over, as the bell rang for books.

John's nearest way home was by our place. Susie went the same way within a few hundred yards of her home. The Allens (Ben, Joe, and Minnie) went part of the way until their road turned off. Conversation was a little strained that afternoon. The only thing we were thinking much about was the very thing to which we made no allusion. That night I laid my troubles before mother. It was my first conflict with the world. She was much concerned. A difference with any of Col. Parker's family was painful in the extreme. Her manner, put into words, would have run about this way: "Why, he's the richest man in the neighborhood! Then, this poor boy, who is he?" She was evidently troubled. She believed I had done right, but shrank from the situation as something to be deplored. Father was made of sterner stuff. He said: "Son, do right, all the way through, and you will come out all right." This advice I determined to follow.

Next day I went to school with some apprehension. I was fully determined that I would not be a party to any unjust ostracism of John Henderson. But I did not wish the ill will of any of the boys. I therefore looked forward to the playtime with great solicitude. In school I had no time to think of troubles to come. It seemed but a short while when we were called up to spell, and then dismissed for dinner. When we had eaten, we were a little surprised and much gratified at the offer of Mr. Dunbar, the teacher, to join us in our game of ball. He was at once nominated as champion. Dolph was selected as the other. They threw up "heads and tails" to see which should have first choice. This fell to the teacher. Having taken position as if reviewing the whole group of eager boys, he paused as if making up his mind, and then chose John Henderson. The surprise was intense. Dolph looked like a thunderbolt had barely missed him. Instantly the the boys saw the whole meaning, and the approbation was so hearty that they gave round after round of cheers. This rebuke was so timely, and had such happy effect, that contempt for the poor boy was not shown again, openly, for several months. Meanwhile, John made rapid progress in his studies. In fact, in about three months it began to appear that it would require extraordinary diligence to keep ahead of him.  He had long ago left the foot of the class and had been several times at the head, while the general average in his studies was very respectable.  This rapid advance brought John into general favor, was gratifying to the teacher, and quite mortifying to Adolphus Parker.

One feature of the school was of special interest.  This was the lecture.  Every Friday afternoon was taken up by lectures, speeches, declamations, and dialogues.  The teacher generally took part.  These lectures were designed to promote useful reading.  Literature, criticism, philosophical and scientific inquiries were the topics. Books, new and old, were commented on.  To many of us this was the most stimulating exercise in the whole school.  It provoked inquiry, stimulated thought, and led to general reading.  In a few years we became acquainted with the merits of English literature.  The names of the great authors became as familiar as household words. We knew when and where they lived, and something of what they thought and wrote.

It did me good to see the effects of these lectures on John Henderson.  It was like the coming of an ardent and long-baffled lover to the one who possessed his soul entire.  The flash of the eye, the flush of interest on the face, the eager satisfaction so visible in every movement, as new ideas flashed into his mind, was a wonder and a spur to me.  If knowledge was worth so much to John, why should it be worth less to me?

# CHAPTER XV.

DURING all these years while I was growing and learning, one thing constantly impressed my mind. It was the fact that the country was all the time growing richer. The slaves continually increased. Troops of young negroes on our place were every year recruiting the field hands. The children with whom I used to romp and play and hunt rabbits went to the field about the time I started to school, and were now able to do the work of full-grown hands. These had been preceded by others, and were followed by an ever increasing flow.

So on all the neighboring plantations. Constant outdoor work developed fine constitutions. The muscles were so trained to labor that by the time the negroes were fifteen they were efficient hoe hands. This constant recruiting of the hoe force from beneath was followed by a corresponding promotion of the larger boys to the plow. A boy felt a new importance when he could walk straight between the plow handles, and have a mule to ride to and from his work, with the additional privilege of feeding and grooming. The plow force was the measure of importance and respectability. A planter was frequently spoken of as having a

(105)

force of so many plows, ten, twenty, or forty
plows. These were the degrees of dignity and
the measures of credit. These numbers helped to
rate the value of his children in the matrimonial
market. They were a fair index to the number of
bales of cotton he could place on the market the
coming winter.

Nearly every year new hands were purchased.
These were bought from dealers, who kept up a
lively trade by buying slaves from the border
states, where their labors were less profitable, and
selling them down here at a fair profit. Thus,
with the natural increase, and the influx of new
hands, the working force of the country was rapidly growing, year after year.

New lands were cleared to make room for the
larger force, The forest disappeared, and the
fields spread still wider over the country. Where I
used to catch rabbits in the thickets fine crops of
cotton now grew. Each year the number of cotton bales reached higher figures. The wagon
trains had to be increased, and kept longer on the
road. Such was the pressure to get the crop to
market, such the hurry to get off with another load
every time the wagons returned, that I thought
Jack did not enjoy his preëminence as he did in
the early times. The bells on the mules were neglected; the wagons looked more worn and bat-
tered; the wagoners had lost much of their glee.

The love of wealth had evidently grown with the
increase of riches. There was more stir, more

push, more anxiety, all centering in the greater effort to make still larger crops.   This was natural.
Wealth creates its own desires, erects its own stand-
ards, and  demands  tribute, in  some  form, from
every one.   Wealth gets to be the standard of merit and the passport to honor.

It was during our school years at the academy
that a great industrial revolution took place in the
country.   It was the building of railroads.   An
important road was constructed through our section.   This new power brought still more changes.
The important cities had now the means of quick
and safe transportation.   Small towns sprang up
at the depots, and inland cities began to grow at
important points.   The markets came to our very
doors.

Jack's trade went down.   No more wagon trains,
with tinkling bells.   No more camping out.   No
more telling of long stories by bright camp fires at
night, while the mules are munching their feed
and the owls are hooting in the neighboring wood.
No more great loads of groceries to be stored away
as a whole year's supply.   No more new stories of
the great river and the fine boats.   Jack must
henceforth, like a retired soldier, content himself
with rehearsing the adventures of the glorious past.
We may pardon a sigh for the return of the better
days, but to Jack those days will come never
again.

With the roads came brisker trade, more travel,
more dress, more fashion.   The newspapers had

greater circulation. With them came a more intimate acquaintance with other localities, and a
more general knowledge of the world. Life was
quickened. Old methods seemed slow. Steam
was now employed for milling, and in some instances took the place of mules for ginning.

The domestic industries, such as spinning and
weaving cloth at home, greatly declined. Goods
from the large factories became cheaper than they
could be made at home. A woman's time was
now worth more in the fields than at the wheel or
loom. All available force was employed to make
cotton. To grow cotton, to make money, to buy
negroes to grow cotton, was the regular orbit into
which the industry of the country had fallen. In
the wild rush after wealth men not only used all
the money they could make to purchase additional
slaves, but in many instances used their credit
also for all it would bring. Under the spur of
such influences the country seemed to be on the
road to prosperity, and to move forward with a
bound.

An innovation which had already obtained in
other places took place about this time in our
neighborhood. It was the custom of hiring over-
seers, a custom hated by the slaves, and one
which greatly increased their labors and lessened
their mirth. Of course it would be unprofitable
to hire an overseer unless the farm made an additional amount to pay his wages. This meant more
work, earlier to the field, and later to the quarters.

It meant dissatisfaction, and often running away, on the part of the slaves. The planters themselves did not much like the custom, but it relieved them of annoyance, and gave more time to talk politics and save the country.

During all these years the controversy in regard to slavery waxed warmer with each campaign, and sometimes the interest grew so warm that there was scarcely a lull, even between the elections. Prominent men, aspiring to high office, became eloquent in demanding our "rights." Every man who wanted the people's votes constituted himself the champion of the people's "rights." He appeared uninvited on the field, as another Don Quixote, ready to do or die for our "rights." But the more our rights were defended, the more restless people became. The newspapers were always ready to come to the rescue, and many were the learned "leaders" on the all-absorbing theme of our "rights." Meantime, while the hustings and the tripod, with equal zeal and discretion, were taking care of our "rights," the country was growing richer every day.

Finally the theme was wonderfully intensified by the crack of the Sharp's rifles in Kansas, followed by the Brown raid on Harper's Ferry, in Virginia. These things had the smack of earnestness, and served to give a very sharp point to the discussion. The "peculiar institution" of the South now had the ear of the nation, not to say of the nations, and was of world-wide interest. The parties to the great controvesy on either side were growing more confident and more defiant. They could afford to be defiant, as they were usually about a thousand miles apart. But the excitement was assuming colossal proportions. The battle of the giants was on the boards of fate, and events indicated an early rise of the curtain.

Now all these things did not disturb me in my quiet studies in the academy. They are mentioned here to show how the country was advancing in making money and taking care of our " rights " while I was advancing in my studies and on to manhood.

# CHAPTER XVI.

## STILL AT SCHOOL.

THE years passed and changes came to us as well as to our school. We grew in size and in knowledge, and the school grew in numbers and in usefulness. Another and better house was added. This was appropriated to the girls. A lady of fine accomplishments was placed in charge. Better methods gradually prevailed, and better work was done by the students. Our teacher was a master in his business, and our school became one of the best.

During the vacation John Henderson worked with his father at the carpenter's trade, that he might have the means of continuing at school. This was the cause of extreme disgust on the part of Dolph, and a few others like-minded. But John's position at school was no longer doubtful. Merit wins, the world over. John felt the need of education, and was putting the sweat of his brow into the culture of his brain, and felt that he had no time to be idle. Dolph soon found that John was pushing him on every line of study. John was a spur to us all. But Dolph seemed to regard it as an infringement of time-honored prerogative for this "poor upstart" to pass him in his studies. He seemed to think that wealth ought to give him the advancement without the labor of brain. But if Dolph's disposition grew murky, John's did not become sour.

He was one of the brightest, most cheerful, and manly boys in school. As the years went by he grew in manly beauty as well as in all the accomplishments of the mind. It is hardly necessary to say he was one of the most popular boys in school. First in play, first in study, first in the hearts of his companions. Thus he had at least some resemblance to the great "father of his country." For one to be a leader in any group, community, or nation, he must excel in what his fellows want most to do. John met these requirements; he was foremost in study and in every sport on the playground. It was in the third year after we entered school that Dolph's continued dislike for John came to an open rupture. John was then about sixteen, and Dolph was about one year older. The boys had fallen into the habit of abbreviating a great many words, especially each other's names. In this they were simply following the genius of their mother tongue. The tendency is to shorten words, and to use short words in preference to long ones. This is seen in nearly all the best writers of the language. Words of half a dozen syllables have a slim chance to live in English. The Latin races may delight in long, sonorous words; the Saxon never. Well, one day on the playground, when the game of ball was at its highest pitch, John, wishing to get the ball in time to cross out a boy on the opposite side, in the glow of excitement shouted to his companions: "There it is by Dolph Park!" Dolph straightened himself up to his full height, and swelling his breast out to its largest dimensions, exclaimed; "I'll have you to know, young upstart, my name is not Dolph Park." John was so intent on the game that he did not see that Dolph had taken offense, and went right on playing till his attention was directed to Dolph. Then in the most complete good humor, in the abandon of excitement, while his face wore a hearty smile, he said: "What is it, Dolph Park?" Thus unwittingly he committed the same offense the second time. Dolph's anger was at white heat. He almost hissed the words: "I ll make you know, you scoundrel, my name is not Dolph Park." John was taken completely by surprise. The colors chased each other over his countenance for an instant, then the look of determination which was habitual to him when in earnest settled down to about a three-ply thickness on his visage. He faced his wrathful assailant and with a bow of mock humility and obeisance, and with manner and tone most defiant and provoking, he replied: "Mr. Adolphus Parker, your humble servant begs a thousand pardons." The manner was so dignified and the ring of the voice so significant that the boys gave a lusty cheer. This was the "unkindest cut of all," for Dolph most highly prized his influence over the boys. This, he saw, was about to be lost. He was furious. But just then the bell rang for books, and that ended the matter for the time.

That evening as we were going home, when we reached the fork of the road where the Allens were to leave us, we were thrown into a state of perturbation by the rapid approach of Dolph Parker along the road on his pony, overtaking us. Dolph frequently rode to school. He had done so that day. It is evident that he stayed about the schoolhouse till all were gone, and then set out to overtake us. There was no time to do anything, not even to get Susie and Minnie out of the way. John saw we were all excited, and asked us not to interfere, but to let him manage the case. He was so calm, and talked so much like business, that we were all tolerably well assured, and awaited events. I had made up my mind to interfere if necessary to prevent John from being badly hurt. Feeling some concern, I looked around for Susie, but found she was about as much composed as any of us.

When Dolph came up he dismounted with a most self-conscious flourish. "Well, Mr. Henderson," he began, "I feel it my duty, sir, to administer to you a severe chastisement." This speech had evidently been prepared for the occasion. It was delivered with a pompous air, in accord with the pompous language. That's the way his father talked. He was putting on the parental style with as little regard for fit as if he were donning the parental wardrobe. The average schoolboy never talks that way. His language on such an occasion would have been, " I'm going to give you a lickin' " or " one of us has got to be whipped." Not so Dolph; he was to administer " chastisement."

When John saw that a fight was inevitable, the same determined look settled on his face. His eye was a study. He assumed the same manner of mock humility. His voice was so near the natural tone that one not well acquainted with him would be in doubt whether he meant what he said, or the exact opposite. He pleaded that the rules of school forbade fighting; that fighting was not to his liking; was not the best way to settle difficulties; and that no offense was intended on the playground. Dolph replied: " Think not, sir, that your pusillanimous hide can escape through the regulations of the school. Offended honor knows no such regulations." Without further parley, as if afraid his resolution would escape through his long words, he made at the object of his wrath. John partly dodged and partly parried the intended blow with his left hand, while with right he planted a clear square blow right about Dolph's ear. The blow came straight out from the shoulder, and with such force that Dolph staggered under it. This advantage was followed up with blows which came so fast and with such effect that Dolph was completely unnerved. He could do nothing but stagger about, and would have fallen had not John checked up. Seeing

that Dolph could make no further resistance, he
stopped. "Why, Dolph," he said, "is this the
way you administer chastisement? Is this the way
pusillanimous hides are tanned in your shop? I
suppose offended honor is now satisfied." But
Dolph had no time for chatting just then. He
made for his pony, which, by the way, had fed off
at some distance, wholly unmindful of his master's
adventures. Never was a boy more surprised
than Dolph. He was older and larger than John.
To "administer chastisement" to him was evidently considered mere pastime. But John's right
arm had not pushed the jack plane and wielded
the handsaw and hammer for nothing. There
was in his make-up a combination of mind and
muscle that was admirable to witness.

After Dolph left we held a counsel and agreed to
keep the fight a secret, provided Dolph said nothing about it. Next morning Dolph was in school
like nothing had happened. Fortunately, his
bruises were not hard to hide, and no one had any
suspicion of the fight. I never knew anything to
improve a person like that whipping improved
Dolph. He almost became amiable! His politeness and deference to John were shown on all occasions. To the few who had and kept the secret,
this was a source of constant amusement.

By the fourth year of our school life John was
fairly ahead in all studies. He was an earnest
speaker, a shrewd debater, and an exact thinker.
He was a recognized leader in all our mental

labors. The speaking every Friday afternoon proved to be of great advantage to us all. We learned to express our thoughts readily and without embarrassment. On these occasions the two departments were brought together. The presence of the girls was a great stimulus. Likewise, when the girls had concerts, as they did nearly every week, we were not only expected to be present, but to take part in the singing. Every girl was taught music. To perform well was regarded as the highest accomplishment. Therefore the girls were put to music early, and kept at it throughout the school course. When they were sent off to finish their education, as was often the case, it meant mainly some extra touches in music. With or without talent the girl must be taught to perform on the piano. It was the universal accomplishment.

The years passed rapidly, and almost before we were aware of it we were ready to begin our last year at the academy. The boys in my classes would be ready at the end of the year to enter college. But John, to be able to go to college, found it necessary to spend at least one year at work with his father. This was a great hardship. There was danger that he might not be able to stand his examination. To lose a whole year out of school just at this time was most unfortunate. John was greatly perplexed, but not discouraged. Poverty is inexorable, but John's resolution was equal to the emergency. He determined, by studying at night and at odd times, to keep up with his class while working at his trade, and thus, in spite of difficulties, to be ready to enter college with his class. Whenever opportunity offered, the teacher was to give him help.

Mr. Henderson found very profitable work erecting cotton presses and building ginhouses. This year he had a contract to make important additions to Maj. Allen's dwelling. In all these labors John was his most efficient help.

This last year of our academic life passed without any special or unusual interest. Dolph was now about nineteen, well grown; pompous in appearance and language, and evidently enjoyed a very high opinion of himself. I think he was really glad John had quit school. An unpleasant reminder was thus removed. Then it left him the semblance of his old superiority.

Meanwhile Susie was growing more and more beautiful. This was a cause for congratulation. This was not to be taken as a matter of course. Feminine growth does not always follow this rule. Indeed, whether it is the rule or the exception for pretty girls to make beautiful women, is an open question. The celebrated budding period, when the girl begins to bud and blossom into womanhood, is often the period that brings out hidden tendencies which soon develop into ugliness. The class of pretty " Preps." will not, by any means, turn out a class of uniformly beautiful graduates. Some will be too low, some too tall, others will be too thin, while yet others will be too stout. Some will be stooped and others angular. Some will have rough complexions or coarse features, while a very few will be faultless both in figure and features. Such was Susie. She had, from the first, been a diligent student, and had taken on accomplishments as by natural affinity.

Dick Webb had maintained a high standard throughout. Dolph was at least respectable in his average standing as a student. The brightest one of us all was John Henderson, struggling against hard fate and by extra efforts bringing up his studies in a manner, so the teacher told us, to be able with the rest of us to enter college.

Finally, the academic studies were completed. The last day of the school came, and the teacher had all the boys in my class to come forward to receive his farewell advice. At the close of a good lecture, he assured us we were now ready to enter college. We all felt a new sense of importance. We were sure that fortune was getting ready to open her finest gate for us to enter.

# CHAPTER XVII.

## VACATION.

WE entered upon this vacation with special relish. It was more to us than others had been. It was the gap between our Academic and College studies. We had now arrived at the age when the *genus homo* begins the important task of putting off the boy and taking on the man. This is done on the principle of natural development, somewhat in the same manner that the batrachian reaches his growth, by throwing off and sending out. We were now throwing off our boyish naturalness and sending out beards, the latter of rather slow growth.

I was now eighteen. Up to this time, life, to me, had been as limpid as a mountain brook, secluded from freshets and fed by perennial springs. The one purpose had been to get onward. To reach manhood seemed to be the fruition of all hope. I was now on the borders of that mysterious and long-anticipated period, yet I cannot say that I felt like one who was approaching a haven of perfect satisfaction. The long-desired country was just before me, but obscuring clouds and mists hung over the landscape. A tremor of uncertainty and something like the shadow of a doubt toned the buoyancy of my expectations. " 'Tis ever thus " when the fondest hope, the

(120)

sweetest anticipation of life has not yet become a settled reality.

Susie Brantlett was sixteen, and was as lovable as she was beautiful. The graces of culture were visible in every feature, and added charm to every movement. The elasticity of health was in every finely chiseled member. In her clear blue eyes was the perfect blending of softness and brilliancy. Her hair was dark, soft, and abundant; and when she wore it flowing, it was indeed a charm of loveliness. The delicate tracery of veins made visible by the transparency of her complexion gave proper finish to superior beauty. Hers was a face in which all emotions were plainly visible. She was moderately tall, of medium size, well-formed, erect, splendidly poised. Her voice was clear, soft, musical. The delicately finished hand was a thing of beauty. She was a lady of the finest type, and Southern in every fiber of her nature: a true representative of the type so much admired by Southern men. Of course she was a general favorite. This was gratifying, and yet, it was a source of uneasiness. Her beauty and her intellect, so dear to me, made a prize which others would attempt to possess. The very thought was like a sword of double keenness. The very fact that we were soon to be separated was a source of constant anxiety. I was to go to college and she was to attend a "finishing school." I could not but hope that this would not be the blighting of my fondest aspirations.

During this vacation I became conscious that a great political excitement was agitating the country. Men seemed unusually restless. Gatherings were more frequent. Public speaking was epidemic. The great Democratic party, for the first time in its history, had two candidates in the field for the presidency. This divided neighbors whose political opinions had always been the same. The party became two contending factions. Each faction claimed to be the true party, and tried by arguments, earnest and vociferous, to convince the other. But the noisy disputants only served to make the division more complete. Each faction became more confirmed by controversy. All parties were trying to save the country. This was the theme on all occasions, the speakers becoming more vehement and abusive as the magnitude of the undertaking became more apparent.

Col. Parker was an important speaker. He was going to have his "rights." He had suffered outrages too long already. Patience was no longer a virtue. One day at the village store, when several neighbors had met, he was, as usual, waxing warm on this theme. Mr. Brantlett, in a very quiet tone, requested him to name the rights of which he had been deprived. He was going to have the right, he said, to carry slaves into any part of the Union without danger of molestation. He was determined that the people of the South should have the right to establish slavery in any territory with perfect impunity. Mr. Brantlett replied that by such agitation we were in danger of losing the right to keep slaves at home. But this only provoked a storm of invectives, and for the sake of peace among neighbors Mr. Brantlett said no more.

The very young men, like myself, Dolph Parker, Dick Webb, and the Allen boys, left the saving of the country to the older heads, while we tried to have the best time possible. We frequently had impromptu gatherings at each other's homes. In fact, such meetings were necessary to take up our spare time. True, we could fish or hunt or attend political meetings, which were very plentiful and stormy. We attended church nearly every Sabbath. A good deal of time was taken up in reading. Still we had ample time left for social life.

One beautiful summer day we met at Maj. Allen's. Susie Brantlett and Julia Parker were present. Music and conversation were made doubly sweet by the exuberant life and buoyant hopes of youth. It is not strange that we were having a delightful time. But there was one thought constantly present which brought something like a tinge of sadness to my mind. It was the fact that John Henderson, who had so long been our chum, was hard at work in our hearing. The spacious residence was receiving important additions, and the Hendersons were doing the work. I had learned to appreciate John's noble qualities so highly that his isolation from our society made me sad.

The parlor door opened out on a pleasant veranda. By the most natural impulse we all walked out to enjoy the cool breeze and look at the flowers. Just beyond the fence which divided the back yard from the front, and in easy speaking distance, we saw John, in his shirt sleeves, soiled with labor, carrying on his shoulder long planks to be used in the building. I did not look to see, but suspected that Dolph's lip was curled in scorn. I heard him ask Miss Minnie if she was not annoyed by the carpenters. There was a peculiar accent on *carpenters*. I thought I discovered a slight blush on Miss Minnie's face, as she replied: "No, I rather like the noise, and I frequently go in to see the work progressing." Dolph bit his lip and said no more.

But if I felt commiseration for John, he certainly seemed to feel none for himself. In a suit evidently kept for the purpose, he appeared at the dinner table, the gayest of the gay. Not one of us could talk with more intelligence. It seemed strangest of all that he could come from rough work into our circle without the least embarrassment. He did not underestimate himself because of hard conditions. Nor did he overestimate others on account of accidental advantages.

His manners were exceptionably fine. He was ever watchful for the convenience and happiness of others. In those delicate attentions and in the chaste and elegant conversation so much appreciated by ladies, he was especially gifted. He told us how he was progressing with his studies, and that he was hopeful of being able to enter college with the rest of us.  Mrs. Allen commended his diligence in overcoming difficulties.  His reply was characteristic: "One who receives little from the labor of others needs to be doubly diligent in his own labors."

When dinner was over, and while we still lingered at the table, John rose from his seat, remarking that it was time for him to go to work, and, asking Mrs. Allen to excuse him, took leave of us with a dignity that would have done honor to Chesterfield.

In the afternoon Dolph and Minnie strolled among the flowers in the front yard.  Dick Webb and Julia Parker found retreat in the summer house, while Ben and Joe solaced themselves with books or a nap.  This left me alone with Susie. I thought she never looked so beautiful.  Her vivacity was perfectly charming.  She was as cordial as I could expect, but somehow I felt that she was more distant.  I felt my own manner restrained.  The truth is, we were no longer children.  Susie was now a young lady.  This very fact seemed to make her coy, and made me awkward.  I realized that, without any estrangement of feeling, an invisible barrier had risen between us.  I began to see that a woman cannot be claimed on the ground of preëmption.  Though we had been playmates from earliest childhood, and though the tenderest feeling had always existed between

us, she was now as free as she was lovely, and
must be wooed and won if she was ever really to be
mine.   Every woman wants to be courted before
she consents to be married.   When she makes the
most important gift that a woman can make, the gift
of herself, she  wants to feel that it is by her own
volition and in response to the most earnest and
honest solicitation.   We walked among the shrubbery and toyed with the flowers, unmindful that
the long afternoon had passed and that the evening
shadows were already settling down upon us.
Her every movement was a model of grace; her
words were more than music; her laugh was the
ripple of ecstatic sweetness.   I felt that she was
the very soul of purity, the essence of loveliness.
To possess her was to have an inestimable gift of
Deity.   I instinctively felt that to bring anything
less than the purest motives to such a shrine as
this would be wounding to the highest attributes
of my nature.   In the glow of this love my ideal of
life was heightened, and I had a higher conception of womanhood and manhood than ever before.
To measure up to this ideal, and become worthy
of the object of my adoration, and to possess this
treasure of womanly loveliness, was the resolve
deep down in my nature that quiet evening. ·

With such feeling and such resolve life had now
a  new  meaning  and  a  grander  purpose.   In a
dream of ecstacy I returned to my home after escorting Susie to hers.   That night I slept on the
borders of enchanted ground which must be akin

to heaven. Next morning in the very exuberance of life I walked through the forest and seemed to have a sweeter communion with nature than ever before. Why I went toward Mr. Brantlett's the reader can probably guess, but I did not set out with that intention. To go by there would probably have been the nearest, or at least the best, way anywhere. I took that direction, and kept it, till I found myself passing the house. To my great joy, I saw Susie, even at that early hour, out in the flower yard. In her straw hat and white apron, her cheeks aglow with the fresh air and busy work, I thought that of all the daughters of Eve she was surely the most beautiful. The flowers were gay with rich profusion, rejoicing in the morning light. In vain they tried to rival the beauty of the nymph divinely fair, who was teaching them the art of superior loveliness. It was a picture not to be disturbed, and so I passed by unnoticed. Under the inspiration of that hour my thoughts fell into rhyme, and this was the result:

MY NYMPH AMONG THE FLOWERS.

When lovely summer's finest tone
  Had deeply touched the leafy bowers,
The poet's charm was o'er me thrown
  By my sweet nymph among the flowers.

The morn in beauty's fairest sheen
  Had wrapped this lovely land of ours,
And walking forth in nature's green
  I saw my nymph among the flowers.

The shades of light in dewdrops glowed,
  The birds made music in the bowers,

And life's sweet symphonies there flowed,
  Around my nymph among the flowers.

And nature's beauties climbed to sight
  Like corals in the ocean's dowers,
And greeting, filled the waving light
  Around my nymph among the flowers.

In vain their charms of beauty flowed,
  In grass or blooms or leafy towers,
The sweetest of life's graces glowed—
  My lovely nymph among the flowers.

Of all that's rare by nature brought,
  When winter's storm no longer lowers,
There's naught compares with that that's wrought,
  In my fair nymph among the flowers.

What if the poet, lucky shrimp!
  While pleasures speed on golden hours,
Does charm and hold that lovely nymph,
  The nymph I saw among the flowers.

And now my little song I'll close,
  And leave it to the fair one's powers,
To guess both where and when it was
  I saw my nymph among the flowers.

But should she wish to see the elf,
  She need but try the mirror's powers,
And there she'll see the nymph's own self,
  The nymph I saw among the flowers.

It was charming to witness the shy blush which, in spite of her effort to conceal, spread in lovely wavelets over Susie's features as she read these verses, and pretended not to know who was meant by the "Nymph among the Flowers."

# CHAPTER XVIII.

## MR. WILSON.

DURING this vacation the young men were pushing forward a social revolution that for some time had been progressing. It was no less than getting the young ladies out of the aristocratic family carriages and taking them to church in single buggies. Why this had not been done all the time, I do not understand. But having a taste of the better method, we, by persistence, so far succeeded as to carry our point, and the girls too. So I had the inestimable privilege nearly every Sabbath of escorting Susie out to church.

The young men had now two reasons for attending divine services. First, they could have the girls with them, going and returning. It must be confessed that this was a potent reason. We were now all punctual church-goers. I was especially zealous! But, in the second place, the earnest eloquence of our new pastor, Mr. Wilson, was attracting great attention. This is saying much, for just at that time it was difficult for anything outside of politics to gain much notice. It was well to have something to divert the mind from the all-absorbing themes of the hustings.

The lectures at school had especially prepared us to appreciate Mr. Wilson. Mr. Dunbar was

9                                         (129)

himself a lover of nature. He had pointed out the existence and all-pervading influence of her laws. He had dwelt on her beauty and unfolded to our minds the relations of her forces. Thus the desire for knowledge had by being partially satisfied become doubly eager.

Mr. Wilson's capacity for presenting ideas in attractive form was truly wonderful. He was remarkable for breadth of view and beauty of imagery. Whatever his theme, he never failed to catch the rays of relation which showed connection with all else. Faith, repentance, conversion, or holy living, did not stand off isolated. These were acts and relations in perfect accord with all life and all being. We touch and are touched by the infinite variety, and are parts of the grand unity which embraces all. Spiritual life is as much in accord with the universe as natural life. He claimed that it is misleading to say natural life as distinguished from spiritual, for all life is natural.

One sermon impressed me very much. It was the "Vision of Divine Glory, or the Picture of Providence," based on the first chapter of Ezekiel. I was surprised that so much thought and beauty could be drawn from the prophecy of Ezekiel. I had thought that the book was well symbolized by its own valley of dry bones; but, listening to Mr. Wilson, I concluded that the dryness was in my own mind. The prophet, he said, was in captivity; his own land and venerated city were in ruins; the chosen people languished under the rod of the oppressor. It was natural that he should study the mysteries of Providence. By the river of Chebar he was engaged in the most intense devotion. His mind was all aglow with the prophetic fire. He was prepared to see visions. A whirlwind, the harbinger of revelation, came out of the north. He saw a cloud the color of amber, having the appearance of fire infolding itself. The fiery cloud seemed to be dissolving, but still kept entire. Such is providence. Things seem to be held with an unsteady purpose. Apparent wastes are everywhere seen. Chance and accident seem to fall to the lot of men, and largely to influence the course of things. Yet nature holds entire.

Nothing, however small, ever falls out of nature's grasp. Combinations are forever changing. Organisms grow and decay. Old races die out and new ones spring into life. But nature never grows old. She loses none of her freshness, none of her potency, by the lapse of ages. When vast eras pass before the mental vision, and we see that the wholeness of nature is still unimpaired, we perceive that chance and accident have no place in the allotment of things. As the eye of the mind passes along the ages, we take in the great fact that laws stronger than fate and gentler than an infant's breathing control everything in the domain of being. As the grand procession of things marches along by us, the mind is impressed with the absolute unity of all that exists. A combination of purposes is perceptible in all being.

In the cloud was the appearance of four living
creatures. These were cherubim, symbols of
divine glory. They were composite beings to de-
note the different qualities of divine government.
Each had four faces: that of a man, a lion, an ox,
an eagle. These indicated intelligence, strength,
patience, movement. Such are the elements of
providence. Intelligence that never makes mis-
takes, never experiments; strength that never
fails; patience that never wearies; and movement
never out of time.

By the living creatures were wheels whose
height was " dreadful." There was the appearance of a " wheel in the middle of a wheel." Nature is orbital, circular, globular. The worlds
move in orbits; life and being have circulation;
matter naturally forms into globes. Good words
and works go forth to bless the world, and then
return in blessings to those who sent them forth.
Efforts to injure others are apt to return, like the
boomerang, on those who gave them horrid birth.
Thoughts and actions, like chickens, come home
to roost. In these circles of influence all human
lives are ground to powder or rounded into gems.

Above the crystal was a throne of sapphire, and
on the throne the appearance of a man. Here is
the symbol of enthroned intelligence and controlling power. All things bear testimony that they
are controlled by one power. A power which dis-
plays intelligence infinite, looking to the ultimate
good of all. Through all the mysteries and intri-

cacies of nature, we catch glimpses of purpose,
" a labor working to an end."

From such " stepping stones " of thought the
mind adores the God of all.

Such are the main thoughts of the sermon.
The impressive tones of voice, the enforcing ges-
tures, the flash of the eye, and the personal mag-
netism of the man are all lost on paper. The sermon was a tonic, a means of grace to the body as
well as to the soul. I felt the effects on myself,
and noticed them on others. The step was more
elastic, movements more springy, the manner more
animated, more graceful.

The sermon was followed by a love feast, at
least so far as I was concerned, for I took Susie
with me in the buggy, and was soon lost to all else.

# CHAPTER XIX.

## PLUM CREEK CHURCH.

ONE Saturday morning, while with small prospects of success I was casting about for a pleasant way to spend the day, I was greeted by the cheerful salutation of John Henderson, "Good morning, Sam. Well, old chum," and his voice with merriment rang, "we have knocked off for the week, and I'm going home. Mr. Wilson preaches at our church to-day, and I have come to invite you home with me, and we can attend church."

"Certainly, John," I replied, "I am delighted to go with you." Calling Dick to saddle my horse, I invited John to a seat in the hall, while I made ready to start.

We were soon on the way. At once there was a complete change of scenery. The broad level fields of growing crops were left behind. Hills and valleys, or "hollows" as we called them, all covered with heavy forest, while wild flowers and singing birds added charm to the deep shade; such was the scenery through which we rode.

Youth is always in sympathy with the woods. This may be a trait which has survived since the time when our ancestors lived in the wilds of undisturbed nature. Inherited instincts play an im-

(134)

portant part in every human life.    The instincts of wildness inherited from remote times, are felt more in childhood and youth, while the later tendencies to civilization come to us in our maturer age.

Riding over these giant hills and down into the deep, narrow vales, feasting the eyes on the wild luxuriance of nature, and inhaling the soft air of summer, we felt all the zest of life and glow of health.    Our studies in botany came to our aid in giving names to the plants we saw.

In a deep valley, where the forest was unusually dense, and the rich vegetable mold of ages, like a soft carpet, sank deep beneath the feet, we found a rare and beautiful flower.    It was a " lady's slipper."    Moved by a common impulse, we made a perceptible halt to admire this gem of the woods. It hung like a tiny lamp of beauty, in pleasing contrast with the deep, somber shade.    Here was a place to muse and talk; a place where the pleasant fellowship of congenial minds was softened and elevated by the wider communion of nature. It was a restful place; a place where Pan, in ancient times, might have inspired his devotees; or where, in later ages, fairies might have danced with delight.

Looking back over the experience of the past, it appears to me that life and responsibility never rested with lighter burden on the mind than on that bright morning of my ride with John through the woods to Plum Creek Church.    But even then the brightness was not without a shadow.    By some

occult law of our nature, something like a veil of
sadness seems to wave always in conscious near-
ness to our minds, even in the seasons of our most
untarnished delights.  A sense of unrest, it may
be a prophecy of evil to come, casts a shadowy
tinge of sorrow over the brightest scenes and
sweetest experiences of life.

The people who attended church at Plum Creek
were a study to me.  They contrasted strangely
with the congregation at Conway Chapel, only a
few miles away.  No fine carriages with likely
drivers were on parade.  Most of the people came
on foot; some on horses, often two or three on
the same horse.  In some cases the head of the
family, with two or three boys,  came afoot, while
the family, packed on the family horse, came slowly on behind.  Some families came in wagons.
Some of the men who walked came in their shirt
sleeves, carrying a thin coat which looked like a
strip of cloth or a napkin, thrown across the shoulder, ready to be donned before going into church.

The boys and girls were brusk, ruddy, and shy;
manifesting in their easy awkwardness a strange
mixture of timidity and independence.  They acted as if oppressed by a sense of rudeness, and yet
animated by a feeling that worth is greater than
polish.

The people met and commingled with very little
ceremony.  There was an absence of all studied
politeness.  They seemed to be wholly natural,
and did and said things as whim, fancy, or feeling

prompted. As compared with the people at Conway, I made these observations:

They had broader faces and thicker bodies. They had larger waists, and were consequently nearer the same size all the way from shoulder to hip. They were more angular both as to body and features. Civilization long continued tends to change the shape of the body, as well as the character of the mind. It gives a finer chiseling to the features, and a milder color to the complexion. It has a decided tendency to raise the forehead and retire the cheek bones. To give the mouth a backset, and the back head a forward drive. It gives to the general outlines more symmetrical curvatures, giving more of a heartlike shape to the bust. All this is working the animal out and working manhood up. Civilization, so some of the wise men think, is the sea on which the race is drifting away from the monkey type. Their manners were more eccentric, and consequently gave greater variety. Each was a law unto himself when it came to manners. Their speech was uncultivated; consequently retained its unsophisticated force. About Conway the gentility perspired this warm weather; down here, at Plum Creek, these fellows "sweated," because it was hot. A small percentage of the people about Conway had auburn hair and pimples; down here a larger per cent. were red headed and freckled faced.

In fact there were two civilizations here side by side; one based on slave labor, highly cultured,

ease-loving, and self-satisfied; the other struggling with free self-labor, stinted, restless, and
and without the means of culture.

As I have since learned, similar conditions might
have been found in many places throughout the
country. There was a marked difference between
the planters who worked slaves, and the small
farmers who worked in competition with slavery.
All the best lands had been bought up for slave labor and the hills and narrow valleys left to the "po'
white trash." Between these populations there
was very little communication, and less sympathy.

All these facts did not occur to me that day while
I was watching with keen interest the people who
were my near neighbors, and yet very distant
strangers. They have come to me as the result of
further observation and study. I have noticed
that different localities, with different conditions
of soil and surroundings, have people of different
individualities. But for the fact that people are
constantly changing localities, neighborhoods of
people would be as different from each other as
are the localities where they dwell.

I was much interested in the conversation of the
elderly men. The directness and the quaintness
of their talk was to me novel and amusing: "How
goes it, Brother Shaw?" "Just middlin', Brother Smith; how's all your folks?" "Wall, able
to eat all they can git." "How's the craps?"
"All settin' up, 'ceptin' the late corn; that's 'bout
gone up the spout."

This, with much more similar talk, occurred out in the church yard in the shade of a tree, while the congregation was gathering. It was at least refreshing to get where the political elements were not stirred, and to find men who had something to do besides saving the country. The sisters in the house were having a lively time, discussing the neighborhood gossip, while among some the snuffbox was slyly circulated from hand to hand. The young men were mostly content to cast sly glances at the rustic maidens, while the maidens took refuge behind their mothers, as if they thought it would be a bold sin to be looked at too closely. Finally the hour for preaching came, as did also the preacher. There was now a hush; the old brethren all had on their coats; gossip was allowed to rest; all traces of the snuffbox were smoothed out; and all seemed ready to enter on the serious business of the occasion. Mr. Wilson was evidently a favorite here, as among the more cultured congregations. A feeling of eager expectancy animated the entire assembly. The preacher's theme was the supreme law of God: "Thou shalt love the Lord thy God with all thy heart, and with all thy soul, and with all thy mind, and with all thy strength;" and "Thou shalt love thy neighbor as thyself." This law of love has two divisions, expressive of our twofold obligations; to love God and to love man. The full extent of our capacity is the measure of our obligation to love God. The love of self is the measure of obligation to love our fellow-man. Self-love is the measure of fellow-love. The obligation is put in another form, which may make it easier to be comprehended. "As you would that men should do to you, do ye also to them likewise." The simple requirement is that love to our fellow-man should be wholly unselfish. This meets the whole case, solves all the difficulty. A man blinded by selfishness cannot understand the law. Eliminate selfishness and a man would naturally practice the requirements. Let all the relations in life be regarded as reciprocal, and always, when it is your time to do, put self in the other place, and then do to the one in the other place as self would in that place like to be done by.

It is in accordance with the eternal fitness of things that the supreme law should be the law of love. The least thought will convince us that this is right and best. Love is the strongest, gentlest, and most enduring quality of which we can be possessed. To make our eternal welfare hinge on its exercise is therefore the policy of both infinite wisdom and supreme goodness. It is the one thing that we can do best, and best continue to do. It is the one thing in the doing of which we are most highly blessed.

This law expresses our natural and only safe relation to both God and man. It is the law that can never be replaced by another. It exactly meets the case. In all the thoughts of Supreme Wisdom there can evidently be nothing better, nothing wiser. It is the law that must be supreme in any world, even in the highest heaven. Through all time and throughout all space where created intelligences live, this is the first great law. It was born with the creation of the first responsible beings, and must continue while such beings continue. Its observance is eternal life, its violation is eternal death.

These thoughts, made attractive by the beautiful imagery and enforced by impassioned eloquence made a deep impression. These " common people heard the message gladly." I never saw a more appreciative audience. Though I think they were enthused not so much by the literary, as by the moral beauty of the sermon. They drank in the truth with a relish which must have been a source of inspiration to the preacher. He evidently preached with more feeling here than he was accustomed to do at Conway. Good hearers have a powerful tendency to make good speakers.

When the services were over, and John and I were on the way to his home, I asked him why they had preaching on Saturday. He said: " It is because the Sabbaths are claimed by the wealthy churches, such as Conway Chapel and New Prospect. It does look strange, and a little hard, too, to have preaching all the time on Saturdays down here, where everybody has to work; and all the time on Sundays in the wealthy neighborhoods, where people have nothing to do but go to church every day in the week, if they wish to. But," he

continued after a moment's pause, "they pay
nearly all the expenses, and it is probably right.
At least, the people down here, who can pay the
preacher but a little, feel like they have no right
to complain.    The preaching on Saturday is worth
a great deal more than they can pay."

" So it is still true," I replied, " that the poor
have the gospel preached to them, provided they
can find time to lay aside their toil and go out to
church during work days."

John smiled, and invited me to alight, for we
had now reached our stopping place.

The true nobility of John nowhere appeared to
better advantage than in his own home.   The
years of study at the academy and the superior
brilliancy of his own mind had given him a polish
to which the rest of the family were entire strangers.    It was beautiful to witness the loving simplicity of manner by which he drew them to himself, effectually preventing even the beginning of
any caste barrier between him and them.   I learned
from their conversation that John had been in-
structing the children and furnishing them with
useful books.    John at home was not a case of
the diamond in the ash bank, but rather like a
precious aromatic imparting its own fragrance to
all surrounding objects.

Having spent a pleasant day, I returned home
in the dusk of evening.

# CHAPTER XX.

A S the summer wore on, the political firmament became overcast with the signs of the coming storm. Agitation became more general. The speakers gathered momentum from their own vehemence.

Never before was there such a clamor for "rights." Public speakers wanted "our rights." Newspapers demanded "our rights." Groups of earnest men in consultation said that we must have "our rights." There was speaking on all occasions, and nearly all of the same kind, a cry for "our rights." The men who felt that "our rights" had not been invaded, or who thought it prudent to accept the present situation rather than risk the consequences of so much excitement, had nothing to drive them to the same earnestness. Their protests were mild, and consequently disregarded.

All the anger, passions, vehemence of a most stormy campaign were expressed in the one word, "OUR RIGHTS." Our rights must be maintained at all hazards. The man who will not contend for his rights is a coward or a fool. Nobody wanted to be considered either. Conservative men grew doubtful and weakened in their purpose. Men

(143)

who disliked pressure went with the current rather
than try to stem its force. The prolonged agoniz-
ing cry for "our rights" was gaining additional
volume every day. "Rights, rights, rights! Give
us our rights or give us death!"

A few men saw danger ahead and tried by wise
and temperate council to call a halt. They were at
last aroused to a sense of danger. The love of
country, the blessings of peace, the evils of agitation, the dangers of division, the fate of other nations were all pleaded, but in vain. As well try to
stop an avalanche. The movement was constantly
gaining momentum.

The constant agitation became painful. There
was unrest throughout the country. The feeling
would have been more depressing but for the general belief that the excitement would die out after
the election. Whatever the result, it was hoped
that the minority would submit, and that things
would resume their usual course. There would
then be no further cause for contention. In this
hope my fears were somewhat quieted.

It was now time to get ready to leave for college.
With mingled feelings of expectancy, hope, and
fear I went about that duty. I was to go to Virginia. This was good. I wanted to see the old
state, the home of my ancestors. Then I wanted
to travel, as I had been but little from home, and
had seen but little of the world. College life also
had its charms. I had looked forward to this as the
crowning period of young manhood and the door

to all honors beyond. I was glad of the prospect of collegiate honors and advantages.

But the separation from home and Susie was regarded with a feeling of sadness. I could in due time return with welcome to my home. But my claim upon Susie was not so well established. Always with this thought came something like an aching care close about my heart. Then, in spite of all my reasoning and efforts to assure myself to the contrary, a dread of disaster to the country grew heavy upon my mind. So many prophecies of evil, spoken with so much earnestness, were enough to cast a gloom on the horizon of the future.

But if the distant future appeared misty, I had at least the privilege of looking at it through a silvery sheen, the nearer lining to the distant cloud. Such is life. The brightness is never without a shadow, the darkness is never without a glimmer of light. The silvery lining that was now so bright to me consisted mainly in the fact that I was to take Susie as far as Nashville, where she was to " finish." This was especially gratifying. It was an evidence of confidence on the part of her parents, which I thought stood for a great deal. Then we were to spend one more Sabbath at home, and I was to take her out to Conway Chapel.

I was in serious doubt, just at this time, whether it was best to avow my love to Susie and ask her to be mine. As it would be a long time before we were to be out of school, I was afraid that the pro-

posal would be considered premature, result in
postponement, perhaps indefinite, and might
weaken my chance of ultimate success. Then,
unless my suit should meet with prompt and favorable response, it might interfere with my taking her
to Nashville the next week. This I could not but
regard as a calamity. So halting, doubting, trusting, misgiving, I wavered for awhile in poise between desire and prudence, and finally concluded
to abide my time for a more auspicious opportunity. I was in sight of the pearly gate of my earthly paradise, but was afraid to sue for admittance.

Sunday morning was delightful, and so was
Susie. As I escorted her from the door of her
beautiful little home that bright morning, I am
sure that my eyes never before feasted on so much
loveliness. Her conversation was vivacity put to
music. Her smile was the play of sunshine over
the ripples of my agitated nature. Her presence
was like a rainbow of promise to me amid the
stormy elements of our political sky. Driving
with her to church through a country unusually
blessed with growing abundance, and the smile of
peace resting on all the landscape, it seemed to me
that our rights could hardly be in danger. And
especially did it appear that a country so blessed
with peace and so highly favored with heaven's
rich abundance could never become the scene of
cruel and bloody war.

A dashing turnout came into the road just
ahead of us. It was Dolph at his best. He was

dressed in unusually fine style. His span of horses fairly glistened in the sun, while his silver-mounted buggy became a reflector to all surrounding objects. This was evidently a special occasion with him, as it was with me. He was going with Miss Minnie out to church, as I was going with Susie. "A fellow-feeling makes us wondrous kind." I felt like extending the hand of fellowship with hearty good wishes for the success of us both.

Mr. Wilson was in his happiest mood that morning. His subject was, "The Presence of God in All His Works," based on the idea several times expressed in the Bible: "God is all in all." He held that God could not be absent from anything or any place; that he is actively present everywhere, and because of that presence the appropriate work of nature goes on; that the proof of his presence is inherent in every phase of being. The laws of nature are his methods. Their force is his force, working out the ends of nature or providence. The divine force, that which sustains the universe, is but the action of divine will. "He spake, and it was done; he commanded, and it stood fast." Nature is God's thinking made visible.

Such laws as polarity, gravitation, cohesion, and motion are inherent in the divine plans, because they express the exactness of the divine mind. Because of their interacting forces, everything, from the largest world or system of worlds to the smallest mote or atom, is in its right place and doing its appropriate work.  In this great physical universe, this  divine thinking made visible, we see dovetailing into every part the evidence of spiritual existence.

We see everywhere evidence of a first great Cause.  Not a primordial force by which things exist, but evidences of a spiritual personal being with intelligence and individuality.  Not the soul of nature, but of a Being infinitely greater than nature; one who by filling nature full, loses none of his personality; one whose individuality would remain unhurt if all nature could be destroyed; one sufficient to animate a million universes, or remain just as great without an atom of matter.

Can we believe that the universe consists only of matter?  Our minds instinctively shrink from such an idea.  The unbiased mind naturally believes that matter could never have been without an adequate cause for its existence.  But granting its existence, there is manifestly nothing in it to produce all the life, thought, and spirit that we see and feel about us.  There can be no cause for these things, except in the one Supreme Intelligence.  Our minds are absolutely insulted by an invitation to believe less.

The God whose image is reflected to our minds from the beautiful fabric of nature has all the attributes of wisdom, power, and spirituality to stand as the eternal cause of all that ever did or ever can exist.  In him there is no tendency to waste or decay.  The laws of his nature work to eternal stability. The making of worlds does not make him less; their decay does not add to his greatness. He remains ever the same, unchanged amid all changes.

He changes not, because absolute perfection is essentially unchangeable. We are commanded to strive after a like perfection. "Be ye therefore perfect, even as your Father which is in heaven is perfect." It is the will of God that we should always advance toward his perfection. This cannot be if decay is the ultimate law. Therefore we are invited to the belief that some of the laws of God tend to eternal advancement. That there is a realm where the laws work not to decay, but to eternal life. Such laws secure immortality. The boundary is between the natural and the spiritual. All organisms in the domain of nature tend to ultimate decay; all in the spiritual domain tend to perpetual existence. When the laws of spiritual life are not violated, the being lives in happiness coeternal with God.

Would not an eternal God desire eternal creatures? It is certainly reasonable that he should. The more like himself they become, the better he would be pleased. The desires of God become fixed realities. If it is reasonable to believe that God desires such beings; it is still more reasonable to believe that such beings do and must exist.

To my mind the belief in God is a mental necessity. I cannot believe in an intelligent and spiritual universe such as I am in contact with every day, without believing in an intelligent and spirit-

ual God.   Then it is easier to believe that this God
would surround himself by immortal beings, par-
taking to some extent his own nature, than it is to
believe that he remains forever alone amid the rise
and decay of transitory beings who could only, as
through a glass darkly, catch glimpses of his glory,
utter feeble praises for a moment, and then pass
into silence forever.   The existence of God implies the existence of immortal beings to adore that
God.

Thus reason and revelation combine to establish
the main points of religion, the existence of God,
and the immortality of man.   The immortality of
man implies spiritual relations, a spiritual domain,
governed by spiritual laws.   The word "universe"
should be extended not only to embrace the physical, but also the spiritual, in one harmonious
whole.   There is no impassable gulf fixed between
the physical and the spiritual.   What we know of
the perfection of the laws of nature warrants the
belief that a like perfection pervades the entire
unlimited domain of God.   "God is all in all."
This applies to all and makes a unit of all.   The
spiritual and physical are one complete harmony
of existence.   What we want is a genius broad
enough, with towering mind and vigorous faith,
whose hand of cunning, trained to methods wise,
shall be able to sweep all the chords of wisdom,
and show the harmony in all the works of God.

Such were the main thoughts around which the
preacher wrapped the beautiful sheen of poetic

verbiage, and held us in the thraldom of attention rapt and sweet. After services there was more than the usual amount of social good feeling, in which country congregations are apt to indulge. So many young people were now to leave for college, it was a time for general hand shaking and farewells, with good wishes. Susie, Minnie, and Julia, to say nothing of the half dozen young men, were now mingling with friends before a long separation.

# CHAPTER XXI.

## OFF FOR COLLEGE.

LIKE an April cloud which weeps in the sun-shine, and gives the beautiful bow of prom-ise, such was Susie the morning of our departure. Her smiles and tears sported with each other, as lilies laugh and weep in the summer shower. The mental picture which I received of her that morning has been a souvenir of joy in many a hard hour since. In regard to the gambols of smiles and tears, Susie was not specially different from her companions. But the smiles rapidly gained the ascendency, and brightness held the sway. We were a company of gay and light-hearted young people, with just a flash of transitory sadness. The homes we left were as bright and cheerful as were ever blessed by nature's genial sun and showers.

With never a thought of disaster, or a sigh for endangered rights, we boarded the train and were off to our places of study. Dolph Parker, John Henderson, Dick Webb, Ben and Joe Allen, and I, were bound for college in Virginia, while Susie Brantlett, Minnie Allen, and Julia Parker were going to " finish " in Nashville.

Railroad travel was new to us. The rapidity with which we sped over the country seemed to us

(152)

perfectly marvelous. The sensations were new and exhilarating. I remember how vivid was the impression that the land outside the car window was running back. Fields, fences, trees, and houses seemed to be flying past. But as I looked farther out this apparent motion ceased; a center was reached, and the distant landscape was moving with the train. The land had an eddying or cyclonic motion. The great broad fields seemed to be winding round and round. The size of the eddy varied with the different landscapes.

A question sprang in my mind that morning which has often since come up for consideration and still waits an answer: What is to be the effect of this rapid and easy transportation over hill and dale on the mental constitution of man in the coming ages? How it adds to the continuity of view! How it aids in generalization! It is a new and mighty factor in the acquisition of knowledge. What is to be the effect on the thinking faculties? None of the great thinkers of the world ever sat by a car window and saw the world flit by them. Will the future thinkers show the effect of railroads in their mental wares? Will their reason be more accurate, or their poetry more sublime? Will their conceptions of truth be broader, or their tastes more refined? What is to be the literary product of a railroad civilization?

But why should I be musing in speculations like these while Susie is here to claim my entire attention? Aye, certainly she is here, and must have

my attention. But why is it that we so often let
our talk run in one channel and our thoughts in
another? When conversation assumes a many-
cornered phase, so that all parties can take a hand,
as we do in "town ball," one can give a few
strikes or catches when it comes his turn, and still
have time for speculation. Youthful wit and wisdom were playing a high game, and I could pitch
a thought, or strike at an idea, or miss a meaning,
especially the latter item, with as much facility as
the rest, and still have time to observe the passing
scenes and muse on their meaning.

The scenery through which we passed was of
the most familiar kind. The country was mainly
devoted to cotton. Vast fields joined each other,
presenting to view miles and miles of cotton farms.
The plants at this season were three or four feet
high, and spread so as to meet in the "middle of
the rows," thus completely shading all the ground.
The bolls near the ground were open, and picking
had begun. The white bolls, green leaves, and
yellow or red blooms presented a variegated expanse of vegetable luxuriance peculiar to the
South. Nothing approaching to this in magnitude
was to be met with in any other land. It was a
vast sea of green, underlaid with white, and sprinkled all over with yellow and red.

While I was making these observations on the
country without, the play of wit and wisdom still
ran on within. But both were disturbed by a conversation near by, which had for some time been

growing louder and more earnest. Some gentlemen were discussing the problem of supreme importance: the political situation of the country.
The group was constantly growing larger, as one
after another left his seat and went up to take part
in the discussion. This had gone on till now most
of the men in the car were drawn into close and
earnest debate, each one more desirous to speak
than to listen.

Only two of the men were for Douglas. One
of these, as I gathered from the boisterous dispute,
was a Douglas elector, and he had with him one
faithful friend. All the rest, save one elderly gentleman, evidently "an old line Whig," who was
for Bell and Everett, were for Breckinridge and
Southern rights.

"I tell you, gentleman," cried the elector in
earnest and excited tones, "we must not be sectional. No sectional man can be an acceptable
President to the whole people. Mr. Douglas is a
national man, and a true representative of the old
national party."

To this there was a vociferous reply by at least
a half dozen eager disputants, each trying to get a
hearing. The replies were nearly all of the same import. But the one who spoke the loudest is the one
whose answer I remember. He was a man of commanding mien; face florid; eyes prominent; wore
side whiskers; and gesticulated vehemently. He
said: "Mr. Breckinridge is not sectional. He is
national, because he is for the Constitution. No man

is national who does not demand the enforcement of the Constitution, with all the rights in that instrument guaranteed to us by the fathers. We want our rights under the Constitution, and we intend to have them. We demand the repeal of all laws contrary to the Constitution. The man who is the friend of these unconstitutional laws is purely sectional. Mr. Breckinridge is opposed to all unconstitutional and sectional laws, and stands for the untrammeled Constitution now and forever." With this he brought his fist down on the seat with a striking emphasis.

"I grant you," replied the elector, "that Mr. Breckinridge is for the Constitution as we all interpret that instrument. But he is the nominee of a section, he is supported by a section, and is regarded by all out of that section as a sectional candidate, and as such cannot be acceptable to the whole people. We must grant something to the views and feelings of people in all parts of this great republic."

"Yes," retorted he with the side whiskers, " we have yielded to these abolitionists until they have grown so fanatical that they no longer have any regard for our rights, or even for the Constitution by which these rights are protected. We should yield not another inch. The time has come to demand our rights." Again the fist came down as if to drive the idea home with tenfold force.

Just here the elector by a gesture and attitude of peculiar earnestness, secured a hushed and respected attention, as he replied with a calmness in his voice which indicated clear and decisive conviction: "I tell you, gentlemen, you mistake the strength of the enemy. If we fail to elect Mr. Douglas, Abraham Lincoln will be the next President of the United States." This fairly raised a howl of indignation. "The idea! the man who is the representative of only a small fanatical faction, the man whose party hates the Constitution because it protects Southern rights." But the elector, still composed, managed to project another sentence into the confusion. "If we set the example," said he, "of voting for a man who represents our interests and views, and who is supported by no other section of the country, we should not be surprised if we are beaten at our own game."

Just at this point in the controversy the whistle blew a halt. This was not intended for the argument, though it had the good effect to bring it to a close for the present. The brakeman on the platform began working vigorously to slow up the train. No air brakes in those days. So after much tugging at the brakes, the train finally came to a stop, with laborious jars and thumps.

We had reached a town where there was to be a joint political discussion, and our disputants began to make preparations to leave the train. A vast and excited throng was awaiting the arrival of the train. Hats and handkerchiefs were waving in all directions, while from hundreds of throats came the cry, repeated again and again: "Hurrah for Breckinridge! Hurrah for Breckinridge!" I really felt sorry for our elector. Looking over the vast crowd outside, he could hear but few and feeble huzzas for Douglas. But almost immediately a committee of reception sprang into the car to bid him welcome.

The elector went out with his friends and for a moment stood on the platform, looking down on a sea of upturned faces. He was a fine specimen of cultivated manhood. He was at once greeted by a good-natured laugh. As the leader of a forlorn hope, the innate love of fair play came to his relief. This great assembly of politicians evidently felt that they had nothing to fear from the cause that he was representing, and could afford to be magnanimous. A volunteer spokesman in the crowd seemed to express the general feeling when he said: "Come on, Colonel. We admire your grit, and will give you a hearing." The great throng surged away toward the place where the speaking was to begin.

After this we had a lull in the political discussion. But all along the way there were evidences of great excitement. The people who came on the train talked politics. At all the stations were groups of men in earnest consultation; and whenever we overheard a remark to indicate the topic of interest, it was sure to be politics. The whole country was agitated as never before on a similar occasion. It was on the eve of a most eventful election, and people felt that the destinies of the country were largely concerned in the result.

In those days railroad travel was not so rapid, and connections not so close as at present, and we were more than two days reaching Nashville. But this appeared to us as marvelously fast traveling. Besides, we were in no hurry. We were young, free from care, and fond of each other's company. Travel was new and delightful. There was no reason why we should hurry through scenes where we might linger with delight. We had plenty of time. Time with us had always been plentiful, because we had always been supplied with all that was necessary for our well being. When desires outrun ability, then time is scarce and valuable. The chase after these desires gets many people into a rapid race through life. The man whose wants are supplied has ample time. How few such men!

We had plenty of time! In view of experience since, how strangely this sounds! How delightful it is to have plenty of time! O for the occasion when I can let loose the tissues of exertion, and once more float with the tide, having plenty of time! But few men ever experience that pleasure. When we have once taken hold of the realities of life, we are apt to find that it is like grasping the electrodes of a battery: unpleasant to hold on, and hard to let go.

As a rule, the men who have plenty of time are those who have let time severely alone. It is like strong drink: when a man has begun to use it in earnest it is hard to stop. The Indian, when he is full, and can lie in the autumn sun, while the squaw gathers in the scanty crop and dresses the game, has plenty of time. The man who has inherited an income sufficient to meet all his wants, and who is making no effort to increase the patrimony, has plenty of time. The man who from any cause is letting the world drift, and is making no effort, has plenty of time.

A few people have too much time. It hangs heavily on their minds. It wrinkles up around their spirits in the form of *ennui*. This is a disease from which American business men are very far removed.

We spent two days in Nashville. We saw the young ladies comfortably situated in their new homes. My leave of Susie, while it had a tinge of sadness, was full of hope and joyous expectations. We again boarded the train and were soon following the iron horse, whose head was to the east. Without any mishap or experience worthy of note, we reached our destination.

# CHAPTER XXII.

## In College.

IN college! This is the goal to which years of labor had been directed. An air of culture pervaded the place. The manners and language of the people indicated refinement. The importance of education was the constant theme with the Chancellor and professors. The desire for education took possession of my energies and aroused my ambition. I had never before so fully appreciated its supreme importance. And a feeling of its importance has been growing on me all the years since. Yet the full import of the idea of education cannot be realized. The time has not yet come for any man to grasp the subject in all its fullness. Indeed, the time may never come when any one mind can possess the amplitude of range to estimate all the delights and advantages of truest culture. However vast the stores of the mind, there are vaster stores for other minds to gather. However bright the stars, and noble the constellations that cluster in our mental sky, there are yet brighter heavens below the horizon, nobler stars of light in clusters of richer glory, to rise on the minds of generations yet unborn.

The grand object of education, the ideal of excellence which floats in the van of our noblest en-

11                                         (161)

deavor, is to interpret to the human intellect the relation and nature of universal being. It is to enable man to comprehend the wonderfully complicated construction of nature, and to appreciate the illimitable tissue of interacting forces by which all created existence moves responsive to the will of the great Creator. It is to enable us to appreciate God in all his works and ways.

Such culture not only unrolls nature to the mind, but it unrolls the mind itself. As a flower spreads its petals to the life-giving influences of sun and shower, so the mind unfolds its convolutions to the sweet influences of proper education. Culture continually enlarges the range of mental vision. The mind gains point after point of the rising peaks of truth, and is gladdened with an ever expanding view. To the growing mind, knowledge is a growing picture of beautifully blended truths, bounded by a constantly retreating horizon. To education, therefore, belongs sources of blessings to man, which are inexhaustible in supply and infinite in range.

To educate is to add to the stock of mind, and thus give to the world more of man. It gives to the world more intellect, more integrity, more religion. It adds to the precious stock of soul which our world is continually pouring forth to God. Education, in its widest range and ultimate end, looks to the elevation and regeneration of our race. The pivotal utterance of the world's greatest Teacher is contained in the great commission, the command to go and teach the nations.   When this shall have been fully done, done to the extent of the meaning, then our planet, as she threads her ethereal way amid the throng of sister worlds, will bear her due amount of consecrated intellect as acceptable incense to God.

Of course education, as we here use the word, does not consist wholly in mental drill after the manner of schools, but is the unfolding and development of all the resources of good in man; the unfolding and proper growth of mind; the drawing out and training of the affections; the health and discipline of the body.   Education is to secure the full vigor and well-being of our intellectual, moral, and physical faculties.   It adds strength and polish to the whole man.

To accomplish this in its fullest sense, we must begin with the children.   If the state is to have citizens competent to superintend the delicate machinery of government, we must educate the young.   If the Church is to have ministers and members fully qualified to guard the ark of truth and lead the world to a better life, we must begin in the primary school or in the nursery.   If the mists of ignorance and the fogs of superstition are to be dispelled, we must educate the young.   If we would have our broad land to glow with the splendors of intelligence, we must educate the young.   Finally, if we would have our world to come up to the high import of her divine mission, wrapped in the glorious influences of culture, glowing with the gems of intellect, and enlightened by the stars of genius, like the diadem of God, we must educate the young.

The destiny of every man hinges on the kind of education he receives; not on the kind attempted to be given, but on the kind actually received. This is often very different from the culture offered in the school or attempted in the home. It may be that of the streets, or even of the gutters. But the kind that is received, no matter where it comes from, is that which carries with it the destiny of the man. Then it is important to begin early, begin right, and be constantly persistent. The efforts should begin far down toward the sources of the formation of character, and be continued far into manhood. The set time to be educated does not suit all cases. One takes on education rapidly in infancy or early childhood, another in youth, and still another in manhood. The first and last of these classes are apt to be neglected. The first takes on a corrupt education before the parents are aware of it; the last, after parents and teachers had supposed the education had been finished. Those of the last class are more numerous than is generally supposed. Education comes almost as frequently to the bearded man as to the beardless boy.

Those who seek to educate children, whether by founding schools and colleges for that purpose, or actually engaging in the labor of teaching, are among the great benefactors of mankind. They confer the greatest blessing on multitudes by saving them from a life of ignorance and inefficiency, if not from one of grossness and crime.  To lead the young mind along the beautiful path of knowledge, to admire the wisdom and goodness of God, is an act like charity, twice blessed; it blesses both the giver and receiver.  Education brings out the genius of the heart as well as the strength of the intellect, and yokes them together in the service of man.

These or similar reflections came to me, suggested, no doubt, by the talks of my instructors during my brief career at college.  Years of observation have only confirmed their truth.  "The mind is the measure of the man," and education, correct or perverted, is the measure of the mind.

I had just begun to enjoy the musing of soul which one feels while pursuing studies in the classic shades of college life, when I was startled one day by a letter draped in mourning.  What a flutter of dread went to my heart!  I saw in the next instant that it was from my sister in Louisiana.  With nervous haste the envelope was broken and the letter read.  The little babe had died. When about six months old, the little fellow was taken with the croup.  The skill of the physician and the arts of the nurse were alike unavailing. Just after daylight, having suffered all night, the babe became quiet.  Its features assumed their natural cast, as if in the repose of slumber.  It was, indeed, the last long sleep of death.

That night I sat in my room and thought of the saddened home on the great river.  Every feature of that home, with its elegant appointments and spacious surroundings, was so vivid in my memory. I had there spent pleasant days in delightful reverie. While I could not, of course, feel the pangs of grief as my sister expressed them in her letter, yet a sad and hopeful sympathy connected me with all the sorrowing household. I entered into their disappointment, their hope. I thought how each one would be affected by the great sorrow. I was confident that religious faith would come to my sister's relief. To her the smiting hand would be wrapped in the soft folds of loving designs.

Then I looked out into the region of the stars and mused on the mysteries of life and death. It was a time to think of the knowledge, the ignorance, the doubts, and the hopes of mankind. The mind hung over the problem of existence, and felt for the chord of sympathy which binds all beings in the bonds of a noble purpose. What is that purpose? Can it be other than beneficent? Is it not wiser and better to " trust the larger hope?" The man must be heartless who could wish to clip the wings of faith or check the flight of hope when the soul would rise above the ugly realities of sorrow and tears. My reveries took the form of verse, and I penned the following lines, which I sent to my sister:

THE SWEET LITTLE BABE THAT DIED.

It broke, the light of morn,
The haunts of earth to adorn
Bright as a dream newborn;

And night unrolled her gloomy folds
    From bud and bloom and thorn,
And nature glowed as from new molds.

    It flowed, the stream of time,
    To song of being's rhyme,
    As rang the morn's sweet chime;
Like crystal, winding ever bright
    Beneath the bending lime,
It flowed in morning's waking light.

    Ere yet the sun of day
    Had chased the dews away,
    Whose drops on every spray
Hung like angels' quivering tears;
    And beauty's mantle lay
On all the scenes of hopes and fears;

    I saw a bud of life,
    Ere yet the pruning knife
    Had waked the pangs of strife,
Just o'er the pearly waters hung;
    With flush of being ripe,
Its fragrance on the zephyrs flung.

    Its petaled robe of light,
    In beauty woven bright,
    Like an angel's wing in flight,
Was barely to the eye unfurled;
    We caught but hasty sight
Of beauty as it onward whirled.

    I looked; an angel came;
    Her eyes showed love's pure flame;
    A light was round her frame;
A holy purpose stayed her flight.
    Our joy of heart grew tame;
Why came she from the realms of light?

    She plucked with hands of white
    The bud of human light;
    Then fell the weight of night;

Then rose the storm with sorrow fraught.
'Tis but a cherub's flight
To haunts of beings' nobler thought.

Above the storm cloud's roar,
Beyond the eagle's soar,
To heaven's lovely shore
The angel in her homeward flight
The life bud kindly bore.
It blooms in realms of endless light.

Bright in the home on high,
Where never breathes a sigh,
And all the good are nigh,
That bud of life so pure above
Matures where angels fly
Its fruit of intellect and love.

# CHAPTER XXIII.

## WAR.

LIFE at college was now running smoothly. From the papers which came from home and from other sections of the South we knew that excitement was constantly at fever heat. But as this now seemed to be the normal condition, we had become accustomed to it. We were out of the current, and glad to let others take care of the country. Aside from the papers we heard but little of politics in our quiet retreat. The young men, especially the seniors, frequently had the subject up for debate in the societies, but this made little or no impression.

I became every week more deeply interested in my studies. The letters constantly received from Susie, for we kept up a regular correspondence, were sprightly and witty, full of hope, and teeming with good sense. Those letters were to me a source of inspiration for good.

John began his course with some disadvantage. A whole year out of school could not be entirely overcome, even by the most extraordinary diligence. But he was rapidly regaining his lost prestige, and we all knew it was only a matter of time when he would again lead in the classes. Indeed, he was equal to the best of us now. Dolph, Dick, and the Allens were getting on well.   We were all ambitious to make a good record at college.

We had, in fact, become so intent on our studies that we were to a great extent oblivious to the outside world.   But in the midst of our abstractions we were startled by an announcement which seemed to shake the whole fabric of society.   It was the election of Mr. Lincoln!   The Faculty were unusually concerned.   As the students nearly all took their home papers, they to some extent shared in the state of public feeling.   These papers showed that excitement was now reaching white heat.

Secession was then the vital question.   Vital because the lives of a million men hung upon the issue !   The legal right of a state to secede from the federal union was the all-absorbing question.   In its discussion all other differences were forgotten.   After a few weeks' discussion the great majority of the people South seemed to be convinced that they had the right to secede.   Behind that was the question of expediency.   On this there was a more decided difference of opinion.

Our home correspondence now greatly increased.   We had made common property of the letters so far as they brought the eagerly sought news.   By this correspondence and the flood of papers, which flowed in from every part of the South, we had ample means of knowing the state of feeling and the drift of the arguments used.   From Will Benson I had a full account of events in our neighborhood. Col. Parker had taken the field in favor of secession. Our usually quiet neighbor, Maj. Jones, represented the other side. Col. Parker contended that " secession is the only way left us to protect our rights. Our rights have been so long disregarded and violated that we have absolutely no security that they will be respected in the future. We have, in fact, every assurance that they will be purposely and persistently violated. Things have been getting worse and worse for years. Our rights have been despised and trampled on in every possible way, every day for years past. These things have been done while the government has been friendly, or at least indifferent. Now with the government hostile to our peculiar institution, there is nothing left us but to form a government of our own; a government in which the rights of the federal Constitution, so long violated, shall find safe and permanent guarantees. There is no use to disguise the fact that a strong and growing faction North are determined to break down the Constitution left us by our fathers. They intend nothing less than the destruction of slavery. They have been constantly growing in number and power till now they have a President to occupy the high and honored place of Washington and Jefferson. We must act now or tamely submit to insult, and cowardly look on while the grand bulwark of liberty formed by our fathers, and cemented by the blood of patriots, is pulled down before our eyes; our children despoiled of their rightful inheritance and left to beggary. Secession cuts the Gordian knot. Once severed from these agitators, peace will reign supreme. It is admitted on all sides that we have the right to secede. Then, if we have the right to secede, no government has a right to object. We only do what we have the right to do. It is the right which adheres in a sovereign state. We went voluntarily into the Union; we can go voluntarily out. Of course there will be no war. The government has no right to make war on a state. The state is anterior to the government, and has rights superior. She is independent and can do as she pleases. All we have to do is to put on a bold front. The Northern people have no interest in slavery, and have no idea of fighting about it. I will agree to drink all the blood that will be shed in this quarrel."

Maj. Jones replied: " The argument for the legal right of secession, viewed from the platform of state rights, seems very plausible. But what we claim and what others will admit are likely to be very different things. I do not believe the government will concede the right of a state to withdraw from the Union. To do so would be to consent to its own destruction. If one state may secede, all the states may withdraw, and leave no government. To admit the right of secession is to give up all power of constraint, and at once deprive a great nation of all nationality. It is not the nature of governments to tamely submit to dismemberment.

This fact is attested by all history. When did a government ever consent to disband? Self-preservation is the first law of nations, as well as of nature. We have in common with all people the right of revolution. But that is a desperate venture. It is an appeal to arms, and should only be resorted to in extreme cases. Certainly we have no cause now for revolt. The government has done nothing to justify revolt. And there is no probability that it will attempt to interfere with our peculiar institution. If it does, then will be time enough to try the expedient of forming a new government. I am sure that such an attempt at any time will be attended by a bloody war. It is extremely unwise to provoke such a calamity. This is a time for cool, clear-headed wisdom, and not for passion; a time for patience and forbearance, and not for precipitant haste."

When the account of this debate was read we could almost see Dolph swelling with importance. He threw his shoulders back and walked the floor with learned and pompous airs. He at once procured the letter, that he might take in and mentally assimilate every syllable of his father's speech. It was amusing the next day to hear him holding forth to a squad of boys gathered around, who evidently regarded him as a marvel of political wisdom. How he rolled the sentences! What a volume of meaning there seemed to be in the sonorous words! " Yes, gentlemen," he said, " a sovereign state has the inherent right to secede.

The states were anterior to the general government. They were sovereign then; they are sovereign now. Voluntarily they went into the Union, and voluntarily they can go out. The states having the right to secede, no government has a right to object. Then of course there will be no war. Gentlemen, I will agree to drink every drop of blood that is shed in this quarrel.'' Dolph put his thumbs in the armholes of his vest, as his father would have done, and walked around with the consciousness of having merited distinction. But his countenance rather fell when he saw John and Dick standing behind the bower, laughing at his eloquence.

Similar discussions were going on all over the country. The wildest enthusiasm prevailed, and the most absurd things were said, with the most provoking earnestness. Some of the papers contended that if we had a war it would be gloriously short. It would be a mere breakfast spell to whip out the whole Yankee nation. Some of the orators could whip them, one against ten. One said: '' It will be short work when every shot counts a pigeon.'' The speeches were calculated to make the impression that if we did have a slight brush, it would not be worth while to go over and count the enemy's slain, unless we naturally had a mind to; it would be just the same to count the number of shots from our side. These utterances, in the light of the history that has been made, give fresh meaning to the ancient proverb:

" Whom the Gods wish to destroy they first make mad."

While these discussions were waxing more and more fierce, and passion was everywhere gaining ascendency, matters were still more complicated by the secession of South Carolina. It now looked like the die was cast. This brought unusual stir to the college. Discipline was almost impossible. Profitable study was out of the question. The South Carolina students held a meeting and asked permission of the Faculty to return home. The Faculty promised to consider the matter, and advised the young men to be patient and await further developments. These were not long coming. The wires soon flashed the news that Mississippi had followed the example of South Carolina.

Each week brought new developments. State after state went out. Soon the representatives of these states met in Montgomery, Ala., and organized the Confederate States of America. Thus, before we could fully realize the fact, our homes were in one country, and we in another. The Virginians, good-naturedly, called us foreigners. To make the impression still more real, some papers down South placed under the head of " Foreign " the news from the States outside of the Confederacy.

Thus we had two governments standing face to face. The attitude of the new government could only be defiant; that of the old was of bold watchfulness. Thus, like two ferocious beasts, they

eyed each other before making the assault. It
was the fearful pause before the deadly struggle.

"Will there be war?" was the all-absorbing question which quivered on every lip and burned in
every heart, during all this time of terrible suspense.
As if to give sharp point to the question, military
companies were forming all over the country.
Fiery speeches were made; burning philippics
filled the papers. The drum and fife were everywhere used to inspire the martial spirit. The forts,
arsenals, and munitions of war in different parts of
the South were taken charge of by the Confederate Government. Only one fort held out against
the demand for surrender. That was Fort Sumter, near Charleston, S. C. The attention of the
whole country was now directed to that fort,
standing as it did like a faithful sentinel in the
midst of universal alarm. During all this season
of warlike preparation, we heard of negotiations
going on between representatives of the two governments. How many hopes hung on these ru-
mors! How soon were they dashed to pieces!

These days of suspense, like everything else,
must have an end. So, when winter was gone,
and nature was putting on the peaceful livery of
spring, the wires grew hot with the terrible news
that the war had already begun. The Confeder-
ates were firing on Fort Sumter.

This completely demoralized the college, and
put discipline at an end. The Faculty at once gave
permission for all the young men from the seceded

states to return home. Having advices from our parents to the same effect, all from our neighborhood agreed to start home in two days. Thus suddenly and sadly our college career came to an end. That day I learned by letter that Will Benson was forming a company. This brought the matter near home.

Only a few months ago our country seemed the very abode of peace. Now war was at our very doors. So we have seen the calm afternoon, when all nature drooped in the quietness of peaceful repose, when all at once the forces of the storm began to gather. The wrathful lightning in fearful flashes was only equaled by the deep-mouthed howl and roar of "heaven's loud artillery." Thus the storm of war was now rushing on with fearful potence. The tempestuous sky was every hour growing more lurid. None could foresee the results; none could tell who would make up the hecatombs of victims.

Our little company in its homeward flight was seemingly gay and happy. But back of all our coruscations of wit and humor plainly stood the background of apprehension. We returned by Nashville for the young ladies. Susie, as I now saw her, through the gathering mists of uncertainty, looked more charming than ever.

As soon as we crossed the line into our native state we could see everywhere the evidences of high enthusiasm. "The banner with a strange device" was floating in all the depot towns and from many

12

private houses.    Ladies on the train wore the min-
iature flag pinned to their dress fronts, while gentlemen sported the same colors on their hats.    We
saw  several  companies  drilling  to  the  martial
strains of  drum and fife.    People were unusually
gay and sprightly.    It looked as if a universal holiday had been proclaimed.

# CHAPTER XXIV.

## A Soldier.

WHEN we reached our native state and saw the new flag floating in every breeze, we felt that we too were out of the Union. The old country was left behind; our allegiance was due to the new. But the division of the country into two governments was to me a humiliation. I had loved my country, admired her greatness, gloried in her future possibilities, revered her flag. My bosom had swelled with emotion as I thought how that flag was respected by all nations.

Now this was all passed. Instead of a great government respected by all the world, we are now to have petty states. As there is no supreme law to hold the states together, we are likely to have endless division; for the least dissatisfaction, of which there is generally a good supply on hand, will be sufficient at any time to cause any number of states to withdraw from either of the governments now established, and form still another. American unity is likely to be even a greater impossibility than German unity has been.

With all this there was sure to come insignificance. We would no longer have a government great enough to claim the proud title of America. America would still be a broad land, but no longer a great nation. But a jumble of petty states whose good opinion nobody would be concerned to court. And I gave to the waning glory of America a sigh profound as it was sincere. It never occurred to me that it was otherwise than my duty to stand by my native state at all risks. Nor did I have an idea that since the states were determined to secede, that they could ever be prevented from doing so. I simply had to be reconciled to the new order of things.

Are we to become soldiers? This question had been one of growing interest from the time we left college. I noticed that the military enthusiasm of our party rose rapidly after we got under the domain of the Confederate flag. It could not have been otherwise. Martial enthusiasm was in the very air we breathed. Everybody was elated. The whole country was buoyant. Men were exultant over the fact that the Gordian knot had been cut once for all. We were to have no more agitation about slavery. That question is at last settled. And if we do have a little war, it will soon be over. Thus everybody was hopeful. Some even went so far as to say that war is necessary to cement the new state. To gain by arms what is ours by right will be the fitting laurel of glory with which the new government is to be crowned. "Hurrah for the Southern Confederacy!" "Hurrah for Jeff Davis!" "Hurrah for the brave men who will defend our rights!"

These and like huzzas we heard all along the

way. They came from the lusty throats of strong
men. They fell from the dainty lips of lovely
women. Of course we caught the fire. Dolph
was especially zealous. He was only afraid that
the war would be over before he could get a chance
to fight.

I was glad to get back. But the dear old home
was already changed. A deep shadow rested on
its threshold. I came to a saddened household.
While peace still lingered, the sunshine of hope
was dim. I was surprised and grieved to see father look so careworn and broken. Mother, too,
was sad. Both looked much older. I just now
realized the fact that my parents were rapidly
growing old. The prospect of war was already
telling fearfully on their declining strength. I
here tasted the first bitter fruit of the war. Their
son-in-law, Will Benson, had been elected captain
of a company. So he was in for the war. This
was to them a source of great anxiety.

I found that father by no means shared in the
hopeful view as to the shortness of the war. He
said that it would be a desperate struggle, and in-
volve a terrible sacrifice of life and treasure. And
all to no purpose. He was clearly of the opinion
that the war would be the end of slavery. He and
mother were very averse to my going into the war.
They needed my help at home in their old age.

According to my father's gloomy view of the
war, soldiering was likely to become a serious
business. The startling developments every week

seemed to confirm that view. Military enthusiasm
was not one of the noble weaknesses of my nature.
I was a lover of peace. I most heartily wished
that there was no war. But what was I to do?
This was a practical question. It did not consult
my preferences nor hinge on my theories. The
state was calling for troops. My parents really
needed my help. Which is the first, the family or
the state? Perhaps always the family. But in
great emergencies the obligations to family and
state blend into one, and the family is best served
by serving the state.

I was certain that most, if not all, of my associ-
ates would enlist. What will they and the community expect of me? What do my parents expect
of me? Their sadness would be greatly increased
by my going. But do they really expect me to
stay? Thus by judicious weighing of motives, I
was balanced on the line of uncertainty. Was
this a balance between inclination and duty, or
between inclination and pride? Motives are very
subtle, and often wear strange disguises.

Deep down in my nature I was conscious of a more
powerful incentive, an oracle whose word would
at once have decided the case. What would
Susie expect of me? I could face any danger
that Susie approved. I could "run through a
troop or leap over a wall" for Susie. I could stay
quietly at home and be regarded as a coward by
the world, if only by this Susie would be drawn
closer to me. Here the stiff-featured moralist

who sees an imp of Satan perched in every smile
loses all patience and exclaims: "Duty! Duty is
the only criterion of action!" Yes, verily; but
what is duty? Are we likely to deviate very far
from the path of duty when we make the purest human love of which human nature is capable the criterion of our action? In the great emergencies of life
we often can find no direct command telling us to
do this or that. True, the great principles are given
for the guide of conduct. But these principles
have to be interpreted by our consciousness of
right. The interpretation of principles by consciousness gives conscience. Trueness to conscience gives character. When are we more likely
to follow the leadings of conscience, and thus be
true to ourselves, than when we are true to our noblest human loves? Is not even our love for God
developed from the human side? Can we suppose
that God is displeased when we yield to the
strongest feeling he has planted in our nature?
To sacrifice everything to the noblest, purest love,
gives to man the grandest type of character. I
could not but believe that Susie was like most other
women; that while she would shrink from the
danger involved, she must admire the courage and
applaud the heroism that stands firm in the hour of
danger. So I resolved to be a soldier.

Capt. Benson's company was not so full but
there was room for the "College Brigade," as we,
the returned college boys, were called. We at
once became important. From the state of school-

boys, at one stride we became men. Yea, in common with all the members of our company, we became distinguished men; the country's brave defenders; the heroes to defend a nation's greatness; sons of the noble sires of '76. What a power is war to make one great! How easily one steps from the seclusion of private life into the glare of military glory!

About one-third of our company were from Plum Creek neighborhood. These sun-browned sons of toil, unknown before, were now toasted and praised by the *elite* of the great plantations. Their awkward manners and rude speech no longer shocked the tender nerves of wealth.

The artificial grooves worn in the stratum of manners by the long years of peace are obliterated by war. The entire basis of respectability is changed. Bravery becomes the passport to every distinction. Consequently war brings new men to the front. Indeed, war erects a new front of its own, and the brave only are conspicuous on its crest.

As our courage had not been tested, our heroism was taken for granted. Everybody thought or said we were brave, and we thought or pretended to think so too. Many were the flattering remarks that we heard. We were the men to make a short and glorious war. We were to hang the chaplets of victory around the brow of the young giant among the nations. Generations yet unborn are to rise up and call us blessed. Thus the old men gave us encouragement. Thus the matrons inspired our fortitude. Thus the maidens smiled us on to victory.

Our company was ordered to remain at home and drill for the present. Special stress being laid upon the drilling. An old veteran of the Mexican War was at hand to teach us military tactics. We could have remained at home and drilled every day, but it was thought best to go into camp to inure us to the hardships of a soldier's life. As it was now balmy spring weather, our military life was delightful. It reminded us so much of the camp hunt or the fishing frolic. Then if we had rain and things about the camp were wet and unpleasant, it was so easy to get furloughed and go home, or go and see our sweethearts, and be toasted as heroes around the family circle. We began to think "soldiering" a delightful business.

It was a time of high enjoyment. Our camp was the center of gay festivities for the whole neighborhood. The old men came and told all the anecdotes they knew of martial adventures of other days. Many of these anecdotes were greatly mutilated by time, still they were much enjoyed by the narrators. Every one who had a speech, however old and musty, was now expected to hand it round. Great was the feast of antiquated wit! But it was all made fresh by the foam of unfermented military enthusiasm. The matrons of the neighborhood came, and by their motherly solicitude touched our hearts with a new love for home and native land.

The young ladies came, and by their confidence
and hope inspired us with new incentives to nobler
endeavor.

It was delightful, and sometimes amusing, to see
these young ladies trying to bridge the chasm
which wealth and culture had deepened between
the aristocratic slave-owning population and the
white toilers of the neighboring hills. "My dear
Mr. Smith, do have some more of this lemonade.
It is some of my own mixing; spiced with elixir
and dashed with sherry." "I know hit's powerful
good, Miss Fannie. I do b'lieve, though, I've
drunk mighty nigh a quart already. I reckin
though it won't hurt a feller." And the unsophisticated soldier drained the glass. While the lus-
cious drops of the liquid were still hanging on the
rich luster of his lips like officeseekers around the
door of patronage, he said: "Am! that's mighty
good, Miss Fannie." "I'm so glad you enjoy it.
Let me prepare you another glass, Mr. Smith."
"No, thank you, Miss Fannie; I'm plumb full
now."

Thus war laps the extremes of society. The
love of country and the sense of common danger
welds them together. Thus patriotism becomes
the band which draws society into closer union,
and holds the state together.

But if our Plum Creek volunteers were un-
taught in the amenities of plantation society, we
were all at equal disadvantages in the matter of
military discipline. Our "line" more often de-

scribed the section of a circle. It was sometimes serpentine. And at all times we found it hard to " dress."

At the command, " Forward march! " some boys would start in advance of others. The command seemed not to reach at once all the centers of activity. Like a boy setting off a row of fire-crackers, he fired all at once; yet, because the fuses were of different lengths, the popping was irregular. A dozen boys scattered along down the line would start together; then another lot would get themselves in motion; then still another; and a few would lag entirely behind. Our line in motion was something like a shaft in a machine shop, with cranks or eccentrics set at different angles: while some were coming up others were going down. But a little practice gave us the " step," and in a few months we could drill like veterans.

# CHAPTER XXV.

## FIGHTING.

WE had been in camp over a month when we were ordered to a camp of rendezvous about seventy miles north, where the regiment was to be formed. We moved toward the front.

My farewell to Susie was sad. No feigned martial enthusiasm, no assumed gayety of manner befitting a soldier's life could hide the fact. Susie saw through the pretense, and instead of military alacrity saw only a reluctant compliance with the demands of duty.

Maj. Allen had a very trusty servant named George who was to go and look after his two boys; and as it was unnecessary for us to have more than one, it was arranged that George was to be cook for our mess.

As we were leaving camp the news of the victory at Big Bethel greatly excited our ardor. We were more than ever afraid the war would be over before we could cover ourselves with glory. In all speeches of this kind Dolph was the spokesman for our mess.

After the organization of our regiment, drilling went on more vigorously than ever. The news of the great victory at Bull Run almost set us wild. The boys clamored to be sent to Virginia, as all

(188)

the fighting was to be done there.  " It is unjust to hold us away from the field of glory.  The great battle of the war has already been fought, and we are kept here ingloriously idle."  Such were the impatient murmurs.

But we were to some extent pacified by a move toward the front, and the promise of a fight in the near future.  The more thoughtful men among us were of the opinion that we would soon have fighting enough.  The unprecedented calls for soldiers by both governments, and the widespread enthusiasm North and South, indicated a bloody struggle.  The giants were arming for the contest. The work of organization was vigorously pushed all along the line from Western Missouri to the Atlantic ocean.

Our first service was on the Tennessee River in defense of Fort Henry.  It was a beautiful day in autumn when we pitched our tents on the shore of that placid stream.  Its rippling waters gave no sign of the coming storm.  If we had been on a pleasure excursion and camping out for recreation, no more appropriate spot could have been chosen. It was a place to commune with nature, and study the lesson of peace on earth, good will to men.

One day the officers sent the " College Brigade " down the river to reconnoiter.  I suppose they sent us for exercise, for there was no evidence of an opposing force within fifty miles of us.  But we were entirely ignorant of that fact, and went on the lookout for real Yankees.

The situation was novel. Never did a company do more genuine looking. Every distant stump, especially if it had a broken limb to represent a gun, became an object of special scrutiny. A one-horned cow, blazed faced, with head erect, in the distance, looking right at us, demanded very careful observation. The further we went the more nervous we became. About two miles from camp a homesick feeling came over us. We were moving along close to a little slough, looking intently as far as we could see in the forest, when a bullfrog, disturbed by our invasion of his privacy, gave a keen, characteristic screech, and went head foremost into the water. We jumped like a rifle had been shot at us.

This broke the spell. We laughed a dry grin, and held a counsel of war; agreed to say nothing of the frog panic on our return to camp, but to lay aside this childish nervousness and be soldiers.

Our mettle was soon put to the test. We had stubborn fighting for nearly two weeks. During this time, Fort Henry and Fort Donaldson both surrendered, after the most heroic resistance. We retreated to Nashville.

Our next position was at Corinth. Everything indicated an important battle near that place in a short time. We scarcely had time to get ourselves in order before we were put on the march to meet the Union forces which were gathering at the landing on the Tennessee River about twenty miles distant. The battle of Shiloh is a part of history. I am now interested only in the part taken by our company.

About 6 o'clock, April 6, the action began. For a time we were held in position, waiting orders. The smoke of battle filled the air. The roar of the guns was growing more terrific. We could see the line of ambulances to our right carrying back the wounded. The bullets were whistling close about us, and bombs were bursting not far off, while cannon balls were shattering the trees, sometimes directly over us. Inaction under fire was a trying ordeal. The order to advance was a relief. We advanced rapidly, still reserving our fire. All this time we could hear the sharp clicks as the bullets were hitting objects about us; then a dull thud as a fellow-soldier was struck. The order to fire came and had the effect to steady our ranks.

Before I realized the fact we were under a heavy fire, and comrades were falling from our ranks. I was almost blinded by smoke and deafened by noise. The command to charge was barely heard, amid the din of battle. Our advance became a run. I knew by the dense smoke and increasing noise that we were close on the Union lines. I thought I heard the word bayonets, and all the company brought their guns to a level, as we still charged onward. I thought we would be right among the opposing forces. But the noise ceased and the field before us cleared. We had routed the enemy from that position. We were com-

manded to halt; and when drawn up in line, I saw
for the first time that we were fearfully thinned.
The "College Brigade" was still intact. While
we were standing there an officer of high rank, I
think he was the brigade commander, rode by, and
waving his hand, said: "Soldiers, that was a brilliant charge. I am proud of your gallant daring."
That was to me the first intimation that we had
distinguished ourselves. There was too much to
be done to think of what had been accomplished.
The fighting was not so severe with us for some
time, but there was scarcely a cessation in the
firing. Our foes fought stubbornly all the time, as
they fell back, till they took a decided stand, as
they did again and again; then they fought des-
perately. In a great battle we take little note of
time. During a pause in the struggle I looked at
my watch, and was surprised to find it was past 12
o'clock. In the afternoon we came in range of a
battery on a rise several hundred yards in front of
us. The battery was well supported, and was
dealing death and destruction to our ranks. Several unsuccessful attempts had been made to silence these guns. Our brigade, now not larger
than a regiment, was ordered to take that battery.
That was a fearful command. But we were flushed
with victory. The thought of failure, or of living
to see a failure, never entered our minds.

The charge had to be made over a deep ravine,
now muddy from recent rains. We hastily drew
up in line and went off at a brisk march, reserving

the charge proper till we could get nearer the battery. Aided by the smoke and a feint made at another point, our purpoše was not suspected until we had made half the distance. The fire was then directed to us, and we charged double-quick, or quicker! We raised the rebel yell as we dashed into the blaze of the cannon and the more destructive bullets of the small arms.

Our ranks were fearfully thinned, but our officers kept them closed as we advanced. Those who saw the charge from the rear said the line grew sensibly shorter as it charged so fearlessly into the jaws of death. I kept by the side of John Henderson till we were in thirty feet of the battery. How he got ahead I cannot tell, unless it was on account of better muscle.

The battery showed no signs of wavering. We were in very touch with the blaze of the guns. John silenced the first gun. The bayonets gleamed right across the touchholes, and the gunners just had to give back. The battery was ours, and we had a little time to think and observe. I noticed that John was smoking—not comfortably puffing a cigar—but his clothes were on fire, having caught from the blaze of the cannon.

Our company was the first to reach and silence the guns, and John was its gallant leader, with bayonet presented. His conduct was noticed, and he received a captain's commission for bravery on the field. Our company was warmly commended, as was also the entire brigade, for this gallant charge.

13

It was glory at a fearful sacrifice. When Capt. Benson drew us up in line, more than half the men were missing, among them Ben and Joe Allen. We hoped they were only wounded. But even that hope was of short duration. They had fallen near together, apparently without a struggle.

Night came at last, and the first day of the Shiloh contest was over. We had been through the thickest of the fight, but had seen little of the battle. Men who fight in the ranks have no time to observe the movements of a great battle. That night we slept on the field of victory, in the tents and camp of the enemy. Exhausted nature must sleep, despite the cries of the suffering or the torrents of rain. Why is it the general rule that rain follows a great battle? Is it because of the concussion of the atmosphere so akin to thunder? Does rain come as a help or hurt to the feverish wounded? That night I thought it might be that heaven, in pity, was relieving by absorption the burning thirst of the wounded and dying.

As the pitiful cries of pain fell on my drowsy ears, and the loss of companions weighed like lead on my heart, the thought which burned into my very soul, as tired nature sunk to rest, was that war is man's shame, and never can be his glory.

During the night the Union army was reënforced by the arrival of Gen. Buell's command. Next morning we were attacked by an energy born of desperation and returning hope. The fight of yesterday was reversed to-day. We disputed every inch of ground, but were forced back, and dark found us at Shiloh church, just where the battle began the previous morning. The loss in our company was not as great as it was the day before, though it was considerable. Dick Webb had received a severe flesh wound, but kept with us.

When we had settled down for the night, George found our camp. It was the first time we had seen him since the death of Ben and Joe. As he came up and stood in the dim, weird light of the camp fire, he looked the very image of distress. Sorrow spoke in every feature. He stood silent for a moment, as if mastering his emotion, so as to speak intelligently. He began: "I wants you, please, to help me bury my young massas. De las' thing ole massa tole me was, if de boys fell on de battlefiel', to bury dem whar de graves could be foun'. 'For I want,' says he, ' to bring 'em home to de ole cem't'ry.' "

Dolph was the one to speak: " Why, George, it is impossible to get to them. It is a mile and a half to where they fell, and the whole Yankee army is between here and there."

"No, massa," George replied, " dey's right down dis hollow, not more'n a half mile off. I brought dem back las' night, an' to-day, when I seed our army wus comin' back, I moved 'em ag'in, an' kivered dem wid leaves, an' I tuk an' blazed trees, an' looked how de logs lay about, so I could be shore to fin' de place. An' late dis

ebenin', when our soldiers passed by I was hid by
my young massas, an' hit was so late I thought
de Yankees wouldn't come dat fur.  Dere picket
line is on dat hill [pointing in the direction],
an' our picket is on dis hill (pointing again), an'
young massas is down dis hollow between de lines.
An' by goin' down dis branch we can git dar
widout comin' to either line."

Before George had finished speaking, I saw that
John had fastened his shoes, secured his blanket,
and seemed to be impatient to go.  But Dolph replied: " How can we bury them without a spade
or anything to dig with.  Then there is every
chance of being shot by either army, or captured
by the enemy and killed as spies."

"Massa," said George, "I foun' a spade dis
mornin' an' hit's dar whar I can git it."

It needed no words to convince me that John
was going.  I determined to share the danger with
him.  Wishing to relieve the embarrassment of
Dolph, I remarked to him that it would hardly be
right to leave Dick without a nurse, and suggested
that he remain.  That was a soothing potion to
Dolph's sick spirit.  Dick said he could take care
of himself, but Dolph developed at once a com-
mendable alacrity in administering to a fallen
brother.

George was, of course, mistaken about reaching
our camp without passing a picket line; he had
simply gotten through in the dark without attracting
attention.  John said he himself had placed the

guard and knew that in the direction we were to go the sentinel was a good friend of his from Plum Creek. Whether it was strict fidelity, the reader must determine; but this sentinel, after earnest remonstrance as to the danger, let us pass.

The picket line came in a curve, and crossed a little run at that place, and from here on, as George had reported, the picket lines were on either hand just on the brow of the hills, with this deep valley and little stream between. George led the way. We three kept in close touch of each other and moved noiselessly, so as not to awaken suspicion. We could in the stillness hear the soft tread of the sentinels of the two great armies. The thick darkness in this deep valley was a covering to make us glad.

The magnitude of our undertaking grew upon me as we advanced. How we were to dig a grave in the hearing of these lines without being discovered was a problem. We came to a fallen tree. George placed his hands on it and closely scanned the surroundings. Finding that another fallen trunk lay in a certain relative position to the first one, he got over between these logs and felt his way along till the bodies were found.

Right between those fallen trees, the grave was carefully marked off by moving the leaves and trash from the surface of the ground. John's forethought was now apparent. He had brought a small tin bucket, from which, to prevent noise, he had broken the bails before leaving the camp.

This served a good purpose in moving the soft, *humus* soil. Fortunately, we encountered only small roots, and a good pocketknife served to cut them away.

What with spade and bucket and hands, the work of moving the dirt went on rapidly. In an hour the grave was sufficiently deep. The bodies, each wrapped in a soldier's blanket, were laid side by side, and the grave was carefully filled. The remaining part of the task, that of getting back inside of our picket line, was soon accomplished. We found our picket still on duty, and he warmly congratulated us on the success of our mission.

Both armies appeared to have had fighting enough for the present. We marched back to Corinth in good order. Here our decimated ranks were to some extent recruited, and a partial reorganization took place. John was assigned to duty in another regiment. I regretted very much the separation from him.

When we broke up from Corinth, John's regiment was ordered east, where, at Murfreesboro, at Chickamauga, at Chattanooga, and at many other places of less note, he won distinction and rose to the rank of major.

George was a hero in our regiment after the affair at Shiloh became known. He voluntarily remained with us most of that year. The question of cooking dwindled to nothing in the presence of the more important one of getting something to cook. Having done his duty well, George retired from the army, and enjoyed the reputation of a hero in the shades of private life. His devotion to what he considered duty was remarkable. Not even the superstitious dread of haunts and ghosts, characteristic of his race, could shake his fidelity.

The wound which Dick Webb received at Shiloh proved to be more permanent in its effects than was at first supposed. It disqualified him for infantry service. He went home, raised a cavalry company, and became its captain. In that capacity he served with credit through the war.

One great battle effectually cured Dolph's propensity for hard fighting. Col. Parker had sufficient influence to have him placed on a general's staff, with the nominal commission of lieutenant. In that position—a kind of life insurance policy—he stuck the war gloriously through to the bitter end. With these removals the " College Brigade " was lost to history.

Our regiment went south, in front of Gen. Grant's forces, as he was trying to push along the line of railroad to Vicksburg. Having gone about seventy-five miles below Holly Springs, the destruction of the supplies at that place, by Confederate cavalry, caused Gen. Grant to change the plan of attack. The Mississippi River was chosen as the most feasible way of reaching Vicksburg. As we could not have the honor of marching ahead of him, as a sort of vanguard, all the way down to Vicksburg, we hastened down to give him the warmest reception we could on his arrival. We

were there in good time, and paid our regards to
him when he crossed the river below the city and
landed on our side.

We gave a small entertainment at Port Gibson,
and something more at Raymond. When the
general insisted on visiting our capital, we insisted on going with him. But we had no disposition
to violate any of the proprieties, and strictly ob-
served " regulation distance." When he and Gen.
Pemberton were greeting each other with such
warmth at Champion Hills and Big Black, we were
playing court a little in the rear; and when the
general invested Vicksburg, we on the outside invested him!

This is the strain in which the soldiers who had
seen service at Shiloh were wont to speak of our
experience in the rear of Vicksburg. But the fall
of that devoted city is too serious a matter for jest.
That historic town was the scene of devotion and
daring excelled in no part of the world. When
the surrender was made, I felt a deep conviction
that the war was practically over in the West; and
that the Confederacy, born of so much enthusiasm
and defended with so much devotion, was doomed.

The proclamation of Mr. Lincoln freeing the
slaves left no doubt as to the intention of the vic-
tors. Sitting on the ground at the root of a tree,
by our camp, I faced the conditions, hard and in-
flexible as they were. To hold on grimly to the
end, and then meet the new problems of life bravely, was all that could be done. The remainder of

this year (1863) was employed in marching, watching, and fighting, to prevent as far as possible, the devastation of our native state.

Military operations with us had degenerated into a kind of guerrilla warfare. We were no longer able to attack the main body of the enemy, no longer able to prevent the movements of large forces. But we could prevent the country from being despoiled by small bands of armed men. In this way we kept the Union forces in closer quarters, and thus saved to our people much that would have gone to support the army of invasion.

# CHAPTER XXVI.

## THE CAVE OF FUTURITY.

ONE bright morning in the spring of 1864, the scouts brought in the news that the enemy's foraging party were devastating the country to our left. As this was the section from which most of our own supplies came, it was important to stop the depredations. A cavalry command was sent to surround and route them. To our company was assigned the difficult task of getting between the raiders and the main force, and thus intercept them on the retreat, and, if possible, capture the wagons.

We marched rapidly for some time. The road led toward my home. Home, sweet home, now not more than thirty miles distant, and yet so far beyond my reach. How my heart went out toward the loved ones there! How I longed to see them all! My solicitude was all the greater because word had from time to time reached me that my parents were in feeble health, my father especially; he was now no longer able to leave his room. And they were at any time subject to insult and spoliation, as the whole country was now overrun by hostile troops. This sent a pang of sorrow, indignation, and humiliation to my very heart.

(202)

I had managed to keep up an irregular correspondence with Susie. Her letters, through all the years of war, years of hardships and dangers, hunger and thirst, cold and heat, had bound me to hope. How vivid was her image before me as we marched in silence that morning. Her constant sympathy and words of encouragement had more than ever bound to her my very soul. I thought if I could but secure an honorable peace, with Susie left as my own, I could ask no higher boon. The more I realized the sad decadence of worldly prospects, the more this one treasure of my hope filled the entire circle of my desires.

But my thoughts were soon demanded by present emergencies. The scouts sent out had failed to report. I saw that our captain was getting uneasy. Nothing could be heard of the cavalry which was expected to overtake the raiders in a few hours. We marched on, expecting every anxious moment to hear from our reconnoïtering party. Their failure to keep us posted was certainly ominous. The whole company shared the uneasiness now too plainly visible in our officers. Our march became slower, and we became silent and vigilant.

All at once we were startled by a rush of troops from the brush to our right. We saw at a glance that we had been surprised by a superior force. But we had been through too many hard places to become panic-stricken. The command to surrender came clear and distinct on the morning air. The case seemed so hopeless for us that our gen-

erous foe did not fire, no doubt thinking it unnecessary.

Capt. Benson never exhibited cooler bravery.
His words of command were spoken too low to be
heard by the enemy, but in such earnest tones as
to be instantly obeyed. The road at this place
was on a ridge. To form in line and retreat backward down the declivity into the thick woods was
the work of a moment. We at once had the advantage of position. We were under shelter of
trees and brush, and the elevation on which the
road was located was nature's own breastwork.
Charging over this, the foe was exposed to our
fire.

Though we were outnumbered three to one, we
were making such use of our advantages that we
might have held our position had we not been
charged upon by a cavalry force equal in numbers
to that we were holding at bay. Retreat was out
of the question. Surrender was all that was left
us. I plainly heard the order to " stack arms! "
and heard the stacking. Then there was momen-
tary darkness. When I came to myself, I saw as I
lay on the ground the trunk of a fallen tree, which
had been burned out till it was a mere shell. Into
this I crawled out of sight. Lying there concealed,
I heard the command given for my company to
march off. Then I was lost in slumber or uncon-
sciousness. When I roused up, it was late in the
afternoon, and I was all alone. The mounds of
fresh earth showed too plainly the work of the

morning. How many of my comrades had been killed and how many captured, I knew not. I was conscious of having received a terrible blow on the head; but as I was not very bloody, I concluded that my wound had been made by the butt of a gun, and not by a bullet.

When I had collected my thoughts the best I could, I tried to fix in my mind, by the aid of the setting sun, the cardinal points, so that I could get the direction home. To get home was now the all-absorbing thought. I concluded that it was best to follow for many miles yet the plain road that we had come. Wounded, weak, and dizzy, I pulled myself up for the important task of reaching home. It was nearly night; but this was fortunate, as my chances for escaping the enemy were thereby increased.

For some time I saw no sign of dwellings. When I did come to houses, they seemed to be deserted. The people had either hidden out or were afraid to have lights burning. A fight in the neighborhood makes the people very cautious. As I toiled on I began to have terrible thirst and to feel the pangs of hunger. Finally about 10 o'clock at night I reached a house where I heard voices. The people were very slow to heed my calls, but I finally got a hearing. When I explained that I was a soldier in the Southern army, and that I had escaped from the fearful fight and capture of the morning, I was received with hearty welcome.

Water to drink and water to bathe in; what a luxury! I found an old man in charge of the home. He and his wife and two daughters would under other circumstances have completed the household; but now a widowed daughter, whose husband had been killed in battle, was, with her several children, living there for such protection as she could find. Then there were two daughters-in-law, whose husbands were in the army. They and their children swelled the responsibilities of the aged couple. They had a sad tale of woe, but I was too tired, sick, and foot-sore to listen long. They had evidently been well off, but now the great plantation was a wreck.

There was but little to eat on the place, but they freely gave the best they had. For the first time in many months I enjoyed the luxury of a bed. It was broad daylight when I awoke. The old gentlemen gave me directions as to the way home, and the probable whereabouts of the enemy. So I had but little apprehension of being captured. I walked on slowly till about noon, when I called at a house and got dinner. Here, as elsewhere all along the way, I saw dilapidation, devastation, and ruin. All the able-bodied men were in the army. Only the old and infirm, the women and children, and such slaves as chose to remain, were to be found. The plantations had shrunk to patches; the fences having been drawn in, and the greater part of the fields abandoned to weeds.

But I was glad to see fewer evidences of devastation as I reached nearer home. There were no indications of the enemy in this section at present. And as I had time, for it was now not more than twelve miles home, I rested an hour before starting on the way. I knew all the country and most of the people on the way home, so I could afford to take my time.

But as the afternoon wore away I became tired, gloomy, and apprehensive. I became strangely nervous. Everything appeared distorted and painfully dislocated. I could see only the dark side, and everything was fearfully distinct and augmented on that side. I was now approaching home under very peculiar circumstances. I had no papers, no visible excuse for my absence. Wasn't I liable to be arrested and carried back? Suppose I should meet with an officer who should refuse to believe my version of the capture? Then, was the capture of my company a valid excuse for my coming home? Was it not my duty to report to my command the fate of my company? Suppose I should be accused of desertion and tried for that cowardly offense? The very thought seemed to freeze my blood.

Strange all these things had not occurred to me before. Now every question seemed to be pointed with a dagger! Could I face Susie under these circumstances? Then, am I really sure that my company was captured? I was evidently in poor condition to know what was going on. Stunned as I was, how do I know but the capture was the mistake of a disordered brain? What if I should be accused of desertion, and my story of the capture should prove false?

My head grew dizzy and my heart grew faint. I reeled to a log beside the road, where I sat down. Resting my throbbing head in my hands, I groaned aloud. Surely I could not go home. I was not more than two miles away, and was likely to be recognized by any one passing. What was I to do? Plainly it appeared to me that I had no proper showing to explain my absence from the army. To go back now in my feeble condition was almost out of the question. Without any definite purpose, I took a dim path which led me from the main road. I was just then hardly capable of any definite purpose.

I needed time for reflection; and yet reflection was goading me to despair. The whole prospect was gloomy. The country was overrun and desolate. We seemed to be fighting in a vain cause, only to meet inevitable defeat at last. Already our levies had drawn out the entire manhood of the country from eighteen to sixty. We have no other recruits, and still we retreat and give up the country to devastation.

Then, to crown all other misfortunes, I am here liable to arrest for desertion. Disgrace may be added to defeat, and the loss of character go with the loss of all besides. How I wished that there was some way to surround the present difficulties! If I could only go around one year and come back

into the path of life! That would be like surrounding an impassable mountain. I remember the
distinct wish came into my mind that I could discov-
er here in these woods a cave of futurity that would
in some mysterious way lead out into future time.

That wish seemed to be the forerunner of the
reality, for just before me was a bluff with a
cave opening into its side. I stopped to consider.
I looked far into the cave, and all the way the bottom was smooth and covered with beautiful moss.
The sides of the cavern were regular and came together overhead, leaving a space of about eight
feet from floor to apex. The moss growing around
the mouth of the cave had such a peculiar appearance that it attracted my especial attention. To
my surprise, I could trace in large letters of living
moss the words forming an arch over the mouth of
the cavern: " The Cave of Futurity."

What did it mean? Surely there was no such
cave here when I used to ramble over these woods.
This was the hill country to the north of our home
where I used to hunt rabbits. I was familiar with
it all. But here is the cave. How can I have such
a dreamlike experience in daylight, when I am
conscious of being wide awake. I felt a strong
desire to go in and explore. Afraid to go home
or to be seen by any one, and too weak to return
to the army, there was little inducement just then
to stay out. I saw from a glance at the sun that it
was nearly night. Here was a chance, too, for
undisturbed rest.

14

So I went in. The floor of the cave all the way as I went was covered with soft, beautiful moss. I was astonished to find the passage light enough to walk without difficulty. The cave was level and straight all the way. It seemed to me that I must have walked a mile, when it began to grow dark. It was night. Just to one side I saw a mossy mound about the size and shape of a couch. I was safe here for the present. There was no evidence that any one was in the habit of penetrating this seclusion. So being tired and sleepy I laid down on the soft bed of nature's own making and felt so calm and pleasant, the tension of my nerves completely relaxed, and I was soon in deep, restful slumber.

It was broad day when I awoke. The cavern looked even more light and airy than on the previous evening. I could see more than a hundred yards either way. The cave seemed to be a straight tunnel as uniform in size as if made by human skill. A desire to still further explore this strange passage led me to go on. As it was not more than a mile back to the mouth of the cavern, I could easily return after making further search. So I walked on very briskly for some time.

I was thoroughly rested. The mental gloom of the evening before was all gone. I felt again the elasticity and hope of youth. When I walked far enough to count about one mile, I saw an opening before me. The light grew brighter, and it was soon apparent that I was reaching the end of the

tunnel.   I walked out into the bright morning sun-
light.   The sun was about two hours high, and the
day was beautiful.   That such a tunnel as this, at
least two miles long, should exist here in the very
neighborhood of my home, and never heard of,
was marvelous.   It came out of the side of a hill.
At this end it looked like an ordinary cavern, with
nothing to attract special attention.

The tunnel had led me under a range of hills in
such a direction that I thought I must be about the
same distance from home I was the evening before.
These were the same hills over which I had ridden
with John Henderson years before down to Plum
Creek Church as recorded in this faithful history.
I was confident of my whereabouts, and knew there
was a road on this side the hills leading up to my
home.   It was now my purpose to find that road
and go home, see my aged parents, and greet my
lovely Susie, and then report to the command.   I
had done no wrong, why should I be afraid?   So
finding a little path leading in the right direction,
I set out through the brush to find the road.

But what a surprise when I reached the road, to
find it skirted by an elegant iron fence.   How came
such an improvement in war times?   A beautiful
gate let me out, only to find still greater surprises.
For instead of the old dirt road, here was a paved
highway smooth and level as a floor.   Still greater
was the astonishment to see a country beyond the
road dotted with splendid country residences, great
barns, neat schoolhouses, elegant churches, and

busy windmills, all well constructed and elegantly
painted.   As far as I could see there lay before me
such a country as I had never seen before.   What
I had read in books of travel about the most highly
cultivated parts of Europe was the only thing of
which I had ever heard approaching this scene in
the splendor of its elegance.

I knew this country was covered only a year or
two ago either with forests or cotton farms.   Mr.
Benson's farm lay right along this range of hills.
The morning I set out with mother and mammy on our trip to Louisiana, we went right along
this road, with the plantation on one side and these
hills on the other.   But now here are green meadows smooth and beautiful; luxuriant pastures with
finest herds of cattle grazing on them.   Then
what elegantly painted houses!   How artistic the
fences, delicately dreamlike in beauty, dividing
land from land!

But when I had time to collect my thoughts a
little, I noticed that all the fences were made of
iron.   The posts were semicircular half-tubes
about four feet high and set alternately in the
ground and in transverse bases about three feet
long.   The fences presented little surface to the
wind, and stood firmly.

I thought this must surely be a land of enchant-
ment, where wonder succeeds wonder.   I could
not believe such improvements possible in so short
a time.   Yet everything looked real.   Why should
I doubt my senses more here than I had been ac-

customed to doubt them all through life? As I stood lost in wonder and wrapped in thought, my attention was arrested by a passing carriage. It was fairylike in its elegant lightness. I was surprised at how little noise it made. The gentleman and lady were large and fine-looking, with an air of distinction, but I knew them not. Hardly knowing what to do, I started toward home.

# CHAPTER XXVII.

## The Strange Country.

I HAD gone but a short distance when the woodland from which I had emerged gave way to the same high state of cultivation. On both sides of the road were the richest pastures and rarest herds, with green meadows, elegant houses, fairylike fences, with intervening fields for crops. Everywhere were evidences of the highest type of civilization. Here was a joint reign of peace and plenty. Wealth and culture had united in the production of the best.

This country north of the road had been considered too hilly for successful farming. It was covered with heavy forest timber. But here were the same hills with not a trace of timber on them. The hills were terraced, and green, level swards and cultivated areas, one above the other, presented a most lovely appearance. I was amazed at the number as well as the elegance of the residences. The whole country was full of people. Again and again while I was making these observations, the elegant carriages of different patterns and various sizes rolled by, each maintaining a cultured silence. But every human face was strange. The people had a strange if not a foreign appearance.

I had never before seen such cattle as were graz-

(214)

ing in herds far and near. Each herd was uniform in general appearance. They were of distinct breeds. Some were black, some white, some of variegated colors; some had peculiar horns; some had no horns; but each had well-defined characteristics. I had never seen thoroughbred cattle, but I knew them at once.

But what most attracted my attention, and which made the strongest impression on my mind, was the fact that the people were so much larger than those I had known. I was, among my companions, of more than ordinary size; but here I felt diminutive. Then they were so uniform, both in size and appearance. As I afterward learned, the average weight of the men was about two hundred and twenty. And few varied much from this standard. There were no giants and no pigmies. I concluded that the people, like their stock, must be thoroughbred. The ladies especially had this appearance. They were large but delicately rounded, smooth-featured, easy and graceful in motion. They had every appearance of being highly cultured, independent in thought, yet womanly in every fiber of their nature.

Passing a piece of land devoted to crops, I noticed a highly polished machine, of compact build, at work on the margin of the field near the road. At the distance of about four hundred feet down in the field was another machine of the same kind. I would have thought that they were steam engines, but they were making very little noise and producing no smoke.  They were used for plowing.  A wire rope band, working on pulleys, was stretched across the field from one engine to the other. The pulleys were four feet in diameter and ran horizontally.  Thus the two sections of the band were four feet apart and equal distances from the ground.

The plows were attached to frames and arranged in pairs—that is, with points in opposite directions so as to plow either way.  There were plows enough on each frame to plow out a row at a time. These frames were pulled by the opposite stretches of wire rope, and so arranged that the plows reached opposite ends of the rows at the same time. Thus two rows were plowed at once, the plows moving in opposite directions.  Trucks at each end of the frames served to regulate the depth of the plowing, and made the work lighter.

As soon as the plows reached the engines they were lifted entirely out of the ground by an automatic attachment.  The machines then moved up just eight feet, and the plows came down in exact position to work two other rows.  The work went on rapidly.  The two men with their machines could easily plow from twenty to thirty acres per day.

I asked the man in charge what the machine was called.  He stared at me with such an expression of astonishment that I felt embarrassed.  But I persisted in my questions until I succeeded in making him understand.  His reply was nearly as puzzling to me as my question had been to him.

But making allowance for a strange dialect and stranger pronunciation, I made out to interpret his reply thus: "It's a mo, of course."

Just then the plow had reached the end of the row, and he turned to his work as if he was more interested in his "mo" than in my strange speech and grotesque appearance. As soon, however, as the plow started back, he turned to have a better look at the uncouth stranger. This encouraged me to ask further questions. I asked if he knew an old gentleman living near here by the name of Williams. To my astonishment he said there was no such person living in the country. He thought there were some young men of that name in the city. I asked about the Brantletts. He knew a family of that name living in the city; none in the country.

I was completely stunned and dumbfounded. But I finally asked the name of the city, and how far to it. The name was "Comos," and it was three miles off. The name sounded a little like that of our depot, and the distance was what I expected. As one in a dream, bewildered, I started toward where I used to have a home.

This short conversation, while it, like everything else, seemed to indicate my removal from all familiar scenes and persons, was still to some extent reassuring. For really the transformation had been so great, and the people were so strange, that I was afraid I might find them speaking a language entirely strange to me. I was glad to find, therefore, in my venture with the man at the "mo,"

that I could, though with difficulty, convey and receive ideas.   I had caught a few items in regard to
the pronunciation and the construction of simple
sentences, and was determined to make the most
of them.

But the people I passed seemed to be unap-
proachable.   They were well-dressed, fine-looking
people, not to be annoyed by simple or unintelligi-
ble questions.   It is embarrassing to stop a man
who seems to be going somewhere, the man with
an object in view.   It is the loitering man in shab-
by clothes, with nothing to do, whose position in-
vites questions.   How I longed to meet a "common
man in vile raiment" who would have time to sit
down and chat!   Or, best of all, if I could only meet
a plantation negro.   Then I could learn all about
the situation.   Not a thing going on in the neighborhood but I could know it all.   What has become
of the slaves?  This country certainly should be alive
with them, yet not one is to be seen.

But everywhere I could see only the same type
of man.   These thoroughbred people, as I had
come to think of them, seemed to fill the whole
land.   And how multitudinous they were!   Walking on, my attention was attracted by a strange
building by the road.   It seemed to be a tower
having an open space near the top just under the
roof.   Around the lower part of this open space,
covering the banisters, was a web of white cloth
over a yard wide stretching entirely around the
building.

A man up in the tower, projecting his head over the canvas, looked down at me with a kindly expression of countenance. A narrow flight of spiral iron steps around the outside of the tower led from the ground to the space above. As this offered a good view of the country, and as I knew that I was near home and yet could not recognize a single feature of the landscape, much less any houses or other familiar evidences of my whereabouts, I determined to venture up this stairway for observation and inquiry. When I reached the landing above, about sixty feet from the ground, the man kindly swung back a little door, which also supported its portion of canvas, and invited me to enter.

By this time I had concluded to be more discreet, and to find out the meaning of my present situation. So I said to the stranger: "I am in the strange condition of not knowing where I am. I find myself among strangers whose language I can scarcely understand. Every object is strange. And all this just where it appears to me that I am in the immediate vicinity of my home, where every object ought to be familiar, and I should know every man I meet." I told him my name, and asked about my father and neighbors. No such people lived in that country. Completely dejected, what could even a soldier do but give way to grief? The man was moved with sympathy. He questioned me closely as to how I came into the country.

I told him the whole truth, as it was surely

mapped on my memory. The reference to the
war and to the battle two days ago, as well as to
the story of the cave or tunnel under the hills only
a mile or two off, were to him such marvelous ab-
surdities that he could only regard me as out of
my mind. I showed him my wounded head as
evidence of the truth of my story. This still more
confirmed him in the belief that my mind was
wrong. But it furnished him, as he thought, with
a clew as to how I came in the country. Scanning
me with closest scrutiny, he asked me if I had not
fallen from the airship which had passed over the
country yesterday. This furnished me with equally good grounds to doubt the normal condition of
his wits. But I had experienced so many surprises that I was ready to accept anything, however
wonderful. I simply inquired about airships, stat-
ing that I had never seen one and did not know
that such things exist. This proved to him more
clearly that I was the victim of some mental de-
fect. I had the appearance of being worn and
tired, and the kind-hearted man suggested that I
might need food. This was a timely hint, and I
told him that I had eaten nothing since yesterday
at dinner. He said that he and his chum kept
some confections and fruits to while away the
tedium of their watch, and at once, going to a large
closet, he produced a bountiful store. Never food
came in better time. Having satisfied my hunger,
I rose up to make observations. The first thing to
be seen was the great city, now in full view. The

city was regularly laid off, the broad streets crossing each other at right angles. The streets ran
entirely through the city each way, being about
four miles long. They were broad and beautiful,
and so set with trees that the city looked almost
like a forest. I concluded that I had as well accept the situation, for understand it I could not.
Such changes as these could not by any means
have taken place since I was at home. I was involved in mystery beyond all my powers of reason
to unravel.

Having looked long at the city, I began to make
inquiries, and soon learned the character of some
of the largest and most conspicuous buildings. I
finally asked how old was the city. My companion replied: "Well, the country has been settled
about thirteen hundred years; the city, I suppose,
was founded soon after the settlement of the country. It was first a village, then a town; probably
the city proper is not more than seven or eight
hundred years old." I was more than ever con-
founded. Where have I been cast? I know no
country this side of the ocean could claim such an-
tiquity as that, and here are all the marks of an old
settled country.

Having surveyed the city all over, I turned
to take observations of the country. The beauty
of the scenery was fascinating beyond description.
From our elevated position we could see five or
six miles in every direction. The country was
gently undulating in every direction except to the

north, where it was decidedly rolling.  But everywhere was the same high state of cultivation.  The
same kind of elegant improvements in all directions gave an artistic beauty to the whole landscape.
The airy fences, in particular, stretching over the
wavelike unevenness of the land; now going
down in the depressions; now scaling the distant
elevations; now running along the valley; now
marking the center of the ridge; other strands in-
tersecting or crossing, like border traceries in an
endless garden; now stretching in pairs, indicating roads or lanes; now in single strands, dividing
meadow from pasture and pasture from crops;
now inclosing beautiful yards, now bountiful gar-
dens and lovely orchards.  Surely no painter's
brush or poet's pen ever described a scene so fair.

While I was admiring this scenery, a train of
cars came in view.  As I knew there was no road
in that direction when I left home, I uttered an exclamation of surprise.  "Yes," replied my companion, "the train on the Northwestern is coming
in also," and suiting the motion of the hand to the
words, waved it toward the northwest.  Sure
enough there was another train.  "The trains,"
he said, "make the same time to the city, as does
also the northbound train on the Omaha and
Pensacola," and pointing southeast, said, "you
see the train coming now."  I did see the train
coming on the old familiar track I had always
heard called by another name.  I was so dazed
that surprise had almost ceased to be astonishing.

I had now tarried here till politeness required I should move on.   But where was I to go?   From this tower I had surveyed the whole country where I had expected to find my home, and not a vestige of the home is left.   It seemed that I had no home and no friends, nowhere to go and nothing to do.   Adrift on the tossing waves of the world without an anchor,   I had somehow lost my identity, and with it all my connections.

The old adage that we should hunt for a thing where it was lost  came to me, and I resolved to go back through the cave.   Thus I hoped to regain my proper position, establish my identity, and with it my true connection with the world.   But common politeness required me to be affable to the gentleman who had befriended me.   So I inquired his name, that I might return his kindness should opportunity ever occur.   I also asked him what was the use of the tower he had in charge.

"This is a signal station," was the reply.   But as he saw I did not understand, he explained: "This is a weather signal station.   We have all the instruments to indicate changes of the weather: when it will rain, when it will be stormy, or when it will be cold.   By a proper display of bunting of different colors, the people are forewarned of these changes.   When the display is white only, as it is now, this indicates dry weather.   We make observations every two hours; and if a change is indicated, we make the proper display of color.   By the way, it is now time to make an observation."

Examining his instruments, he said there was a call now for a strip of yellow bunting. Opening the door of the closet again, he brought out a strip of yellow cloth about twelve inches wide, with hooks on one edge. This he proceeded to hook on around the lower part of the white canvas. As this afforded me something to do, I gladly offered to help. This was cheerfully accepted, and we very soon exhibited to the farmers twelve inches in favor of rain.

My companion explained that if the indications of rain increased other strips of yellow would be added; and when the whole space is covered with yellow, rain is expected to begin at any moment. He said that if wind is indicated this is made known by black cloth. Before severe storms the whole space is covered with black. Then no citizen should venture out. These stations, he explained, are places at such distances apart that all the people can have one constantly in sight.

Thanking my new friend for his information, I was taking leave when he detained me to ask where I was going and what I expected to do. I told him frankly that I was so bewildered that I had no well-defined purpose; that I had some hope of meeting with friends by going back a few miles. He then told me that he was to make his last observation at 18 o'clock, and would then walk into the city, and if I did not meet my friends and would be back by that time, we could go in together, and he would show me a place to spend the night. I thanked him very heartily, and started back to find the cave, which I hoped would lead me back to the world of my acquaintances.

I walked very rapidly like a man who had business, and was going to give it attention. The woods soon came in view, and I took courage. I went at such pace that I was in a short time at the gate where I had come out but a few hours before. I found the little path and made rapid steps toward the cave's mouth. But what was my disappointment on reaching the hill to find no sign of a cave there. Again and again I went back to the gate to take a new start, and tried over and over to find the cave, but always with the same disappointing result.

I felt like one fairly caught in a trap. I had taken the fatal step from which there seemed no retreat. Shut out from home and Susie! The woods were searched thoroughly, and found to be only a small reservation of about fifty acres. In the evening people came leisurely in at the gate seeking recreation. I approached a young man and asked him if he knew of any cave in these woods. He was surprised at my strange speech; but after two trials I made him understand the question. "O no," he said; "there is no cave in this reservation." As there was nothing else to do, I returned to the signal tower and went with Mr. Dorman into the city.

15

# CHAPTER XXVIII.

## The Strange City.

IT was dark when we reached the city. Mr. Dorman conducted me to a small boarding house, where he said I would have a comfortable rest. To say that I was tired, hungry, exhausted, was hardly doing justice to the case. I had taken but one light repast of confections and fruits since yesterday at noon. Mind and body were alike worn out. A delightful supper was spread, and I did full justice to its excellence. I retired early and had a good rest.

As soon as breakfast was over next morning a difficulty arose on account of the Confederate money I offered in payment of my bill. I told the straight truth about the matter. I was at once regarded as insane. Quite a number of persons were present, and they all expressed the same opinion. Mine host said it was his duty to report the matter. Mine host no doubt is a conscientious citizen and intends to perform his duty to the state. As soon as he was off on that mission, and I thought it safe to do so, I stepped aside and made my way back to the signal station to take counsel of the only person to whom I could appeal. I told Mr. Dorman the trouble I was in, and showed him the money I had offered.

(226)

He scanned the money very closely, and directly exclaimed: " Why this bill is a thousand years
old."

I showed him that it bore the date of 1864.

" That," said he, " is what I see."

" Well," I replied, " don't you see the money
is fresh from the press?"

" I see," was the answer, " it looks new enough
to have been printed yesterday. But here is the
date," and his finger was pointing to the figures,
1864.

" Certainly," said I, " that is the date, the date
of this very year, and the money came direct from
the Capitol at Richmond, and was paid to me not
two weeks ago."

The look he gave me was one of astonishment,
mingled with compassion.

Changing the subject abruptly, he said pleas-
anly, " I rode out on my cycle this morning, and
I can readily go into the city, and sell the bill as a
curiosity. Such things are much in demand."
Then calling down to a friend at the house near
by, he added: " I will get Frank Love to take my
next observation, and I will have ample time to
look after your matter. If you so desire, I can
pay your bill out of the proceeds of sale."

I thanked him very much.

Stepping to one side he remarked: " I will send
the elevator after Frank."

He touched a little knob and the platform of the
elevator descended with great speed, and we soon

heard the merry voice of Frank; "All right, Tom;" and Frank was landed in our midst.

I was introduced as a stranger from Spanish America. Mr. Dorman gave me a meaning look as he rather emphasized the words, Spanish America. I had no motive to deceive, but thought it best to be silent. And I found it greatly to my advantage to be regarded as a stranger, as that would account for my strange speech. Frank readily agreed to stay and take observations, and Mr. Dorman stepped on the elevator and waved us adieu as he descended out of sight.

He was soon speeding along the smooth road on his cycle to the city. I was surprised to see that he was not using any visible means to drive the machine. His feet rested in stirrups, and he seemed perfectly at ease. I asked my new friend what propelled the cycle.

"It is magnetic force," he answered. "The weight of the rider brings the magnets in position; and his position in the saddle regulates the force; the speed being increased by sitting further back."

Indulging the hope that a time might come to examine this machine, I resolved to make use of the present opportunity to inquire about the signal service, from whose station we were now keeping watch. Frank was at once full of the subject.

"The object of the service," he began, "is to warn people in advance of the kind of weather we are to have. As everybody knows what kind of weather to expect at least twenty-four hours in advance, each day's work may be intelligently planned.   The service has a very good idea of the weather a week in advance, but for practical purposes the display on the canvases at the stations is for twenty-four hours ahead.   Any one wishing to travel or to plan work which requires several days of sunshine may consult the agents at the stations, and so be informed of the weather several days in advance.   Whenever a severe storm is arising, or a disastrous cold wave is coming, the fact is published at once, with the date at which the crisis is to be expected."

I expressed surprise that the changes should be known so far in advance.

" No  trouble whatever, he replied, " we only have to hear from the source of the storm.   Then knowing its momentum, and the track it is on, we readily know when the disturbance will reach any section of the country.   We know as well when a cargo of flour leaving Winnipeg will arrive here, as if it started only at the next station."

As he said this he pointed along the track of the Northwestern, indicating the way the cargo would come.

When I asked him how news could be had from the source of the storm, he replied: " By having a man at headquarters.   Every disturbance must begin somewhere, and by having men everywhere, we are sure to have one at the right place.   Reports of storms often come first from some of the outlying West Indies, Barbadoes, Grenada, or

Trinidad, and frequently from stations further out. From equatorial Africa and the Indian Ocean come reports of disturbances to be dreaded."

" Why," I asked, " is it possible the government has men stationed so far off?"

" O," was the reply, " the service is international. All nations are alike interested, and the expense is equitably borne by all."

I did not like to appear so very ignorant, but I reflected that it was better to show my ignorance here to this youth than for it to appear to all whom I may meet. To reveal ignorance at the proper time is the way to have it cured. So I ventured to ask how long the service had been established.

" Hundreds of years," he replied. " For a long time each nation had a separate service. But as this was manifestly deficient, the present plan, embracing all the leading nations, was at last brought to its present high state of efficiency. Our country claims the honor of leadership both in discovery and development. Just a few days ago the very learned Dr. Simpson, in an address to the university classes showed that the great Prof. Maury, who lived in this country about a thousand years ago, was the great founder of the system. The doctor was truly eloquent on this subject. It is a specialty with him, as he has written several books to show that Prof. Maury is justly entitled to this honor."

Just at this point Mr. Dorman came in. He had sold my ten dollar Confederate note for eighty dollars, and said, as if apology was necessary, that if he had not been pressed for time he could have sold it for more. He had paid for the night's lodging. He seemed to be cheerful, but there was something about his manner that was not reassuring. I was afraid all was not right.

Frank took leave of us, and then my friend proceeded to tell the real truth. I had been reported as insane.

"The authorities," he warned me, "are very strict in these matters. Dr. Simpson, one of the curators of the university, is the leading man on the Examining Board. I had a talk with him, and assured him that you were not insane; that I thought you had fallen from the Spanish-American ship, and the fall had affected your memory. That I think is the case. Now I want to give you some advice. If you run on about a war and getting wounded, and having money paid you by a government, whose very existence only the bookworms have heard of, they will surely think you insane, and send you to the asylum."

I thanked him and told him I would be discreet. Just then a light wagon drove up to take me before the Board. Before sending me down on the elevator he gave me this final hint: "Dr. Simpson is regarded by many as a crank in regard to memory. He contends that the ideas fixed in memory are stamped successively on different parts of the brain; that, however small that portion of the brain devoted to memory, each new idea is stamped on a new portion, and that under some conditions, each

day of life, just as we lived it, may be unfolded to us.
According to his theory memory has nothing to do
with sanity. All the memories of the past may be
blotted or blurred, and yet the man be sane. The
store of memory being put up in sections, the destruction of any or all the sections may take place
without affecting the reasoning faculties. Your
case has reminded me of the Doctor's theory."

Thanking my friend most heartily, I resolved to
profit by this hint. I was soon ushered into the
august presence of the Board. Dr. Simpson was
occupying a central position. He spoke to me
kindly enough, and bade me give an account of
myself. That was about the hardest thing he
could have asked me to do. but I rose respect-
fully and said: " Gentlemen, I confess to a great
degree of embarrassment. I remember everything
that has happened to me since yesterday morning.
At that time I found myself on the road about
three miles west of the city. If I talk of what appears to me to be the memory of things prior to
that time, it is said I talk at random, and like one
insane. Gentlemen, my memory may be at fault,
but my reason is not." I saw that I was making
a good impression on the mind of the great Dr.
Simpson. This gave me courage.

" Now, gentlemen," I continued, "we are all
liable to accidents. I am conscious of a wound on
the head. That may disqualify me for testifying
as to some parts of my life. One thing is sure;
I have been educated, I have had tutors, I can

read and understand, can consider facts and draw conclusions as well as I ever could."

Dr. Simpson here handed me a small volume and desired me to read. I saw at once it was English, but how changed! It was the strange language of the strange people among whom I had so strangely fallen.

"This," I said to him, "is the English language; but not that in which I was educated. It is strange to me." Then taking from my pocket a small testament which mother had given me, and which I had carried through the war, I said: "Here is the English in which I was educated." I began to read. They were all intent to hear, but only a few seemed to understand.

Dr. Simpson took the book, and looked at the date. "Why," said he, "this book is more than a thousand years old. Is it possible," he inquired, "that you read books of that date?"

I assured him I could read any English book printed about that time. He wished me to name some classic books I could read. I came near halting at the word classic, but after a slight hesitancy named Milton, Shakespeare, Gibbon, and others. He said the ancient versions with the old characters were used in the university; and after a little consultation with the members of the Board a messenger was sent to bring copies of Shakespeare and Milton. As the messenger was starting some member suggested that Prof. Young be invited over, and all the rest bowed assent.

The messenger soon returned, accompanied by
Prof. Young, who handled the precious volumes
with great care. Milton was handed to me, and
for once I astonished a highly cultivated audience
by my profound learning. Milton had been used
in our academy for analyzing. Of course I was
at home in this ancient classic.

Prof. Young was electrified. Various passages
which he thought the most difficult in both the authors brought were pointed out for me to read and
explain. When they saw that I could read any
and all passages with the same ease, they were
completely captured.

After keeping me reading and expounding for a
long time, they finally dropped back to a further
consideration of my case. They were much puzzled because I could give no satisfactory account
of myself. I thought this was the time when silence was golden, and said nothing. Prof. Young
was sure I was a graduate of the great Cowan
University, the only institution which educated up
to the standard which I had attained. But how
came him on the Spanish-American ship? It
seemed settled that I had fallen from that aerial
vessel. That is easily account for, suggested one
of the Board. "An eminent scholar might be traveling to further improve his mind." This was very
satisfactory.

Prof. Young wanted to know with what classic
books I was acquainted. I ran over a long list of
English and American authors. Then, recalling

the conversation with Frank in the morning, I said: " There is a very learned work issued much later than any of the books I have mentioned—one whose influence has been very great in aiding the world's advancement. It has made navigation safe and agriculture more sure. Of course, gentlemen," I assumed an air of great learning, " I can refer to no other than Prof. Maury's Geography of the Seas." Dr. Simpson almost jumped from his chair. He then eagerly questioned me about the methods adopted by Maury, to learn the facts underlying the signal service. I gave an account of Maury's influence in securing an international conference to consider these matters, and how Maury induced all the leading nations to have exact reports from all their ship masters in their voyages as to directions of winds and ocean currents; how bottles were thrown over from time to time containing reports of currents at the place of overthrow, the date and place; how these were picked up, sometimes thousands of miles away, showing the tracks of the great sea currents; how Maury demonstrated the existence, the breadth, and velocity of the Gulf Stream; and how, in consequence of all these labors, the signal service had become possible. During all this time the Doctor's eyes fairly glowed with pleasure. I had met him, and he was mine.

The verdict of the learned Board was peculiar: " In the case of Mr. Samuel Williams we find he is suffering from a concussion of the brain, sup-

posed to have resulted from a fall from a Spanish-
American aerial ship, in consequence of which
certain sections of the memory have been impaired,
or temporarily suspended.  In all other respects
the mind is exceptionally clear.  In classic English he is most proficient—in fact, speaks the language with the ease and fluency that one speaks
his native tongue.  From all the evidence we can
gather he is a graduate of the great Cowan University.  We think his services would be invalua-
ble as lecturer in the department of classic English
in the university.  We earnestly commend him to
the favorable consideration of the Curators.''

I felt like one on rising ground.  Several members of this Examining Board were also Curators of
the university.  My prospects were therefore good.
As I now had some money and quite a roll of bills
yet to be disposed of and some prospects in the
world, I thought it best to lay aside my worn military uniform and dress in a style becoming a citizen of some expectations.  This was soon carried
into effect.  I could now pass about without attracting attention.

Dr. Simpson and Prof. Young soon hunted me
up.  They were accompanied by a venerable man
I had noticed during my examination, but who had
remained silent.  He was now introduced as Dr.
Wise.  I was told that Dr. Wise was President of
the Board of Curators of the university.  They
wished to known if I could serve that institution as
lecturer in classic English.  Dr. Wise said he was

greatly pleased with my examination, and was now better pleased with my appearance since I had put off the strange apparel. Dr. Simpson said he hoped I would consent at once. The university could not afford to miss such services. Prof. Young said my services would be a blessing alike to professors and students. I thanked them for their good opinion, and indicated my willingness to serve the university to the best of my ability. My work was to begin with the next quarter, about two weeks off. I was glad of that little time for preparation.

Dr. Wise here called attention to the fact that nothing had been said about the salary, and rather emphasized what he called the stranger part of the fact that I had made no inquiry about a matter of so much importance. I replied that I supposed they had a uniform custom, and what was satisfactory to the other professors would be so to me. He said they did have a uniform compensation, and that my salary would be three thousand dollars per annum.

After my learned friends had recommended me to a suitable boarding house, one becoming the dignity of a professor, they left me to my reflections. I had reflections. Arrested for lunacy and promoted to a professorship in the same day! I now thought it time to study the situation in earnest. In my room I saw a calendar. This was what I wanted. Astounding! Here is the date 2864. I turned to a small library and took down volume

after volume.  All of them, by their dates, verified
the fact that in some way I had leaped over a thousand years.

Now that I had time to think, the absurdity and
certainty of my situation came to me with almost
crushing force.  I beat myself about trying to
throw off the delusion.  I thought of a dream, a
trance, of mental aberration; but do or think as I
would, the certainty and absurdity were still there,
seemingly fixed and permanent.  The continuity
of thought and experience had been complete.  I
had realized no transition in time.  The money I
had was new, it having been issued but a few
weeks.  My Testament was just as I had carried
it during the war.  My clothes were those of the
Confederate soldier.  Now they are all regarded
as antique curiosities.  I was myself a curiosity.

# CHAPTER XXIX.

## Strange Customs.

THE eloquence of silence is often more effective than the eloquence of words. It had been so for me, and I resolved to court her good office still. I would say nothing of my history, but study my present environments. With this view I immediately ordered the city papers. Then I quieted down for a little restful, sober thought. The loss of Susie, the loss of parents, the loss of all connections by a sudden transition of a thousand years was something to demand thought.

On the shaded walk in front of my boarding house I was looking on the strange scenes of the strange city, when, just at the close of the day, Mr. Dorman came speeding by on his cycle. I hailed him and he rounded up to where I sat. He hardly knew me in my new clothes, but congratulated me on my improved appearance. He at once inquired how I came out before the Board. I gave a full account of the day's work. He was surprised at my good fortune, but seemed to be as much elated at my success as if I had been an old acquaintance, or even a relative. I felt that I had at least one friend in this strange world. He said it was time to drop formalities. I was to be Sam, he Tom, and we were to be chums. To this I most heartily agreed, as I needed just such a friend.

"Now, Tom," said I, "tell me how this is: I see according to the calendar and all other indications that this is the year 2864. But according to my convictions and all my experience and knowledge it ought to be 1864. I seem to be a thousand years ahead of my age."

"Your fall," he replied, "has knocked out a thousand years of the world's history for you. Well," he continued, laughing, "that was quite a backset. It is fortunate for you that it is only an imaginary one; for if you had to live back in those barbarous times of a thousand years ago, so full of wars and outrages, you would likely have a hard time of it."

After much pleasant conversation I finally inquired where the university buildings were located.

"The school buildings," he replied, "are in different parts of the city for the convenience of the students."

"Yes," said I, "the preparatory schools, but where is the university?"

"Why, of course," he answered, "the same buildings are for all the schools."

Past experience had taught me caution. So I asked my friend to regard me as a novice and explain the school system for my benefit. The theory of sectional memory came to the rescue, and he explained: "The school buildings are neat, comfortable, convenient. They are located in every part of the city in the ratio of about one to every thousand of the people. Each building has four departments or rooms, one for each school. There are four schools: the primary, the academic, the collegiate, and the university. Five hours are devoted to recitations and lectures, with an intermission of twelve minutes between each hour, thus making the school day five hours and forty-eight minutes long. This intermission of twelve minutes is for the professors to go from one building to another to meet the classes. It is not necessary for the students to leave their rooms. The different professors come to them in turn through the entire school day. Thus you see the student goes through all the schools within the same building, and that near his home. The only change is from room to room as he advances."

" Is the short space of twelve minutes sufficient for the professors to make the necessary changes?" I inquired.

" Well, sometimes it requires a little undue haste for dignified professors," he answered with a smile, at the same time scanning my undignified person. "There has been just a little friction at that point. The old professors objected to long walks, but it has become fashionable for all the young professors, and some not young, to ride cycles. With them distance is desirable as a means of recreation. With this improvement everything works smoothly."

"All the students do not keep on through the university course. It seems to me," so I suggested, " that these classes would be small."

16

"So they would," he replied, "but for the influx of students from the country. The primary school extends all over the country and comes in reach of every child of educable age. The academic school is pushed out into all the more populous neighborhoods. Then many of the larger towns have a collegiate school, and are called collegiate towns. The university draws from the collegiate schools not only here but over a wide reach of country. There is a constant aggregation of students to the more important centers. In this way the higher classes are kept full."

Seeing that I was deeply interested, he continued: "Of course the same system extends through the entire nation. The university school is located in all the important cities, and these are called university cities. These university cities are from fifty to one hundred miles apart."

"It seems to me," I argued, "that the university thus spread out all over the nation would be wanting in *esprit de corps*. There would be lacking the close competition and desire to excel which would stimulate students congregated in one large building."

"Not at all," he replied, "the *esprit de corps* extends to the whole community. Public opinion, family standing, a potent, all-pervading caste feeling, based on education, bear the students along to great efforts. Then the hope of success in life is added to these influences. While it is true that men are elected to civil offices by the suffrages of citizens, it is also true that the university-bred man comes before the people with vastly better chances than the merely college-bred man. And he who falls below that grade has scarcely any chance. Not one time in fifty will such a man get an important office. Four out of five men holding important offices are university-bred. Then when it comes to government patronage the chances are still more in favor of the university-bred men. Nine-tenths of the government employes in the civil service are of this class. True, the examinations are open to all, but the university course has been largely shaped to prepare students for these various government services. The examinations are based on the supposition that the applicants are familiar with this course. This makes it very difficult for those who have not gone through this highest school to get an appointment. This is true also to a large extent in regard to all government patronage, both state and national. As none can go through the university except those who have come up regularly through the lower schools, you see that every possible inducement is held out from the very start to urge students to complete all the courses. The machinery of government, the influence of private life, the hope of ultimate success, the all-powerful factor of respectability—all work to this end. The pressure is indeed about as heavy as it should be, and when students fail it is generally for the want of ability of body or mind to accomplish the tasks."

I was warm in my thanks to my friend for the information thus given. Assuring me of his willingness to be of service to me at any time, he bade me good night.

The papers next morning informed their readers that the examination of Prof. Williams, of the great Cowan University, before the session of Curators for position as lecturer in classic English had been very brilliant and deservedly rewarded with success. The university and citizens generally were congratulated on securing the services of a scholar so renowned. The papers further said that the learned professor not only had the stores of classic English by memory, but also had a large number of bills of money printed about a thousand years ago. One of these bills had been purchased by one of the museums at great price.

Tom called by next morning on his way to the station to let me know that my fortune was now made. The notice in the papers of my old money would bring any number of buyers. " Now, Sam, don't be afraid to put a price on your goods." He was right. For some time my mail was crowded with applications to purchase these bills. Fortunately, I had quite a roll of them. I remembered Tom's advice, and placed on them what I thought was a high price; but to my surprise and gratification they sold readily. As the desire for money increased with its possession, the price of my Confederate bills went higher each day. Money flowed in till its volume suggested the propriety of a bank account, so I went round to the First International Bank of Comos and became a depositor. I found that this fact soon became known to the business men of Comos.

One very noticeable feature of school life in those very modern times was the absence of all large schoolbooks. The books were all small vest-pocket editions, three by six inches, and about one-fourth of an inch thick, so that a half dozen of them could be carried in a pocket. The contents were very much condensed and the books were printed in very clear type on very superior paper. The more extensive studies were printed in several volumes. When I remembered the great luggage of books the boys and girls used to tire under, I was prepared to appreciate this improvement of those advanced times.

By reading everything in the papers, especially the advertisements, and by constant conversation with all classes on the street, I had a very good use of modern English by the time I entered on the duties of my professorship. The language had not changed as much as I would have expected in a thousand years. Nothing like the change in the thousand years prior to the old time in which I used to live. There was a very noticeable tendency to throw off irregularities both in spelling and construction. Many old words are dropped out and many new words had come into use. Some of these new words were very expressive. For instance, I asked my friend, Tom Dorman, one morning, about the propriety of lending money to Frank Goodloe. He replied with an ominous shake of the head: "Frank is a good fellow, but he is a victim of to-morrowism." That I thought expressed it exactly. To-morrowism! I have known many people thus afflicted, but never before heard the word to give it proper expression. Whole towns and entire communities are down and kept down by this same trouble of to-morrowism.

The other day a jockey, praising the good qualities of his horse, said he was sired by the great Gomorrow and *mothered* by Fanny Dean. There, I thought, is another excellent word. Stockmen in my day much needed that word. Matriced was used by some to express the same idea. That is also a good word, regularly coined from *matrix*, and expresses the thought. But to my mind mothered is the word. It expresses the whole idea of rearing a young animal to a condition to take care of itself. The changes in the language were nearly all in favor of brevity and perspicuity.

Fewer changes were found in church service than elsewhere. The hymns and ritual reminded me very much of my early days. Many of the old familiar hymns were still in use. The names of the Wesleys, of Isaac Watts, of Doddridge, Heber, Ken and other immortal hymn writers were still familiar to the lovers of sacred psalmody. Many of the forms of prayer still survived. This was to be expected. Moral obligation continues the same through all generations. Man's relation to God

remains ever the same. It is to be expected, therefore, that forms of prayer and hymns of praise
would be very much the same in all ages.

An innovation in one particular deserves attention. The length of the services was fixed by inexorable custom. Sixty-five minutes were allowed
for the entire service: ten minutes for prayer, fifteen for praise, and thirty for the sermon, with an
intermission of five minutes between the different
parts. The intermission of five minutes was to al-
low time for any persons to leave who did not wish
to attend the next part, and for others so desiring
to come in. Sometimes, but not frequently, the
whole service was conducted by the same person.
Generally each part had a separate leader. Some
of the worshipers were contented with the service
of prayer alone; others attended only the service
of song. Still others crowded all their worship
into listening to the thirty minutes' sermon. Some
attended prayers at one church, the service of song
at another, and preaching at still another—every
one according to his own inclination. With a ripe
spiritual man as leader the service of prayer was
often largely attended—the most popular service
of the day. Then again the service of song, owing to the presence of fine talent, would have a
crowded house.

It was painful to witness the deflections of the
audience down to one-half to hear the message of
the preacher. But these things were taken as a
matter of course. But the sermon was by no means

at a discount, although the preacher failed to attract, owing to greater attraction elsewhere. If
the preaching was neglected in one church it made
the profoundest impression of the day at others.
It was generally understood that people were entirely free to go where they received the greatest
spiritual blessing. Some preachers benefited a
few, others the many. This innovation, as I call
it, though it was an old custom of long standing,
may not have contributed to deeper piety, but I
think it secured more general attendance on public
worship. Housekeepers, cooks, and nurses could
find time to drop in ten, fifteen, or thirty minutes.
Then there are nervous souls who dislike to engage to be still for an hour or more, especially
when the more is indefinite. But all this reluctance
is removed by the intervals of rest, giving them a
chance to retreat. Such persons will often stay
well satisfied through all the services, because the
gaps were down for them to retire if they wished.
They can remain two or three hours at a political
meeting and think the time short, just because they
are at liberty to leave at any time. A great many
people are like live stock: they dislike to go in
where the gaps are to be put up behind them.

The habit of changing from one church to
another in the brief intermission of five minutes
could not have been indulged in but for the exact
uniformity in time. This leads me to explain that
time in every city was run from one center. The
plant was conveniently located anywhere within

the city limits, but usually where its tower could be seen by most people. This great central clock was regulated so as to keep exact time. It was connected by electrical currents with all the dials throughout the city. These dials were run by magnetic force, and the electro magnets were brought into action by the electric currents from the central clock. But the machinery was so arranged that the current was broken unless the dial was in accord with the great clock. If from any cause the connection was broken, the dial stood still till one entire revolution of twenty-four hours was made, when the connection was reëstablished and the dial again gave correct time. Thus it was simply impossible to have any variation in time.

# CHAPTER XXX.

## Strange Improvements.

As the warm weather came on, people began to talk about refrigerants. The boarders intimated to the host that refrigerants would be in order. Tom came in on his cycle, and applying his handkerchief to his forehead, remarked laconically: "Time for refrigerants." All at once newspapers were displaying advertisements of refrigerants. Each advertiser had the best materials and appliances. All this naturally raised an inquiry, and setting myself to investigate, I found the refrigerant to be a method of cooling and ventilating the rooms.

A small room made for the purpose was a part of every house. The air in this little room was refrigerated mostly by chemicals. A noiseless fan, run by magnetic force, sent the cold air into all the apartments as it was wanted. Fresh air was supplied to the refrigerant by pipes from above the house. The cold air from the refrigerant was sent into the apartments near the floors. It escaped near the ceiling. Thus the rooms were cooled and ventilated by the purest air that could be obtained.

In winter this process was reversed. The air in the little room was heated mostly by chemicals. The hot air entered the rooms near the ceiling and found egress near the floor. The appliance was

(250)

then called a heater.  In consequence of this way of heating and cooling the rooms, the doors of dwellings were kept closed winter and summer. This gave a recluse appearance to the city. There was, in fact, but little stirring about in very warm weather except early in the morning and late in the afternoon.

As I began my labors in the university late in the season, the two months before vacation soon passed.  I now had more time to look about.  I frequently visited Tom at the signal station, and went several times out to the reservation where I first saw the light of this new world; but I could never find a trace of the cave, though I never failed to look carefully over the ground where I thought it ought to be.

The whole country looked more than ever like a well-cultivated garden.  Beautiful and richly developed flowers abounded in great profusion about every dwelling.  The mos were busy keeping the land in a high state of cultivation.  I now saw the great use for the many windmills which were conspicuous on every landscape.  They supplied the water, drawing it from deep wells or cisterns, not only for stock, but for irrigation.  The water was stored in reservoirs located on convenient elevations, so that it could run on all parts of the land where needed.

When the signal service indicated drought, the farmers promptly applied irrigation, that there might be no check in the growth of the crops.

This kept grass for stock and assured food for man. Any one seeing the vast multitudes to be fed could readily appreciate the importance of this provision.

Where so much depends on the crops it is certainly well to have the means of making them sure. Agriculture, no longer depending solely on the precarious rains, becomes a safe industry, with definite income. Tom said the weather had become far more accommodating than it used to be. "But," he added after a pause, "it will not do to trust entirely yet."

I asked him why the weather is more trustworthy than formerly.

"It is," he answered, "owing to the great amount of iron used, in the atmosphere, in the form of fences, railroads, and communicating wires, thus equalizing the circulation of electricity, giving a more general distribution of moisture and rain. The showers become more reliable for crops. The electricity in the air has easy access to the earth by means of the iron posts used everywhere for fencing, thus taking away some of the causes of storms. Tornadoes, and other destructive winds, and hailstorms are less frequent. Away back in the earlier ages these fearful agencies were terrific in the destruction of life and property." I had a very vivid recollection of those terrific storms in the barbaric times of old. But I had learned that discretion often lurks in the silences.

This conversation about taming the weather, and the fact that the weather was that day presenting to us an atmosphere of unusual clearness, suggested to me an inquiry of my friend about aerial navigation, of which I had heard much and seen nothing.

"We are not on any regular line of air ships," he began, "and this accounts for your not seeing one."

"Regular line?" I replied; "I thought air ships could go anywhere."

"So they could, but they do not," was his sententious way of putting it. The ships are apt to follow some bold landmarks, which can be easily kept in sight. This is decidedly more necessary at night. Ships going from south to north, or the contrary, keep in sight of the Atlantic coast or the Alleghany Mountains or the Mississippi River. Further west the Rocky Mountains become the guide. These ships are used mostly for excursions of pleasure seekers. Such parties in this country generally follow meridians rather than latitudes. This leaves us off the line of travel."

"Why," said I, "it was always my opinion that when the navigation of the air was once made successful it would be made the medium of general commerce; that traffic and travel would be almost exclusively carried on that way; that ships would regularly visit every city, town, and village in the whole country; would bring the market to every man's door; thus practically doing away with the interior, by bringing every place to the front in the matter of transportation.''

"That," returned my friend, "was no doubt the dream of many, but it has not been realized. Experience has shown that the more solid the material on which transportation can be made, the better. And for this reason the steel rail has practically the monopoly in the movement of freight. Steel is better than water, and water is much better than air. The air ship does well enough for excursions, as it affords excitement for pleasure parties; but when it comes to moving heavy articles, the steel rail is wanted."

Just at this juncture Frank Love called for Tom to send down the elevator. We looked over the white panels and saw quite a number of young people, each with some kind of spyglass. "They want to make observations," said Tom, as he started the elevator down for them. Soon gentlemen and ladies were landed, and I, being a stranger to most of them, had to submit to the formality of an introduction. However, it was gratifying to my vanity to see that by reputation I was no stranger; and every one seemed glad of the chance for a formal introduction. While we were exchanging civilities, Frank reminded Tom that the rest of the party were waiting for the elevator. So the elevator was sent, and on its return with the other members of the party, a like introduction was given.

This being attended to in due form, Frank in-

quired of Tom if he had seen the " White Eagle."
" ' The White Eagle ! ' " exclaimed Tom, " what
do you mean?"

" Why," inquired Frank, " did you not notice
an account in the papers of the excursion from
Alabama? A corps of scientists are going to the
Rockies in the interest of knowledge and pleasure. Their ship is called the ' White Eagle.'
This city is to be taken in the route. It is to pass
here at 10 o'clock."

Strange we had not looked at a paper. Tom
and I had been sitting there a long time with one
between us, but we had been much engaged with
each other and had not thought of news. Tom
immediately went to his instruments to learn the
whereabouts of the ship. " Sure enough," he exclaimed, "she is coming; just now passing about
three miles north of Haynesville, on the North-
eastern, sailing about two hundred yards high,
heading for Comos."

"Close to the earth," "comfortable height,"
"don't want to waste gas," and "freeze with
cold," "old sailors on the winds;" these were
some of the comments by different ones of our
party.

" Now, Frank," continued Tom, without giving
heed to any of these remarks, "cover the horizon
about ten degrees south of east, and I think she
can be seen."

Frank at once brought his glass to bear as directed, and after scanning the horizon for awhile

said: "Yes; she's in sight. Nine degrees four
minutes south." Glasses were adjusted accord-
ingly, and one after another gave indication of
finding the ship. Frank politely handed his glass
to me, but as he saw I did not know how to adjust
it, said: "Now, Professor, look just to the right
of that most distant windmill."

I saw the object indicated, and leveling the glass
first at the windmill, and then moving it to the right,
I caught sight of the ship. But I would not have
known it but for its motion. "Why, it looks like
it was half buried in the earth," I exclaimed with
innocent surprise.

The ladies were amused. "Yes," said Tom,
"it looks like a huge terrapin working itself out of
its hole." "Rather like the dome of a temple rising out of the earth," suggested an elegant lady by
my side.

As we looked, it rose clear of the earth, like the
sun rises in the morning. After awhile, some of
the party discovered that it could be seen without
the aid of the glasses. To the unaided eye, it now
looked like a speck on the distant horizon. It
rose higher and grew larger. These were the
only changes for some time. As it came nearer,
we could begin to see that its shape was not round,
as it had seemed. The front did not come to an
angle, as in boats designed for water, but had rather the symmetrical finish like the breast of a swan.

About the time she reached the city, steering a
course to skirt along the southern suburbs, all at

once her speed slacked. "She is going to float," said one. "They want to observe the city," responded another. When her machinery stopped, the ship made a graceful descent, till she was not much above the buildings. The wind was gently blowing from the southwest, and the ship floated very much in the same direction she had been steering. She floated out toward our station, and looked like she might pass directly over us. While drifting in the breeze she had headed toward the south, thus presenting a broad side toward us, and close enough for us to observe her graceful structure, more than two hundred feet long. A grand sight to look upon! The visions and prophesies of ages were in that ship! What a privilege it was to me to be projected beyond my age, and look upon that which so many wise men had hoped to see, but died without the sight!

Her mos began to work; she darted forward and glided upward like a bird with folded wings. With a graceful curve she bent her prow to the west, making the arc of a circle around our station almost in speaking distance. We could see the passengers, a gay company of men, women, and children, at the grated windows, looking down upon us.

Our company waved handkerchiefs, and they of the ship answered the same way. It was something to see a little child with its arms thrust through the cross bars to the shoulder, waving in its tiny hands a handkerchief, in mid air!

17

As the ship passed from us, her wheels came in splendid view. They looked like transparent circles, so rapid was their motion. Thus we have seen a swiftly revolving buggy wheel, without seeing any of its spokes. The wheels were on the order of screw propellers, the shafts extending back, and at considerable angle downward. I could now see why the ship descended when the wheels stopped, and rose when they began to work. The pressure was forward and upward. The ship passed on its way, but left its image on the brainy tablet, so vivid that even the caprices of sectional memory will not soon disturb its beauty.

Life was now, during this vacation, running very smoothly. A good position makes the world look brighter. Mine was one of high honor, and also brought me the means of independence. Classic English was held in high esteem, and was assiduously cultivated. The chair which I filled in the university was one of the most popular. I was a welcome guest in any society, and my reputation was growing.

When it came to my turn, according to custom, to address the learned societies of the city, I expressed a desire to deliver the discourse in classic English. This was hailed with delight. I was at once regarded as a marvel of erudition. Each professor in turn was expected to deliver a discourse to the learned societies of the city, pertaining to his chair. This was to refresh the memories of the alumni, that they might keep abreast of the culture in the several departments. It was a kind of post graduate school in which they continued through life.

The social feature of these meetings was delightful. These learned societies were composed of ladies as well as gentlemen; as all the schools, including the university, were alike open to both sexes. The lectures to the university classes were free to all. These addresses to the learned societies served so much to keep alive a desire for learning that the regular lectures through the school session were often attended by post graduates of both sexes. This was especialty true of the chair of classic English. I often found the room crowded with these lovers of the old tongue.

Invitations poured in from the university cities asking me to come and address their societies in classic English. As I had somehow skipped fresh from the English-speaking people of the classic period into this highly cultured age, I had reason to believe that, however deficient in other branches, I really understood classic English better than any other man in the world. Confidence in our own ability is productive of the greatest effort.

All the years of learning at the old academy, especially the lectures on English literature by the teacher, now came to my aid. With an orator standing a thousand years back, and talking of the events of the age in which he lived but yesterday is like looking through a powerful lens; the objects seems to be brought up for close inspection.

He gives with pleasure who is able to give munificently. To feel that you are quickening the pulse of thought: to see from the eyes before you that flash in unison with your own, that you are enlarging the mental views, and helping souls to communion with higher thought, is joy ecstatic, reserved alone for the real teachers of mankind. Such oratory blesses the auditors much; the orator more. In this also, the lesson of the great Teacher holds good: "It is more blessed to give than to receive." That blessing was mine

# CHAPTER XXXI.

## ASPIRING TO AUTHORSHIP.

AFTER an extended lecture tour, one day late in the vacation I went to have a quiet day with Tom at the station. Easy conversation with a congenial friend is restful. I was communicative; Tom was a willing listener. I wanted to talk over my past life and see if any light could be thrown on the mystery of my transmission through the ages.

I began with my childhood, pointing out the place where I thought our house stood. It was now a beautiful garden, adjacent to a magnificent residence. "And there," said I, pointing to a deep depression, "is where the spring flowed so delightfully cool from under the steep surrounding bluffs. In the deep recess of bending ferns, where the arching foliage of the trees hemmed in the perpetual shade, the water came forth dancing with delight. I tell you, Tom, it was a retreat where nymphs might live and love." Tom had before smiled at my enthusiasm, but here he broke into a hearty laugh. His laugh was contagious, and I smiled in spite of my seriousness. The picture which I drew was in sharp contrast with the present reality. There was before us only an ordinary depression, a little deeper than others in the ever varying face of cultivated nature. But in proof of the former existence of the spring I pointed to the busy windmill on the very spot, drawing the water from the depths below and storing it in a reservoir to gladden the fields around.    Then away across the laughing fields and over the tops of beautiful dwellings, and sighting by a windmill, I pointed to the places where the academy stood and where the church was located.    I told about the slaves and about my youthful companions.    Then in tender accents, letting the voice fall to a whisper, for the ground whereon I walked was sacred, I rehearsed the story of my early and continued love; how the great war came and separated me from the object of my adoration.    I told about our last fight, and the Cave of Futurity, and how I had appeared a stranger in the land of my birth.

Tom was inclined to laugh, but my manner restrained him.    When, in answer to his query, I fondly called the name of Susie Brantlett, he looked up with a smile: "Why, Sam, there is a most excellent lady in the city by that name.    I will introduce you to her this very evening.    But I tell you, old fellow," he continued, "you have the best materials I have ever heard for a romance; you must write a book.    It will be a delight for you to live over all this dream of yours.    You must not forget the Cave of Futurity, and how you got away from those barbarous times.    You can end your story by finding a suitable match for your hero among the civilized ladies of this golden age.    That will be a rich solace for the loss of the old love."

I was provoked at his levity, but I checked such feelings at once by reflecting that he could not but regard my story as pure fiction. But I knew it was true to nature, as I had lived it. I began to think seriously of writing the history; to me it would not be a romance—no plot was needed. I would write the straightforward narrative of what I had lived, and how in some mysterious way I "had outrun my age and race, and found myself in the midst of things not dreamed of before." ·

That evening we called on Miss Susie Brantlett. I felt a nervous anxiety as the time approached. In the midst of such transformations how did I know but that Susie had experienced some of the same, and that I should actually meet her in these strange surroundings? I think Tom really expected me to meet my loved and lost, and that memory was about to be restored, and that I would prove not to be a stranger in Comos. He talked as if he thought I was about to pick up the tangled thread of life and unravel the mysteries of my strange career.

But Miss Susie was not my Susie. She was larger and taller; would weigh at least forty pounds more. She was a noble woman, worthy to be a descendant of the old race. She was highly cultured and very agreeable. Her every movement showed that, like all the cultured citizens of Comos, she was thoroughbred. She was very cordial—in fact, her appreciation was almost embarrassing. "I am delighted," she said—" as who is not?—to entertain the learned professor of classic English. I have heard all your lectures in the city to the learned societies, and have been so well pleased that I have attended many of the lectures to the classes. I am a dear lover of classic English."

Of course I was gratified. A taste in common is often a bond of friendship, and I recognized at once a new tie in the strange city of Comos. In this presence nothing was more acceptable than classic English, so I led off for some time in a sort of discussion of the old authors. Miss Susie seemed to be highly entertained, and so far entered into the conversation as to show she had indeed studied the classics of her ancestors. She had found a volume in the city library which she told us interested her very much. It was found in an obscure corner, where apparently it had not been disturbed for ages. "The title of the book," she said, "is 'Ben-Hur.' I hardly know whether it is history or romance. It is sometimes like one, and sometimes like the other. It perplexes me because I have to make such constant use of the dictionary. When I become most deeply interested I have to stop to hunt words and study phrases, and it is hard for me to keep the personages in mind. I suppose this is because the work is so very ancient. It gives an account of things in the time of our Saviour. I did not know before that the English language was spoken that far back. I will be glad to have you give me some assistance in its study."

With this she rose and went for the volume. I

had never heard of the book, but supposed from the name that it was the work of some Jewish rabbi. I was regretting the necessity of confessing my ignorance, when she returned and placed the musty volume in my hands.  I saw at a glance it was familiar English, and felt relieved.  The next thing was to look for the date and the author.  Both astonished and puzzled me.  Seventeen years ahead of time, according to my count, and by General Lew Wallace.  Why, my ears almost tingled at the remembrance of the guns of Lew Wallace at Fort Donaldson.  The idea of that grim warrior writing the story of the world's great Peacemaker!

I was so occupied by these reflections that I had almost forgotten the demands of politeness.  As it would be to me like reading a novel fresh from the press, or, rather, ahead of the press, I remarked to Miss Susie that I would be glad to read the volume with her.  She was so delighted with the proposal, and I was so anxious to read the book, that next day was appointed as a time to begin the reading.

Reading a few passages by way of foretaste, I saw that the book was one of thrilling interest.  It would be all the more so to me because of the author, who, if I did not personally know, I had good reason to personally remember!  Just here I was reminded by the chime of a neighboring dial that it was 22 o'clock (corresponding to our 10 o'clock P.M.), and time, according to custom, to retire. Custom is more than law in Comos.  No explanation was necessary. Tom and I both rose at the same instant and bade her good-night.

What with filling my remaining appointments to lecture, and reading with Miss Susie, planning my book, the few remaining days of vacation soon passed.

In settling down regularly to work in the university, I settled down also to the task of writing my book. But the question soon came up in my mind whether I should write in classic or modern English. Of course it was much easier for me to write in the old tongue. But that would be to write only for scholars. On the other hand, if I should write in the vernacular, the work might be awkwardly done and be little to my credit. I had a reputation to sustain. I noticed that whole classes of words had disappeared. The thousand years that had intervened had been a severe test of the vitality of words. The words of life and power—words whose very essence seemed to be active in the ideas they expressed—had lived. The most living words in the ancient English were living still in the modern tongue. Most naturally I formed the habit of trying to express ideas by the ancient words which were still in the living language. Being understood by both, they were a bond of union between myself and the people of these modern times on which I had fallen. These were the most expressive words. They were the picture words; such words as painted living images in the mind of the hearers. I was convinced that my success as a lecturer was due to the use of these best words. I determined, therefore, to adopt this method in writing. I would use the old language, but try to express my ideas in such words as were still living. When the word would likely not be understood by the modern reader, a modern substitute in parenthesis would make the meaning plain. When something more should be necessary, I would resort to footnotes and brief translations.

It was evident that such a book would be of great service to beginners in the study of the classics, and also to refresh the minds of those who had partly laid such studies aside. If I could write a book that would be a necessity to the university school, I would thereby secure a permanent place in literature. I was enthused with the work, and applied myself with diligence. The manuscript grew in bulk week after week.

Meanwhile my visits to Miss Susie became more and more interesting. Tom said he was sure I would find a solace for the loss of the ancient Susie in the possession of the modern one. "That," he said, "would be a splendid *finale* to your literary production, and also a desirable consummation of your earthly happiness." Miss Susie was no doubt a jewel of rare value, a thorough lady in every sense; but the sigh of my heart was for my own Susie of the olden time.

In the autumn the great agricultural fair was held in the suburbs of Comos. This was an occasion of great interest. The display of stock was immense. The riding, driving, draft, and race horses were entirely distinct breeds. Each breed had such clearly defined characteristics adapted to the uses intended that they might almost be regarded as different species.

The breeds of cows were many, but all belonged to two great classes, adapted to the world's foods —milk and beef. The race had narrowed down to this. In each of these two great classes were many breeds, such as the Kansas, Delta, Texas, Gulf Coast, and Allegheny breeds. They were severally the products of localities where the foods and climatic influences afforded the best development for the purposes intended.

Mississippi sheep produced the finest wool; those of Illinois took the premium for mutton; the Montana goats carried off the palm for kid, and those of Arizona for the best textile.

The poultry department was extensive and varied. The wingless chickens were new to me. The wings still remained as rudimentary organs long out of use. The dry land duck was also a novelty. He was a plump, compact bird, almost wingless. The web had disappeared from between the toes.

The turkey seemed to be the favorite fowl with these prosperous Americans. There were quite a number of distinct varieties: the pure black, the snowy white, the golden hued, and the deep brown. But in all of them I noticed a great change from the bird of my early time. The long, slender, running legs had been converted into thick, sturdy legs for standing; the unused wings had become small and clumsy; the broad breasts, originally intended to sustain vigorous flight, had become massed with the sweetest white flesh. The turkey, like everything else, had changed to meet the demands of man's exacting appetite. The noble bird as I then saw him was round and plump, his heavy breast hanging forward, more resembling the extinct dodo than the slender, graceful, wild turkey of the American forest.

But time would fail me to tell of all the wonders displayed; of the eyeless potatoes, propagated from the seed; of the coreless apples and stoneless peaches produced by grafting; of the strawberries weighing ten ounces apiece; of blackberries of beautifully variegated colors. Inventive genius had found a way to preserve berries and fruits of every kind, so that it was not strange for these berries to have been kept over in good, fresh condition for the fair. The Comoreans were very fond of berries.

Having a natural turn for machinery, I passed on to that department. The motor was almost the universal power, being used for nearly every purpose. It was on exhibition in nearly every imaginable shape and size. The principle on which they were constructed is the same in all. It is the well-known fact that the opposite poles of a magnet attract, while like poles repel. To secure the full advantage of this principle as a motive power, a simple system of electro-magnets was devised. The essential parts of the machine were as follows: A

cylinder whose outer rim was supplied with magnets. This revolved inside of a stationery cylinder, or shell, the inside rim of which was also furnished with magnets. These magnets, those in
the revolving cylinder and those in the inclosing
shell, thus brought in close connection with each
other, were so arranged that attracting poles were
all the time coming toward each other, and the re-
pelling ones always receding from each other.
This was accomplished by an automatic regulation
of the electrical currents.

In all locomotive machines, including the ever
present cycle, the electricity was supplied by storage batteries. These storage batteries had been
brought to such perfection that a battery not larger
than the canteen I used to carry in the war would
run a cycle for hours. Every windmill might be
used as a motor for storing the batteries, so that
they were always on hand in great abundance.
The machine was simple enough in construction
and very durable. It was called a mo, probably
from the well-known tendency of Americans to
shorten names. In this case they trimmed down
to the central idea. Mo is the taproot of motion,
motive, locomotive. It expresses motion pure and
simple. Thus these advanced Americans had
caught and harnessed one of the most potent forces
of nature—the magnetic force—which holds all the
worlds in proper ecliptic position and performs an
important part in the grand machinery of the universe.

My book grew upon me.  The narrative needed no coloring.  Truth in that case was stranger than fiction.  To tell these people the rude methods of their forefathers;  of their native country, when it was supporting its first or second generation of men, while large areas of it were still covered with primeval forests;  of the manners and customs in vogue when classic English was the living vernacular;  of the slaves, whose constant labors made life a perpetual leisure to their masters;  of the gigantic war, whose history is known only to scholars—these were themes which needed not the aid of foreign ornament.

But the most tender, the most pathetic, the most intensely interesting—the part that had heart and soul in it—was that which told of Susie, the loved and lost.  "While I was musing the fire burned." How pure, how unselfish the love which hovered over this broken shrine!  How sweetly varied the phases of her picture to memory's eye, as in the kaleidoscope of affection she passes in review before me from childhood to maturity!  It was almost sacrilegious to expose the shrine of my heart to the gaze of unsympathetic readers.  But what better could I do?  If Susie, by the cold hand of fate, has been separated from me forever, why should I not embalm her memory in the beautiful mazes of story?

# CHAPTER XXXII.

## The Return.

TWO strange facts had been constantly present to my mind since my first appearance in the country. One was the absence of the slave population. What had become of the negroes? Their absence might readily be accounted for on the supposition that a thousand years had actually elapsed. That seemed really to be the case. In fact, that was the only way to account for this and many other great changes everywhere plainly seen.

I suppose that if one could be unconscious for a thousand years, or even ten thousand, there would, on a resuscitation to life, be no apparent loss of time. I could readily perceive, therefore, that the last day I spent in the old state, even though a thousand years ago, would seem but as yesterday. Of course the transmission was entirely mysterious. I had to accept that, just as I had to accept my existence, as a matter above the reach of my faculties. I had about accepted that view of the case.

I inquired of those who it appeared to me should know, where the negroes were; and the uniform reply was that the darker races lived farther south. I could find quite a number of people who boasted of negro blood; it reminded me of the people, always of the first families of Virginia, who used to boast of descent from Pocahontas, and were really proud of their Indian blood.

The other strange fact was the absence of the poor, especially in a city as large as Comos. I noticed the same in other cities where I had been lecturing. Mr. Wise gave the most satisfactory explanation. He said: "There had been a tendency in all ages for wealth to accumulate in the hands of the few, to the detriment of the many. Conditions of society at different times and different places have greatly strengthened this tendency. Under such favoring conditions great fortunes have been accumulated, thus at once increasing the desire and the capacity by which it is gratified. The accumulation of wealth in consequence has gone on with accelerated facility. The poor were the first to be made poorer. Then the smaller fortunes were taken up. Then larger ones were melted and absorbed. Fortunes grew larger and fewer in regular ratio.

"During all this time rich men were honored because of their riches. The money-maker was the hero. This gave tenfold force to the desire to make and possess wealth. Thus people were aiding their own ultimate downfall. They cheered the skill of the man who was making the fetters by which their own limbs were to be manacled. This same state of things exists to-day in the less enlightened countries.

"But the controlling nations of the world have
18

grown wiser. In all self-respecting men there is a principle stronger than the love of money. This is the desire to have the good opinion of our fellow-man. As soon as public opinion ceased to worship wealth great fortunes ceased to be desirable. The opinion became general that the race for money beyond a reasonable competence was unwise, un-natural, and unchristian: unwise, because it de-feats the very purpose in view, the happiness of the money-maker and his family; unnatural, because it takes the rights of the many and gives them to the few, producing an abnormal and congestive condition of the body politic that is essentially unhealthy; unchristian, because such a state of things is utterly irreconcilable with the principles of the great Teacher.

" When the world came to recognize these facts, none were more ready to readjust the financial basis than the very rich. Strange to say, men of small fortunes, whose wealth was most liable to absorption, were the most conservative. The millionaires were ready to relax. A small per cent. income seemed amply sufficient. The great manufacturers were satisfied with a small per cent. on their investments. The employees were at once content with wages which heretofore seemed too small. The surplus, after paying the per cent. and wages, was divided between proprietors and work-men on terms satisfactory to all.

"All other industries fell into line. Everybody was satisfied. The rich were still rich, the poor had no fear of poverty. Very little, seemingly, had been done. The world had simply let go and let the tension relax. Thus the problem of all ages at once melted away. Rich and poor were alike free.

" To be sure, there were still a few skinflints, but they were ashamed of themselves. Fortunately, such men are of small caliber, and consequently of limited influence. Their closeness was rarely transmitted from father to son. Public opinion became very strong against such avarice, and the young being more susceptible to its influence, the sons rarely walked in the evil ways of their fathers.

" Workingmen easily live on their wages. Their dividends are surplus cash. This is almost invariable invested either in the capital stock of the plant where they work or in some desirable enterprise. Thus men become at the same time wage-earners and proprietors. This has, in the lapse of time, done much to obliterate the distinction between labor and capital.

"'This, then, accounts for the absence of the poor. There are now no special tendencies to poverty. Nobody wishes to oppress. Public opinion demands that in some way every man shall be employed: that he shall make himself useful. Then every man who works not only gets fair wages, but has an equable interest in what his hands have helped to produce. He pays but a reasonable price for the capital he uses. He gets a reasonable compensation for his day's work, and a fair share of what that work has added to the world's wealth."

During the winter I was busy with the university lectures and the writing of my book. This latter labor now engaged my most earnest endeavor. Notwithstanding these labors, two evenings per week were spent with Miss Susie in reading old English. These evenings were delightful, and grew constantly more so as the weeks were passing by.

Miss Susie was a remarkably gifted lady. She soon became so familiar with the construction and pronunciation of the classic tongue that we used it almost exclusively in conversation. It was like a return to my previous state of long ago to hear the dear old words pronounced by the silvery tongue of this cultured lady.

Nearly every day I met and had some pleasant words with Tom Dorman. We frequently took tea together; and many a morning we took a cycle race on the smooth road out toward the station.

My relations with the professors were pleasant. Dr. Simpson and Prof. Young were congenial gentlemen. I loved to cultivate the acquaintance of Mr. Wise. He was ordinarily a man of few words, and had to be cultivated to get to the best stratum of his nature. Thus, with pleasant mental labor and congenial companionship, the winter was " over and gone " almost before I woke to a realization of the fact.

One evening Tom and I were taking tea together

when I reminded him of the fact that next day would be the anniversary of our first meeting at the station. The mystery of my appearance in the country at that time came upon me with renewed force. And we talked upon it for some time. As the next day was Monday, and consequently the rest day for the schools, I had a fancy for celebrating the day by donning my old military uniform, which I had kept carefully folded away, and going out to the reservation to muse on the uncertainties of life. Tom said it would be a recreation for me, which he thought was needful after a hard winter's work.

So next morning, bright and early, before the inhabitants were up, we were on our cycles speeding out of the city. I stopped at the station an hour or two with Tom, taking another view of this beautifully cultivated country. The grandeur of its civilization never impressed me more than it did this morning. The landscape was never more charming. The freshness of a bright spring morning, the rising sun, whose rays clustered in the dewdrops, gave additional loveliness to the scene. The charm of poesy and the power of science had united to make a terrestial paradise.

As I looked fondly on the glowing scenes before me, the thought of my mysterious appearance here so entirely out of time came upon me with such force and weighed so heavily on my mind I felt out of place in the presence of my joyous and light-hearted companion. That I might not oppress his spirit with my own abstractions, I took leave of him and speeded along the smooth road which I traveled with so much astonishment just one year ago.

I turned in at the gate, and, leaving my cycle by its side, took my way along the same path I had come the morning of my singular advent into this strange country. The path looked just like it did that morning. When I reached the hill, to my very great astonishment, there was the cave just as I had looked back to it one year ago. I had looked that ground a dozen times over, and had failed always before to see the slightest semblance of that cave.

I went into this opening with a palpitating heart. Beneath my feet was the same soft floor of green moss. I went on almost in a run till I came to the couch on which I had spent the night. Here I stopped and reflected. This is surely leading me back to the old world. If I go on, I will come out into my former life. Is it best to plunge again into war, and cast my lot in a country desolated by strife? I am leaving my professorship, my precious manuscript, my bank account, the most enlightened and prosperous people I have ever known, a country of peace and plenty. This very evening I have an engagement to read with Miss Susie.

But this leads me home: to father and mother; to Susie—not the cultured, the thoroughbred, but my Susie, the Susie of my lifelong love, the idol enshrined in the shekinah of my soul.   And with this thought I broke into a run, and halted not till I had reached the mouth of the cave.   I bounded out, and sure enough here were the old woods, the same old rugged hills.   I had several times traveled over this country during the last year, and these hills, leveled and terraced, were teeming with crops and ornamented with beautiful residences.   I am now just in the line of the great Northwestern.

But here are the old scenes of my boyhood.   I must now look for home and Susie.   I looked back to take a final view of the Cave of Futurity, and, behold! there was not the sign of a cave: simply the bluff which had stood there for ages. There was nothing unusual on its surface.   I thought I must surely be the victim of some strange hallucination.

I now went along the old way by which I had come down to that bluff a year ago.   When I came near the road, I saw a wagon coming.   It was drawn by two old mules which looked haggard and poor.   Wagon and team both looked like war times.   Why, there's Will Benson, Sam McGee, and Joe Conway.   The wagon made a halt for me to get in.   I had seemed as one in a dream.   But now sitting by Will Benson, while the old wagon jolted over the roots, my mind seemed to clear up. Full consciousness gained ascendency.   The road was familiar to me.   I knew just where we were and how far it was home.

Turning to Will, I asked; "What does all this mean?"

Will's face lighted up with a joy I could not understand. "Why, Sam," he answered, "we are going home. Don't you know the road?"

"Yes," I returned, "I do know the road. But where are we from? What have I been doing the past twelve months?" I noticed the other boys, who sat on the back seat, leaning forward greatly delighted.

"For the last twelve months," Will repeated slowly. "Yes, it has been just a little over twelve months since we were captured."

"Since you all were captured," I said, "but what about me?"

"You were almost killed by the cavalry charge," he said. "The captors wanted to leave you on the field as dead, but you were still breathing. We did not know but there was a chance for your recovery, and it might be long before you would be found and cared for if left. We absolutely refused to march till you were placed in an ambulance. In a few weeks you were well, except in mind. Only a week ago I succeeded in getting an operation performed to relieve your brain of pressure. The surgeon said you would probably come right in about a week. To-day you give the first clear indications that you are well again."

I sat and thought in silence. My skip of a thousand years into the future was all the imaginings of a disordered brain. My professorship, authorship, and bank account, my fame for learning, my high social position in the most cultivated society was all a delusion. I smiled at the uxuberance of my crippled imagination. Well, I had a high time. And perhaps that which appeared to me so real, may, in a thousand years, prove to have the flavor of prophecy. I can well lay down my fancied honors if my Susie will but receive my offer of devotion.

I thought about what I had missed of the hardships of prison life, and what a happy exchange I had made. Instead of confinement in the gloomy walls of a prison, I had been living in splendid style and visiting people who lived in mansions. Instead of the haggard and sorrowful faces of my comrades, I had been looking on the chivalry and beauty of a grand country. I had exchanged the hardships and din of war for a land of peace and plenty. Instead of the taunts and gibes of our keepers, "the proud man's contumely," my rapt ear had listened to the long roll of fame.

Just here I roused up from my reverie to remind Will that he was taking the wrong road.

" O," said he, " we are going to my house."

"All right," I replied; " just let me get out, and I can walk home. It is hardly a mile now." The expression on Will's face alarmed me. The very low state of father's health when last I heard of him, and the long time that had elapsed since, at once suggested the worst.

Will saw that explanation was necessary. As gently as possible he broke the sad intelligence. Both parents had died—father nearly a year ago, and mother six months later.

This was a terrible blow. It was almost crushing. I could see that Will, and the other boys also, feared its effect on my mental condition. But I told them that grief was natural and tears were a relief. As to my mental state, I felt that my mind had thoroughly regained its elasticity.

Sister Mary was overjoyed to receive us back home. "And," she said, " you are home to stay. The news has just reached us that Gen. Lee has surrendered, and of course the war is over." This was startling news, and true.

When the ebullition of feeling had somewhat subsided, Will gave an account of our capture and prison life till we were exchanged a few days ago. I listened attentively, for it was as much news to me as it was to my sister. Letters had come through the lines, and sister had heard of my mental condition. Her joy was unbounded to find me completely restored.

The war being over, it was time to estimate results. The one great result most palpable to us was the freedom of the slaves. At one mighty sweep nearly all the property of the South went down in the whirlpool of war. We stood aghast to see the foundation knocked out, and our entire social fabric tottering to its fall. Slavery had become so thoroughly ingrafted into our Southern life that it seemed to be the natural condition. So it had always appeared to me. A firm but mild authority on the one hand, and a confiding obedience on the other: these deeply imbedded principles, all overgrown with the green ivy of peace, made the symbol of slavery as it had always presented itself to my childish perception.

But four years of war had graduated me to manhood. I now stood face to face with the new problem. Having been born heir to property and cradled in the expectation of an easy competence, I now confronted the necessity of making an independent living, either by muscle or brain. And I felt the manhood in me strengthening up to full proportions. I was emancipated. Along the fiery crest of battle God's hand had been stretched out to take the bonds, not only from the negro's body, but from his mind as well. I rejoiced to know that the best qualities of the negro race as I had learned to appreciate them could henceforth develop in a state of freedom. The picture of old Ephraim, standing day and night by the bedside of his dying master, with grief unfeigned, and helpfulness ever on the watch; the faithfulness and business capacity of Jack, tested from young to old manhood; the unfailing kindness and strict fidelity of mammy, the guardian of my youth; the humble piety of Uncle Sam, the patriarch; the eloquence of John, the preacher; the heroic conduct of George on the field of Shiloh: these and other examples stand vividly out on memory's tablet.

A race which can produce characters like these deserves to be free. Let no man henceforth be in position to restrict or dwarf such traits. The world has a right to the best that every race can produce. It is therefore right for every race to be in position to produce the best. I could not but believe that the deep piety and pure faith characteristic of the negro race gives a divine title to freedom. "If simple faith is more than Norman blood," then the time is overdue when the shackles should be taken from the negro's soul. Such reflections reconciled me to the loss of property and helped to blunt the keen edge of defeat.

Another important result of the war I could but regard with a gleam of satisfaction, even in the anguish of defeat. That was the preservation of the country in its entire territorial extent. From my earliest years I had been proud of my country's greatness. I had mourned over the wane of that greatness in the disunion of the states. Now while my heart bled because of the humiliation of my native state, prostrate as a conquered province, with her proud escutcheon trailing in the dust, I yet felt a recompense in the prospect of a grand, united country; a nation which would command the respect and challenge the admiration of all mankind

# CHAPTER XXXIII.

## The Consummation.

THIS was my first day of normal consciousness for more than a year. It is not surprising that, after the excitement of getting home had abated, I felt great lassitude both of body and mind. With solicitude beyond description, my thoughts centered on Susie. Now that my parents were gone, I felt more than ever that my life's happiness depended on her. I desired to go at once to see her, but sister would not at all consent till I had taken a good rest. But seeing that it pleased me, she talked much about Susie; her sweet disposition and noble nature. I learned from her that Capt. Webb had been at home several times during the last year, and had frequently attended Susie to church, and that he was with her only last Sabbath. I am ashamed to confess what uneasiness this news gave me.

This led to a train of gloomy reflections. It had been reported that my mental faculties were permanently out of order. Why should Susie linger over the memory of such a wreck? Besides, we had never been engaged. How did I know that she really cared for me? I had gone through the war without any special distinction. Dick Webb was captain. John Henderson was major. They

had won distinction by deeds of valor; my distinction had been won in the realms of diseased
imagination. Those fancied honors have gone
like the dreams of the South Sea bubble, and I
am poor, maimed, and only a " high private in the
rear ranks." Why should I expect Susie to be
mine? What have I with which to take care of
her? With these gloomy reflections, I fretted myself to sleep.

Next morning Sister Mary led me into a room,
threw open the trunks, and showed me how she
had preserved my best clothes. This was a most
timely discovery. "Now," she said, with a
good laugh, "you can fix up and go to see Susie.
She will be looking for you, and you will be sure
of a hearty welcome." Her cheerfulness was
catching, as was also her hopefulness.

With a renewed confidence, I prepared to go
over to Mr. Brantlett's. My dress would have
satisfied a Chesterfield. Will had the horse and
buggy for me at the gate. As I rode over the short
distance amid the old familiar scenes that bright
spring morning, I felt the joy of a sweet peace
warming in the rays of the mighty hope which was
rising like a bright sun above the horizon of my
life.

Our meeting that morning will ever remain a
bright, sweet center; a metropolis of joy in the domain of memory. Susie looked more mature, having now reached the full-blown flower of womanhood. It was plain to be seen that anxiety had

left a chastened and refining touch on every feature. Four eventful years had brought out the decided marks of character, and every trace bore the stamp of nature's true nobility. She was never before altogether so lovely.

If a single misgiving remained in my mind, it was dispelled by her old time reception, a greeting full of heart and soul. Her joy at my safe return, both to home and reason, could no more be hid than a rose can hide its beauty. When I had made a full confession, and the sweet vows had been exchanged, she looked perfectly radiant. To possess such love is one of the sweetest joys of earthly experience; a joy which comes as a glorious sun on the landscape of life, and warms into beautiful flowers, and ripens into luxurious fruitage all the nobler capabilities of our being.

Here was the consummation of a thousand hopes which had gladdened life from childhood until now; of hopes which had brought gleams of joy into long, laborious marches, through rain and mud, sleet and cold; of hopes which had made luminous the dismal camp fires of winter, or blunted the keen edge of battle during the campaigns of summer. In the grandly luminous satisfaction of such experience, all labor, pains, aches, and disappointments, all the fictitious joys of success among the highbred people of Comos were gladly buried in the grave of oblivion, without a single regret. The past can only be good, since it has led to this consummated joy.

It needed not the herald of spoken language to tell Will and sister of my success. Every motion of my being proclaimed it in every moment of time. The fruition of our life hope, the coming to us of long-coveted responsibilities, act as a powerful spring to project far into plain relief the purposes and energies of manhood. I now felt it was time to plan and work for Susie's welfare. Will was my best counselor.

"We must make the best of our circumstances," he said. "The land is still here, and the negroes are here also. White and black must make a living together. Go over to the old homestead, Sam, and see what is there. Make such contract with the negroes as you think is right. The only thing is to make the best crop we can, and as late as it is we may do very well." He showed what arrangement he had made with the hands on his place, and told me how they had gone to work with glad hilarity.

Thanking my practical brother-in-law for his advice, I went at once. No time was to be lost. I felt the inspiration of purpose, and went as one having something to do, and a will to do it. Jack, the faithful driver, the trusted servant of my father, was the first to see me when I was yet a great way off. I can never forget the unfeigned joy expressed in his honest black face, as he rushed up to me saying: "God bless you, young massa. I's glad to see you." I grasped his hand with a fervor no less real.

He had come so rapidly as to attract the attention of the other servants, and here they came! Old Mike, limping and gray-headed; George, the carriage driver, growing old gracefully; John, the preacher, and Joe, the exhorter, now looking old and gray; Ike, in the prime of life, no longer awkward, with his wife and a troop of children; Dick and Jake, the boys I used to hunt with, now stalwart men. Then far in the rear, limping, hobbling, toddling, "making haste slowly," came mammy. She was still fat and plump, but old and clumsy. Her will was fast, but her locomotion was difficult. She reminded one of a barrel trying to work its way on end, when it might have fallen down and rolled much easier.

I pushed through the crowd and we soon met. "My chile, my chile." This was about all she said, but her tears were more eloquent than words. My heart bounded with a saddened joy as I grasped the old black hand which had led my infant feet in the paths of safety. That hand had ever been gentle and helpful to me. What a rush of memories, sweet and sad, came to me at this hour! Mammy was my earliest confidante, my trusted friend in every stage of early life. That young life stood out before me with special vividness just now.

By this time nearly all the old familiar faces were looking on, each desiring and each receiving special recognition. With this eager, trustful company around me, I felt that the Old Guard was

19

there, and that the problem of a living was already
solved. Not seeing Uncle Sam, the patriarch, I
inquired where he was. This brought tears to
many eyes. "Done follered ole massa an' ole
missus," was the reply.

Under the spreading branches of an old familiar
oak in the lawn, I reminded them that the situation was as new to me as it was to them, and told
them what arrangement Will Benson had made
with the hands on his place. I ran over some articles of agreement, and asked if they were entirely satisfactory. There was an impulsive expression of approval. I knew that almost any contract
could be made with them, they were so trustful;
but I resolved from the first to treat them fairly,
"to deal justly, and love mercy."

I told them nothing more than the truth when I
said it was a great joy for me to return and find
them all free. I promised them that if they would
be as faithful as freemen, as they had been in the
past, I would always be their friend, and they
would find me faithful to meet every obligation.
Jack, acting as spokesman for the rest, said that
he thought they would be worthy of trust. The
years that have passed have witnessed the fulfill-
ment of these mutual promises.

Jack was at once by common consent installed
as leader. He gave orders and all hands went to
work in earnest. I immediately took Jack into
counsel and told him frankly that the question of
rations for the hands was embarrassing. That I

really did not know what could be done. The old man smiled as he said: "Come dis way, young massa." I seemed to have made the very speech that pleased him most.

He led the way down toward the horse lot, where there was a low shelter by the fence, which had been used to house sheep in bad weather. It was now piled around and nearly covered with rubbish. Jack pulled away some of the covering and exposed the ends of cotton bales. "Ole massa," he said, "had dese put here, and tole us not to tell nobody what was in here."

"How many bales are in there, Jack?"

"Jes' one hund'ed, massa."

I fairly caught my breath, but only to take a new start at breathing. Cotton was then worth over a hundred dollars a bale.

Of course this happy find belonged as much to the other two children as to me. It was timely for us all. It furnished the means for a new start, and enabled us to put our homes in good repair. We appreciated it all the more because it was one of the last acts of a thoughtful father for his children.

With feelings of sadness I now opened the old home so long closed. It had been the home of my parents, the home of my childhood. Fondest recollections, all saddened now by the shadow of death, came trooping from the past. So real and vivid were the images of my parents on my memory's tablet that I seemed almost in touch with them as I handled the familiar things they so constantly used.

This was to be Susie's home. It was doubly dear on that account. Memories sweetly sad and anticipations fondly bright blended now as incense rising from the altar of domestic affection. What a joy to me that I now had the means of putting the dear old home in thorough repair! I knew two good Confederate soldiers who were carpenters, and who had come out of the war with nothing but their families and their trades. A job now would be most opportune. A messenger was sent for them, and they were employed to make the improvements.

Mammy looked ten years younger, now that she was installed housekeeper. Aunt Daphne, the old cook, had gone over to join the "silent majority," but a younger servant had filled the place, and was now called into requisition. With my two carpenter friends and occasional visitors my bachelor life was not entirely lonely. We can endure almost anything if we think it is to be of short duration, and to be followed by something better.

Meanwhile, the farm work went on admirably. Cotton and corn were planted and fences repaired afterward. I never knew work pushed with more energy, even in the days of slavery. The hands now worked from a different motive. They seemed to be cheerful and contented.

I sat in the hall one of those beautiful spring days, enjoying the music of hammer and saw, and

listening to the distant song of the cheerful freed-
man, when my friend and comrade, John Henderson, rode up to the gate. He dismounted without
ceremony, and was hitching his horse, before I
could get out to express the welcome I felt. We
had not met for nearly two years. It was a glad
meeting, where heart went out to heart.

"I came by," he said, "to congratulate, and be
congratulated."

To this I made reply: "I am ready to receive
any amount of congratulation, and as for making
return, there has never been a day since our first
acquaintance that I have not felt like congratulat-
ing you."

"There has been many a day," he answered,
"when I felt like I deserved commiseration, but
that is not the case to-day."

As he said this, the bright, exultant soul of the
young man fairly glowed in his eyes. I knew my
friend had met with some good fortune, and I was
anxious to hear what it was. The carpenters and
their noise occupied the house, so we turned to a
seat under a lovely bower in the corner of the
yard. He had a brief and joyous recital. After
a prolonged and doubtful struggle, he had won the
approval of her parents, and now in a few days
he was to lead Miss Minnie Allen to the altar. I
extended to him the right hand of fellowship, and
our mutual congratulations were prolonged and
hearty.

He related how his love for Minnie had sprung

up in his heart away back in the early days at the
academy; how it inspired every blow he gave
Dolph in her presence; how his love ripened into
resolutions stronger than life when he was working on the Major's residence; how, during all
these years, his heart had been wrung on the see-
saw between hope and despair; how keenly he
had felt the yawning social gulf, almost inpassa-
ble, between himself and the object of his adoration.

During all these years Dolph was the welcome
visitor, the favored one whose prerogative it was
to accompany Miss Minnie out to all social gatherings.

"Still," said John, "I hoped on against all
odds. The war came, and I felt this was in my
favor. It would postpone the crisis and give me
more time. Then, as a soldier, I knew that in
the world's estimation I was nearer on an equality
with Dolph than ever before. I went into the war
to make a record which would help me to win the
idol of my heart or die in the effort. That thought
was present in every battle, and sustained me in
every hardship. It made me glad when Mr. Lincoln proclaimed the freedom of the slaves. I then
believed that the war would end with the freedom
of the negroes. Their freedom was the breaking
down of the main barriers in the way. That was
the leveling of the fort I dreaded most to charge.
As the fight went on, the result became more and
more apparent. All I had to do was to bide my

time, and make the effort to gain the parents' consent, as I felt sure I had gained the daughter's love. The old people have for years entertained the idea that Dolph was to be their son-in-law, and their persistence in that idea had made Dolph hard to shake off. But when they did come round, it was done magnificently. This morning the Major took my hand and said with tears in his eyes: ' My son, you and Minnie are all we have now. We cannot think of giving you up. There is house enough here for us all. I want you to take charge of the place and make a living for the family.' I tell you, Sam, I fought the war through on that line, and I gained the victory.''

I remembered the contempt which Dolph put in the word '' carpenters '' on the memorable day of our visit to Maj. Allen's, while John was working on that house. So I said, partly in reply and partly to myself: '' Then the house you built as a carpenter, you are now to occupy as proprietor. Well, you deserve congratulations.'' And again I gave him a hearty shake of the hand.

John rose to start as one who had discharged the business in hand. But before he left, as if to complete the matrimonial news of the neighborhood, he told me that Capt. Webb and Miss Julia Parker were soon to be added to the number of happy unions.

'' Well,'' I asked in a jocular way, '' what is to become of Dolph? It will not do for him to be left out.''

"Dolph is all right," he answered. "He had two strings to his bow. It is always good in such cases to get one of them broken. Miss Sallie Conway will make him a most excellent partner, and we shall have them for our neighbors."

One busy month completed the days of my bachelor life. In the flowery month of May I led my own sweet Susie to the altar, and then brought her to the dear old home to preside over its destinies.

The faithful servants had earned a holiday, even in the busiest period of the crop season. The best feast that could be provided was given. And these old friends of mine had a grand day in celebrating the marriage of "young massa an' young missus." This is the way the older negroes put it. The younger ones toasted "de young boss and his putty young wife." The old darkies invariably said "massa;" the younger ones constantly used the word "boss." Thus the old conservative and the young progressive elements were even then at work. They have both performed important parts in the development of the new life of the race, and are still at work.

As for mammy she occupied as much of the premises as any three persons; sporting a snow-white cloth on her head, she was the busiest and most delighted of the throng. "Git outen my way, niggers, I's takin' keer o' my chillern. Dey's boff mine. Didn' I nuss em boff when dey wus babies?" And the little urchins scampered away, showing their good nature and white teeth at the same time.

Thus the new life on the old plantation began: a life of love and sweet contentment to " de young boss an' his putty young wife; " a life of freedom and compensated labor to those who were no longer slaves.

# CHAPTER XXXIV.

## Conclusion.

THE interest in human lives by no means terminates with marriage. Many writers trace their principal characters through all the mazes of a lover's experience; through the agonies which lie along the borders of despair; then along the half painful gleamings of a trembling expectancy; then into the glowing rapture of a rising hope; thence into the sorrows and heart-burnings of a misunderstanding; and at last bring them out into the clear light just in sight of the altar, leaving the imagination to catch the idea that the chief end of existence is to be consummated by the ceremony of the priest. Such literature may, in part at least, be responsible for much of the silly talk among young people which conveys the impression that their only aim in living is to get married.

Only the thoughtless and ignoble seek marriage as a finality in life. By the thoughtful and loyal mind it is regarded as a means to a nobler existence and a wider usefulness. The marriage of noble, congenial natures is a union of strength for the real purposes and services of life. Both natures are made stronger by the compact. They complement and brace each other. "In union there is strength," especially so in this kind of union:

strength of integrity, strength of purity. It is as if two streams should come together, each holding chemical elements to neutralize and precipitate the impurities of the other. Thence the united stream flows on clear as crystal and sparkling as the very "waters of life."

Marriage is an epoch, a crisis. Life then takes a nobler trend and projects its aims on a higher scale, or ignobly shrinks from the high responsibilities involved and becomes complaining drudgery. Life is thenceforward rounded into beauty and catches the inspiration of a nobler purpose, or is marred into failure and sinks below all purpose. Marriage, regarded as a means of accomplishing the grandest purposes of life, becomes, when properly entered into, the happy consummation by which we reach a richer experience and a wider and deeper life, moving and living on a higher plain of existence.

A true marriage is in the highest degree normal, and therefore brings to us, as nothing else can do, a settled feeling, a sense of fixed and quiet satisfaction. Single life is too much like the wayward comet, moving in an orbit eccentric and uncertain. When two such comets blend in perfect union, they become a planet, moving in a regular orbit and keeping step to the "music of the spheres."

Marriage has in it all the sweetness of divine appointment. What an ecstacy to feel, to realize in our own experience that our strongest earthly desires and heaven's noble plans are moving in the

same orbit! To many noble minds this is a sweetness which far excels that which comes from the
tenderness of love; it is a joy greater than the joys
of loving companionship. The mind, which has
in a high degree the attribute of faith, and feels
the thrill of the divine presence and realizes God's
tender sanction to this union, feels a joy the unbe-
lieving can never feel.

The man or woman who enters into matrimony
on the low level of sordid motives or present gratification, with no thought of high and holy obligations, not only misses the joys of sweet connubial
bliss, but sins against all that is most sacred; and
sins, most of all, against the deluded party, who,
loving and trustful, brings loyalty and purity, only
to be met and complemented with infidelity and im-
purity. What a sacrilege! How "unequally
yoked together!" Such a person thus coming
into this sacred union is as profane as an infidel
high priest who for filthy lucre should walk with
unhallowed feet in the holy of holies! Such a
union is a deception of the worst type, a fraud
heartless as it is blasting, a degradation beyond
the hope of restoration. Such a marriage is a sin
against high heaven and the most sacred interests
of society.

Susie and I have the very great satisfaction of
knowing that we have consummated a union in
which none but the purest motives have entered.
It is a union of hearts in which love has grown and
ripened. This love has grown with our growth

and strengthened with our strength. From infancy it has been the sweet tie of an unbroken friendship. It has been made stronger by waiting; has been sanctified by suffering, and mellowed by sorrow. In the fullness of time we have come together and laid the foundation of a new home: a home that is to be our own. We intend it shall be a real home: the nursery of affection, the dwelling-place of the heart, the dearest spot on earth. We are not concerned as to the pattern of the house or the style of the furniture. In these tumultuous times we are glad to have any house and any furniture. But we are concerned as to the principles which shall be woven into the texture of the home, not of the dwelling, but of its occupants; the same principles which should be vital in all homes —principles which have made thousands of American homes the dwelling place of virtue, of intelligence, of sweet contentment, and of happiness as pure as belongs to earthly life. These, then, are the principles on which we propose to construct our home:

1. The recognition of the supreme authority and gracious protection of an all-wise Providence. We intend to cultivate the feeling that we have a Father, infinitely wise and purely good; that in all our efforts to do right we shall be led by an unseen hand and upheld by an unseen power; that in our sorrows and afflictions we shall have a gracious Comforter; and in our losses and failures, if we preserve the integrity of our motives, we shall have

one who can sympathize with our weaknesses and help our infirmities.

A recognition of the divine presence in the affairs of life is a constant inspiration for good. It develops unflinching courage, giving strength to convictions and fortitude to action. It makes us feel that the right must finally prevail. With this belief we take heart and stand unmoved amid the wrecks of the hopes and the seeming failures in the lives of good people. With a sublime faith " that all things work together for good to them that love God," we are prepared to walk in our sphere and meet the responsibilities of life with brave and trustful hearts.

2. The continued, abiding love of each other. This is the chord of harmony in every home. Without it the glitter of wealth and pride of position are mere travesties on the sweets of domestic life. No splendid building on spacious grounds, nor costly living with courtly display can compensate its absence. Without it marriage is a failure. But with it the humblest home can be made to sparkle with the gems of happiness, and become the arena of grand and noble lives.

3. The love of country. Every home in the land should be the nursery of patriotism. As we stand in the peculiar attitude of conquered subjects, it will require some effort to cultivate this noble feeling. It may be easy enough to lay down the rifle and pick up the Constitution, but it is by no means so easy to exchange at once the destructive spirit

of the one for the preservative feeling of the other. Yet the love of home involves the love of country. The home is doubly dear to us because it is located in the land we love.

4. Love for our neighbors. Much of the happiness of life comes from congenial and loving companionship with our neighbors. This feeling should be cultivated. Every neighbor has a better side, and it is wise to live on that side.

Hoping that the reader, as well as the writer, may have " love at home," and " peace on earth, good will to men," I bid him, for a time at least, an affectionate adieu.

THE END.

www.ingramcontent.com/pod-product-compliance
Lightning Source LLC
Chambersburg PA
CBHW020810060726

47498CB00017B/1429